PENGUIN BOOKS

A Change in the Lighting

Amy Witting was born in Annandale, an inner suburb of Sydney, in 1918. She attended Sydney University, then taught French and English in State schools. She has published two novels, *The Visit* and *I for Isobel*, a collection of short stories, *Marriages*, two books of verse, *Travel Diary* and *Beauty is the Straw*, as well as numerous poems and short stories in magazines such as *Quadrant* and *The New Yorker*. She was awarded the 1993 Patrick White Prize.

Also in Penguin
I for Isobel
Marriages

A Change in the Lighting

Amy Witting

PENGUIN BOOKS

Penguin Books Australia Ltd
487 Maroondah Highway, PO Box 257
Ringwood, Victoria 3134, Australia
Penguin Books Ltd
Harmondsworth, Middlesex, England
Viking Penguin, A Division of Penguin Books USA Inc.
375 Hudson Street, New York, New York 10014, USA
Penguin Books Canada Limited
10 Alcorn Avenue, Toronto, Ontario, Canada M4V 3B2
Penguin Books (N.Z.) Ltd
182–190 Wairau Road, Auckland 10, New Zealand

First published in Viking by Penguin Books Australia, 1994
Published by Penguin Books Australia, 1995
10 9 8 7 6 5 4 3 2 1

Typeset in Baskerville by Midland Typesetters, Maryborough, Victoria
Made and printed in Australia by Australian Print Group

National Library of Australia
Cataloguing-in-Publication data:

Witting, Amy, 1918–
A change in the lighting.

ISBN 014 024937 0

I. Title

A823.3

A Change in the Lighting

• I •

At the moment which became history, Ella Ferguson was wearing nightgown, dressing-gown and slippers.

She did not eat breakfast in her dressing-gown ever again.

Breakfast had been eaten. Her youngest, only unmarried child, Sophie, had left for her job as secretary assistant in a small film company and Ella was now sitting on the edge of the unmade bed watching her husband's reflection in the dressingtable mirror.

Her husband, Professor Bernard Ferguson MB, FRCS, was knotting his tie. That was why she was watching him. For thirty-two years she had taken pleasure in watching him knot his tie, handling the rich, dark silk, sliding the tightening loop under his shirt collar, where it settled into a firm, precisely placed knot. He was still extremely handsome, having stiffened more in mind than in body, but that movement recreated for her the beautiful, earnest young man she had married. Buying him ties as presents, which seemed such a sedate occupation, was for her what the young people called a turn-on.

Usually, he concentrated on the task. This morning his glance met her gaze in the mirror and he said abruptly, 'Ella!'

'Yes?'

He finished knotting his tie. She said to herself later, in fury, He finished knotting his tie!

'We have to have a serious talk.'

'Oh, yes!' she said eagerly.

So he knew it, too. Things had been going badly between them. Now they would get together and talk it over to make things right again.

What she saw in the mirrored face was shock, then a twitch of irritation. She began to feel chilly.

'Things can't go on as they are, you know.'

She stared at him, not understanding his tone, which suggested that she was the one who had been avoiding serious discussion.

Something odd happened to the next moment. It disintegrated. She heard her own voice, sounding weak and far away, saying, 'Solution to what?'

He had said, 'I think divorce is the best solution for all concerned.'

He did not answer her. The look on his face was one she knew, of impatience at not being immediately understood.

'All concerned? Who else is concerned?' she asked with assumed innocence, though of course she had known at once, in a thunderclap of enlightenment.

'Oh, Ella!'

No you don't. Don't you Oh, Ella! me. You don't slide

out of telling me by making out that I know. You say it, every bloody word of it and damn your precious dignity. Dignity indeed. You dirty old man. You old goat.

'Who else is concerned?'

'Well, Louise.'

'What about Louise?'

He had stopped looking in the mirror. He was fidgeting with something on the dressingtable.

'I think you must know how it is.'

'I know nothing. What is this about Louise?'

Say it.

He saw no escape. He took a deep breath and turned to face her.

'Louise and I are lovers. We have been lovers for some time. We want to marry. Therefore I am asking you for a divorce.' He added more kindly, 'Of course we want to give you every consideration,' but the words dwindled when he saw the look in her eyes. That was a triumph if she wanted to count such a small one – and she did. She would seize any scrap of satisfaction she could get.

'Thank you for the information. Now,' she sang, 'get out. Get out of this house and stay out. Take your things and go. Don't come back here tonight. Don't come back here again ever.'

His face went loose with shock, then rearranged itself to the expression of a reasonable mind. The mouth opened, then shut again.

'Out,' she said patiently. 'Go. Go. Go.'

He said at length, 'Very well.'

He got a suitcase from the top of the wardrobe. She stared at the wall while he moved about opening drawers, sliding doors, very slowly, giving her time to change her mind.

Go, she thought. Go.

She hadn't brought up his clean socks from the laundry. They were lying rolled like a clutch of coloured eggs in the laundry basket.

I cannot speak of socks to that person.

He asked, 'Have I any clean socks?' in a neutral tone, as if he were off to a weekend conference after a small domestic disagreement.

'In the laundry basket. You can pick them up on your way out.'

With that trivial, spiteful remark she had reached him at last. She knew it though she still would not look at him. He snapped shut the locks of his suitcase and went quickly down the stairs.

She waited to hear the front door close. She heard the car start. What was he doing?

Of course, it was because of the suitcase. He would not walk down the hill to the station in midweek carrying a suitcase.

It seemed to be a small thing, not worth thinking about. She did not know that it was the first message from a changed world.

Exhausted from the effort of shooing him out, she was glad now not to be dressed, being one step nearer oblivion. She took off her dressing-gown and slippers and got into the bed.

After a while she got up, went downstairs and came back with the bottle of whisky and two glasses. Moving with economy, she filled one glass with water at the bathroom basin, poured whisky into the other, diluted it, set the drink on the bedside table and got back into the bed.

She did not finish the drink. Three deep swallows were enough to induce the torpor in which she lay, not quite awake, not quite asleep. When at last she stirred, she raised herself on one elbow and drank again. This time she slept.

Sophie's voice roused her, calling, 'Mum! Mum! Where are you?'

She was coming upstairs. Now it would all begin to happen.

Sophie was standing in the doorway.

'What's up, Mum? Are you sick?'

'Your father's gone. He's left me. He wants a divorce.'

She hadn't been able to look at him, but she scrutinised Sophie, who stood rigid, then said gently, 'Bloody, bloody, bloody Louise.'

'That's right. Louise.'

Sophie came to the bed, sat on its edge and said briskly, 'This is shock, Mum. You need to stay still and keep warm. Get under the covers. That pillow is a mess. Lift up your head while I straighten it.'

Nothing would ever be simple again. Every moment brought a variety of messages. Sophie was trying to be adult, which was touching. Sophie was wearing a new necklace and a new shirt, a startling shirt of tawny yellow silk. Sophie was upset but she was not shocked, not even astonished.

Now she picked up the whisky bottle and said, 'That was a good notion. Mind if I join you?'

'You're too young to drink spirits, Sophie.'

'I just aged ten years.'

Her face contorted, and she cried, 'I'm trying to play

it cool but I can't. Everything gone, everything gone in a minute.'

Ella shook her head.

'Not everything.'

Sophie bent and kissed her.

'Come on. We'll have a drink. Can you do another?' She held up the bottle. 'You haven't drunk much. I wouldn't have blamed you if you'd wiped yourself out.'

She hadn't needed to. The shock had done that for her.

Sophie went to the bathroom to fetch the tooth glass. Ella was astonished to find herself forlorn in that moment of absence. Sophie brought back the glass filled with water, replenished the water glass and tactfully poured herself a very small whisky.

'Say when, Mum.'

Ella didn't want whisky at all. Her mouth was dry and she had a headache, but she accepted the drink because she needed to share a rite of friendship.

'The same for me.'

She sipped once, lay back against the pillow, now smooth and cool, and said, 'That's a nice necklace.'

'They call them beggar's beads. Rob brought it back from Hong Kong. I just got it today. The shirt too.'

'That was nice of him.'

She roused herself enough to wonder how old Rob was and whether he was married.

'Rob's a female, Mum.'

'Oh.'

She closed her eyes and made a gesture for laughter.

'You've spoken of her, too. Where did I get the idea she was a man?'

'Because she's my boss, you old sexist, you.'

That didn't explain the sheen on Sophie, then, undimmed as it was by shock and grief. There was more to it than a new shirt and a new necklace. That orthodoncy had been well worth the expense, teeth straighter than Nature could make them being a real distinction, contributing to a new glamour. So did the hairstyle, the thick soft hair, coloured like the fur of a blond animal, now hanging in a heavy plait. The other two being such beauties, and Sophie, besides being nuggety in figure, wearing bands on her teeth, Ella had thought her plain. She had sprung up, of course, so that one could no longer think her nuggety.

'I don't think I've really looked at her for quite some time,' thought Ella.

Now she was frowning.

'Have you had anything to eat, Mum? Any lunch?'

Ella shook her head.

'I'll make you a cup of soup, then I'll see what's for dinner in the freezer, okay?'

'I'm not ill, you know.'

Sophie said, surprisingly, 'It's best to play it that way. Call it illness for the moment, that's the best thing.'

Where had Sophie been, to be so experienced in dealing with emotional shock at the age of eighteen? That film place, of course, probably full of suffering actors. It was outrageous that the same suffering had found her out.

Downstairs the phone rang and Sophie answered it briefly. When she came back with soup and toast on a tray, she said, 'That was Mrs Rodd wanting to know why you weren't at the committee meeting.'

'Oh, dear me!'

'I said it was a virus.'

A virus named Louise. Each had the thought, neither expressed it, each read it in the other's eyes. Ella's face reddened. This was like being caught naked by one of the children. The pity in Sophie's eyes made the moment no easier to bear.

'I'll go and forage for dinner.'

Feeling that she must assert herself, Ella said, 'Veal in the blue plastic box on the top shelf. You can heat it in a saucepan. It won't take long.'

'Okay.'

Sophie took the tray and departed.

When she had gone, Ella got up and stripped the bed, fetched clean sheets from the linen cupboard and remade it. She was dismayed by her health and strength and thought with dread of the feelings lying in wait for her. Sophie had been right – better to play sick, to lie doggo for a while. She had promised herself some satisfaction from throwing down the laundry chute the sheets in which that person had spent the night. It was too small a satisfaction.

As she finished making the bed, Sophie was at the door again, looking awkward. She was about to venture an intimacy.

'Mum, do you have anything to take? Tranquillisers or sleeping pills? I could get a scrip from a friend and go to an allnight chemist, but I'd have to say why.'

'No.'

Sophie said with rage and contempt, 'It's a wonder he didn't think to leave you something.'

Ella giggled with shock at the informed hatred in Sophie's voice, and Sophie joined in the laughter without knowing its cause.

She said then sadly, 'It's no laughing matter. No laughing matter at all. I'd better get back or the dinner will burn. It won't be long.'

Preserving the convention of sickness, they ate dinner in the bedroom, Ella propped against pillows, Sophie in the bedroom chair with her plate on her knees. She had brought up a bottle of wine; a glass of it and the shared moment of giggling misery had made her bold.

'Didn't you ever suspect, Mum? Didn't the thought ever cross your mind?'

Ella shook her head.

'But never here and always with her. Out to dinner three times a week.'

'He said they were doing research.'

'Oh, yes.'

Now every word she spoke seemed to have a dirty double meaning. Research into a virus named Louise.

This time Sophie was more discreet about the shared thought, nodding without meeting her eyes.

'Would you like coffee?'

'No, thank you, dear. That was lovely. Nice to be waited on.'

'No trouble.' Sophie summoned up resolve. 'Is it for real? I mean, is it for good? He might get over it, people do. Very likely, really.'

He might get over it, but Ella never would. The look on her face was enough for Sophie.

'Sorry. But we'll have to think about telling the others. Do you want me to ring up David and Caroline?'

Oh God, poor Caroline. How was she going to bear the disgrace of this?

'Time enough tomorrow. Thanks for the dinner. I'll be all right now.'

Sophie stacked the dishes, bent to pick up the tray and was overtaken by a loud sobbing cry of grief and outrage. She shook her head at Ella, discouraging speech, and hurried away.

Eighteen years old, thought Ella. She must see to it . . . see to it . . . it was all too much.

It had been such a tiring day, though spent mostly in bed and semiconscious, that she didn't get up to clean her teeth, but closed her eyes and slept at once.

She woke in the dark, held fast by a fierce rage that came from outside her and was shaking her, dictating curses. She wished them illness, injury, disfigurement, disgrace, she wished them a retarded child, she wished them a beautiful child who . . . no, she couldn't wish that on anyone. The check brought another kind of anger, more her own, from within. Since none of it was going to happen, why couldn't she curse as she pleased? If she had the power to make curses come true, how much harm would she do them? None. Cursing was the privilege of the helpless, not an unlimited privilege at that. She understood now why people used to make wax images and stick pins in them: it was simply the need to move a hand, exist, assert something against the madness of rage.

She switched on the bedside lamp and looked at the clock radio: half-past 3. What she would really like to do was get up and make a cake, fill the kitchen with the good, comforting smell of baking, but if Sophie woke and found her baking a cake, she wouldn't think of therapy, she'd think of breakdown and be frightened. What was a reasonable activity at half-past 3 in the morning? Writing. Not her thing, but it would have to do.

She went downstairs, fetched pen and paper from the sideboard drawer and hurried back to the bedroom as if it was the only safe territory. She looked at the dressing-table and felt aversion, dragged the stool over to the bedside table and used it as a desk.

Dope, she wrote. Dope, dope, dope, dope, dope, he knew what lie to tell me, that's the worst thing, knew me and I didn't know him coming in so dazed and happy saying he'd been doing research I know now what research but I thought that young man was back been waiting all my life for that young man walking on the beach that night after he'd just won his medal asked me if - said to add to the sum of human knowledge that's all didn't have to be anything to make him rich or famous wouldn't matter if nobody else ever knew he would know and be satisfied. Could I understand that, not looking for money or advancement? Is this a proposal? I said, and he said yes. Up at the house they were dancing, the party was a celebration, we could hear the music, I said Yes to you too then, like a kid but I got it out. You can't see the future. Lucky you can't. Always I've been waiting for that young man to show. When he left the hospital for the University I didn't mind about the money I thought this was it. Instead it was dreary dinners with people talking about jobs and who was against you. Dope or not I was beginning to wake up to myself until that night he started me off again with his talk about research. Dirty little adulterer. Dope dope dope dope

She made to tear up the scribbled pages but this was the good linen writing paper that wouldn't tear.

Oh, stop that, she snapped, hearing herself whimper like three-year-old Becky at this small frustration. Nail scissors. That inspiration took her to the dressingtable. Odd, she hadn't touched the dressingtable in . . . seventeen . . . seventeen and a half hours, and it still seemed like enemy territory. He'll never stand there again, she promised herself, as she opened the drawer and took the nail scissors out of the manicure case. They had a cutting edge of one centimetre and a half, curved at that, which made the destruction of the pages a laborious affair. Time-consuming was the word. What was time for but for consuming?

Here I sit, turning writing paper into confetti. Don't think of weddings. Why not? Very suitable, really, a beginning and an ending. It was something like making wax images, after all. Make and destroy.

She kept at it to the last millimetre, the neat curved shreds showering into the wastepaper basket. Then she began to yawn, as if the task had been a spell that freed her for sleep.

• II •

When she woke, rage was waiting. She heard Sophie's voice at the telephone in the hall and looked at the clock. Twenty past 9. For God's sake couldn't Sophie get off to work by herself for once? Did she have to be waited on every minute and dogged every inch of the way? Surely she was old enough now to . . .

She remembered the circumstances and perceived the extraordinary injustice of this tirade, fortunately before she had run downstairs and voiced it. Sophie had proved very responsible indeed and was being responsible still, no doubt. It was reasonable enough to stay until Ella woke.

Go carefully, she said to herself. So last night she had calmed herself by cutting writing paper to shreds. Writing paper was one thing, Sophie was quite another.

Why Sophie?

She wasn't used to this poking and prying at her emotions, like cleaning out a dirty old cupboard with God knows what at the back of it. Tedious, but it had to be done. Why Sophie? Just because she was available and the monster would jump at anyone? Sophie had behaved so well last night and was probably staying home from work on her account.

Sophie hadn't been surprised. She had been upset but not surprised. Sophie, the youngest, had known something Ella hadn't known, that was the rub. You could write the word DOPE a hundred times and cut it to pieces, but you'd never be rid of it.

Showered and dressed, she went down to the kitchen. Sophie had been talking on the phone again. She came in from the hall, frowning, and spoke snappishly.

'Nothing is easy. I rang in and told Rob you were ill and I couldn't leave you. Well, I didn't want to wake you and I thought you might need me for something. Now Rob wants to come out here this afternoon to work on a script. I had to say yes, unless I said you had smallpox or something. Do you mind hiding upstairs when she comes?'

'It's Nina's English lesson this afternoon. I can't put her off. She isn't on the phone, you know. I didn't know you worked on scripts. That's nice, isn't it?'

Indeed, she was gratified at this, but her satisfaction didn't get into her voice.

'Only this one. It's about a young girl and Rob says I have an ear for dialogue.'

Remembering the shirt and the necklace, Ella frowned, then remembered that Rob was a woman. She must be losing her mind.

Sophie was feeding bread into the toaster.

'It's no use telling lies, is it, Mum? It gets too complicated. I'll have to tell Rob the truth. If you're sure about Nina. You don't look up to it.'

Roles reversed, Ella sat at the table and waited to be fed.

'I'd feel worse, thinking of her waiting for me and being disappointed.' Besides, she was important to Nina. It was a comfort to be important to someone. 'I want to be doing something.'

Something other than building up a living head of Louise: long, sharp nose, full cheeks, grape-grey shallow-set eyes, not quite protruding (not yet), mouth a good feature, just right, chin too, slender neck – it was tedious work, brain-racking, intensive study of a text that wasn't there – smooth black hair hanging in wings – once the living image was complete she could twist her piano wire round the neck and tighten it slowly until the eyes began to bulge and the tongue to protrude, swelling and blackening, and her spasm of rage got release.

Ugly, ugly. Better not make a habit of that. It had been one of the images of disfigurement, misfortune, humiliation that had swarmed in the frantic night, the one that had brought some relief, but she was shocked by it now. Besides, it was very hard work.

'I'm sorry, dear. What were you saying?'

She had said to him, kindly, 'I wonder why Louise doesn't marry? She's quite attractive, isn't she?'

Here was that face again.

'About dinner. Do you want me to put it on?'

'No. I'll bring something home, or we'll live off the freezer again.'

'Okay. Mum, I'll have to tell the others, and Pam, if you don't mind. I'll have to go to work tomorrow but Pam might be able to come in, for lunch anyhow. I don't want to leave you alone all day.'

'I'm not prostrated,' said Ella sharply.

'No. I can see that.' Sophie smiled, and the smile showed the wear on her young face. Sophie had been alone with this too long. 'But it's depressing, being alone all day, and Pam's going to be hurt if you put off telling her.' She shook her head. 'There are minutes when I just stop believing it. What about we tell the others to come over on Sunday? Family council, like? Then we can get it all over in one go.'

'Good idea.'

'Unless you want to ring them yourself.'

'I'd rather you did it.'

She resolved, however, seeing again that look of weariness which had disfigured Sophie's smile, that she would ask nothing more of her. Sophie must not become a victim.

• III •

Though the thought of Nina, waiting for her in vain, eagerness dulling into disappointment, would have deepened Ella's depression, there were better reasons for making the effort to find her notes, dress for the outing and take the train to Newtown. Teaching was so orderly, so predictable; her daughter-in-law Martha would not have agreed, probably – Martha survived by pumping up idealism and optimism as a form of adrenalin – but then, teaching Nina was a special case. A bright, untaught girl discovering with joy the power of her intelligence, she radiated what Martha would call positive feelings; Ella looked forward to being cheered by them.

Today, walking through the streets of Newtown, with their strangely compacted dwellings, their air of age and experience, signs in foreign languages and small, exotic restaurants, gave her some of the relief that foreign travel is supposed to bring to the heartbroken. The rejected suitor flies to Africa to hunt lions, the deceived wife takes the train to Newtown to teach English to a young Chinese.

Almost, she smiled.

There it was – it was the prospect of being welcome, of having Nina's beautiful, honey-coloured Madonna face joyful at her arrival that lifted her spirits.

After all, the lesson was disappointing. Nina opened the door to her smiling, but the smile disappeared. She said, 'Hullo. How are you? Please come in,' but without her usual mischievous pride in the achievement. She led her into the kitchen, showed her homework, took Ella's praise without a smile, listened earnestly to Ella's exposition of the present continuous tense of the verb but did not understand it.

'Nina, I cook. I make cakes. I drive a car. I teach English. What am I doing now? Am I driving? Am I cooking? Am I teaching?'

This small failure seemed to Ella enormous. It wasn't the day for it.

Nina was depressed by it, too.

'I am very stupid.'

'No, you are not stupid, but there is something wrong. What is wrong today?'

Nina opened her copy of *My First Picture Word Book* and turned the pages, searching. She stopped to put her finger on a picture, a baby, mouth open, roaring, tears cascading. 'You,' she said. 'Not baby.' She shook her head, reproving herself. 'You are not a baby.' Her finger followed the trail of a tear. 'You. Why?'

'Unhappy.' She hadn't wanted this, she had wanted escape. But why not say it, after all, see how it sounded exposed to the air?

'My husband and a woman.'

Nina frowned over the words as if she were translating a puzzling message, then enlightenment came and brought silent tears. She knelt in front of Ella, took her hand and let her tears fall on it; oddly, she wiped them away not from her eyes but from Ella's hand, as if it shared her weeping. As she dried Ella's hand, she murmured in her own strange, singing language, a sound of lamentation, sympathy, consolation. Ella, listening, shed a tear or two but as if it were for some other woman or for all women who met this misfortune, not with the great burst of weeping which her own required. That was just as well, since she didn't intend to carry a tear-blubbered face home in the train, or anywhere, ever.

'Don't be unhappy, Nina. Enough, now.'

This time, Nina wiped her eyes.

'Yes. I forget now,' she promised firmly.

An apology for the intrusion.

'We do the lesson now?'

Ella shook her head.

'Next week. The same lesson next week. Okay?'

She kissed Nina on the cheek. Apology understood and accepted.

She carried home with her the memory of Nina's weeping face as a charm against that other one.

There was an old VW kombi van standing in the road in front of the house. Sophie's boss was apparently still here – thoughtful of her not to block the driveway.

Dinner. Thinking of Nina, she had forgotten dinner. She was so bored and irritated by the thought of dinner and every other detail of daily life, every small thread that had to be picked up again with effort, that she considered lying down to die. If one could die by lying down, of course – killing oneself would be the greatest effort of all. Besides, people who committed suicide were sending a message. She had no message to send.

Sophie called, 'In here, Mum!' from the dining room. She at least sounded happier and looked up cheerfully from the page she was reading.

'This is Rob, Mum.'

Rob stood up and shook hands.

'Sorry to hear about your problem, Mrs Ferguson,' she said with surprising bluntness.

Her voice was light and rapid, but with a tone of confidence or conviction which made it impressive.

'Thank you.'

Ella looked at her with attention, because of her importance in Sophie's world. She was tall and thin, but broad-shouldered, had short, dark hair and quite beautiful eyes of a light brown that was almost golden, finely shaped features set too far apart in a broad face, like a beautiful face seen under water. She was wearing a silk shirt like Sophie's, of intense blue instead of tawny yellow, and a short gold chain instead of Sophie's agates. Thirty-five, perhaps. Maybe a little more.

She had sat down to her papers again.

'By a freak of fate, which is well known for its freaks, I suppose, this script we are working on is about a teenager caught in a marriage breakup. I had no idea, of course – I'm not sure I should be involving Sophie in it.'

'If you think I'm like that awful Angela who puts funnelweb spiders into people's shoes . . .'

'I don't want to put ideas in your head, mate. Something nasty might turn up in mine. Seriously, Mrs Ferguson, what do you think?'

Ella, who was contemplating funnelwebs and regretting that she hadn't taken notice of the other's shoes, controlled herself.

'I can't see any harm in it. It might be a very good thing.'

'Attagirl!'

Rob looked confused.

'That was a bit familiar, wasn't it? Sorry.'

'You're welcome.'

Ella warmed to her, since it was her own weakness to speak without thinking, but mainly when she was annoyed.

'Did you get your shirt in Hong Kong, too?'

She had intended this as a hint of thanks and was startled at the sharp, wary glance it drew from Rob. One would think she had intended it as criticism.

'Both such lovely colours.'

'Nothing like silk for holding colour,' Rob agreed with reserve.

'Is it all right, Mum, if Rob stays to dinner? We want to go on working tonight.'

Ella sat down.

'I forgot all about dinner. I meant to bring something back. There'll be something in the freezer. Of course, you're welcome.' She smiled, or at least moved the appropriate muscles. 'It didn't sound much like it, did it?'

'I got the subtext. It was fairly welcoming. My cue, after all. I don't want to impose. I'll go out and get something. Is there somewhere I can buy Chinese – if you don't mind Chinese?'

Ella was wondering what a subtext was but could not ask, for fear of shaming Sophie.

'That would be very nice. Thank you.'

Sophie added, 'There's a place opposite the station, the Small Palace Garden. They do a good Mongolian lamb.'

'Small Palace Garden. That's a charming name.'

Sophie chuckled. 'Note it down. It might come in useful. Do you want me to come with you?'

Was she being impudent? That was her boss, after all. Perhaps film people were different.

'Just give me the directions.'

Rob responded to impudence with an amiable grin.

Yes, it was a different world.

When Rob had gone, striding freely, shoulderbag swinging, jeans and sneakers oddly out of harmony with the glowing silk shirt, Ella said, 'She's very informal, isn't she?'

'They're all like that, Mum. And she's brilliant, truly. It's wonderful working for her. Do you mind about dinner? Things were going so well, I kind of forgot.'

'I don't mind.'

'Poor Mum. You look as if you'll never mind about anything, ever again.'

'I'm tired, that's all,' said Ella sharply. 'There are things I mind about and always will. You've always been able to invite your friends and there's no reason to stop that. Besides, it's better to have something going on.'

'I rang up. I told Caroline and Martha. David wasn't back from his football training.'

'How did they take it?'

'Just what you'd expect. They're coming over on Sunday afternoon. And Pam will be down tomorrow. I hope that was right.'

'Yes.' Ella sighed. 'Well, it had to be done.'

Sophie began to clear the table, gathering scattered pages and sorting them into numbered folders.

'It's all very orderly. I thought creative people would be untidy.'

'The orderly part is my job.'

She stacked the folders according to number while Ella watched respectfully, thinking how grownup she seemed at this moment, more so than David who was eight years older. Perhaps it came from doing work she really liked – no, David did like teaching. Sophie was utterly involved, working with concentration. That was it.

'Can I get you a sherry, Mum?'

Something in her tone brought back the feeling of Nina's tears on her hand.

'I can get my own, you know.'

'I'm in training for a gofer.'

'What's a gofer?'

'Go for this. Go for that. I'm Rob's gofer.'

'It's good she isn't embarrassed. Most people would run away.'

'Not Rob. She's not so easily embarrassed. But would they? Do you think people will shun you?'

Ella shrugged.

'Well, Pam won't, that's for sure,' said Sophie. 'I don't suppose anyone else matters much. Funny old world, though.'

She shook her head in wonder at the nature of the world.

Rob had found the Small Palace Garden and also the pub. They ate Mongolian lamb, shrimp sweet and sour with fried rice and drank riesling.

How suitable this seemed, dishing food from cartons at the table. It was like a scratch meal on moving day.

Rob ate quickly, tidily and with great appetite, but drank sparingly.

'Alcohol makes the ideas flow,' she explained, 'but it makes them seem better than they are. Very treacherous.'

Since Sophie's intake of alcohol was so far limited to a glass of wine at dinner, and Ella did not feel inclined to outdrink them both, there would be another opened bottle to join yesterday's claret in the fridge. One result of crisis: cooking with wine.

'That spider. Did it bite anyone? The funnelweb the girl puts in the shoe.'

Rob was pleased at the question.

'Not the one it was meant for. Making emotions visual, you know, that's the thing. Hatred, it is. Hatred of the father's girlfriend. She has it in a jar, calls it Hannah, that's the other woman. Have to find out how long a funnelweb would live in a jar.'

Sophie asked, 'Do we have to experiment?'

'Somebody at the Museum will know, I suppose. There's a lot of detail I won't go into, but she does sneak it into the other's shoe. It's comatose, might be dead; she tips it into Hannah's shoe, then she goes off to college.' Rob paused to chew and swallow a mouthful of lamb. 'The bus trip is really the significant bit, because she keeps seeing the word "murder" in all sorts of contexts, like headlines. WALLABIES MURDER WHOEVERTHEYARE AT TWICKENHAM and so on. Newspaper placards, a man reading the newspaper, headlines on the sports page. I haven't worked it all out yet. I spend a lot of time staring out of bus windows. She gets out of the bus and bolts back, spider gone, frantic search, flashback to the headlines, etc., the word "murder", while she scrabbles among shoes. I think it has to bite her – a bit obvious but we need a spot of delirium to round out the plot.' She said, apologetically, 'Well, you did ask me.'

'I think it's fascinating.'

'It's my first full-length effort. I've made a couple of shorts, did quite well with one of them. I'm fairly wrapped in it. I don't usually talk about work in progress. Ideas tend to evaporate.'

'Money,' said Sophie. 'That's what they talk about.'

'It's the main consideration. Working on the well-known shoestring and frayed at that.' She turned to Sophie. 'I'm trying to get Martin to take an option on a story of William's. That might keep him going a bit longer.' She said to Ella, 'William Anstey. Do you know his work? Very good first novel. He's on a grant but the money's running out before the novel, unfortunately. It puts him in a delicate situation.'

'What will he do then?'

'Register for the dole. Then he'll have to waste his time going for jobs he doesn't want and won't get. Frustrating.'

'Humiliating, too,' said Ella.

'I don't think William humiliates easily. It's a waste of time, that's all.'

'It seems to be a very interesting world you work in.'

'In spots.'

'How did you go with Nina, Mum? Mum's a volunteer English teacher. Nina's her Chinese student.'

'That's an odd name for a Chinese.'

'It isn't her name. It's as close as I can come to it. She breaks down into giggles when I try to pronounce her name so I call her Nina. She doesn't mind, she likes having an English name.'

Why was she talking so much? To forget that odd sensation of Nina's tears falling on her hand? She had set down her fork and clasped the left hand over the right, the weeping hand.

'We have trouble with names. Sometimes they're unpronounceable so they come out as Natalie and Linda and so on. Sometimes they're rude. We have one girl called Weewee – at least it's spelt H-U-I H-U-I but it's pronounced Weewee. Her tutor changed it to Vivi.'

Why didn't she shut up?

Rob, however, was listening with interest.

'It must be a very satisfying job.'

'This one is a bit special because she didn't get to go to school in China. She didn't even know she was intelligent. She was so frightened when she started and now she's so happy. I don't like to build on it, I don't want to expect too much of her, but I can't help having hopes for her.'

'God, how marvellous. For you, I mean. Making her a present of her own mind. Wouldn't that be a wonderful thing? I wish I had two lives. I'd do that with the other one.'

'It isn't always like that. You don't often meet one like Nina.'

She picked up her fork again.

'It gives you a real charge, doesn't it? It would me, too. But to think of intelligent people walking about illiterate, not even knowing they are intelligent – that's another reason for making good films. They reach everyone.'

'So long as they can spell M-U-R-D-E-R,' said Sophie.

'Down, Fido!' Rob said amiably.

Not at all like Ella's first boss, Mr Westerway.

'Why don't you take your work into the living room this evening? We could put the heater on. It's getting quite chilly.'

Rob considered, then shook her head.

'Your living room daunts me. Oh,' she answered Ella's look, 'in a very nice way. It's like a dignified old person I love very much. It might limit my vocabulary. Antiques put me off, usually, but yours have charm. That lovely old sideboard – '

'They call them chiffoniers.'

'Chiffonier.' Rob filed the word. 'I could use that in a film set. And the enchanting clock with the pop-up carnations.'

'Austrian porcelain. It cost far more than we could afford. I saw it in an antique shop and fell in love with it, so Bernie bought it for my birthday.'

Her voice had dwindled. The wake had been going well until they remembered the corpse.

Sophie was wiping her nose. Rob wore the abstracted air of one secretly biting her tongue.

Abruptly and overloudly, she said, 'Any takers for the rest of the fried rice? When I eat, I stoke up.'

Ella shook her head.

'I'll make some coffee,' she said, carrying her memories of that birthday into the kitchen to be dealt with in private.

After coffee, she went up to the bedroom, where the rage threatened, terrifyingly. In haste she built up the face again: grape eyes, full cheeks, swinging black hair, mouth, chin, throat, piano wire, tension, release. She waited a moment, steadying her breathing, then picked up the phone and pressed the button for Pam's number.

Pam had been waiting by the phone.

'Oh, love!'

'Yes. Sophie rang and told you.'

'I'll be down tomorrow. I would have come tonight but Sophie said she had someone coming. Odd, I thought. That's kids for you.'

'She couldn't help it. It's her boss. They're downstairs now, working on a film script.' Her voice brightened, since that was a cause for pride. 'She's a very interesting woman and it's a help for Sophie, to keep working. She's taking it terribly hard, poor kid.'

'Okay. I take it back. Sophie said you'd gone to your student. That seems almost too normal.'

'Perhaps it is. Perhaps I haven't stopped being normal yet.'

Outwardly, at least.

'Look, love. Would you like me to come now? I could come straight upstairs and not disturb them. I could bring sleeping pills if you don't have any.'

After a pause for thought, Ella answered, 'Not tonight. I think it's all catching up with me. I'm dead beat.'

That was no lie. She was yawning widely.

'Okay. Sleep well and I'll see you tomorrow.'

She did sleep deeply until 5 o'clock, then woke tense with rage. Quickly she built the face – that was becoming easier – and performed her ritual murder. The face bloomed like a hideous orchid and vanished. She slept again and woke at 7.

• IV •

At breakfast Sophie said, 'What did you think of Rob, Mum?'

'I thought she was very interesting. So enthusiastic about what she's doing. Did you work late?'

'A bit after 10. I looked in on you but you were fast asleep. Would you mind if she came again? We got so much done and she liked it here. If it doesn't worry you.'

'It's a relief to have something else to think about.'

'It's just the most interesting thing in the whole world.' Her eyes were shining; yesterday's misery was forgotten.

That explained the new sheen on Sophie. She was in love, not with a man, but with a film.

'I'll tell her. Next Friday night, and we'll bring in the food.'

You won't keep that up, Ella said firmly, but to herself.

Kindly meant, no doubt. How many offensive things were kindly meant.

At least Sophie left for work without asking her if she

would be all right. That was an advance.

In the hall, the phone rang. She picked up the handset and heard Caroline in distress.

'Mother? Oh, this is terrible. I can hardly take it in. It's just . . . I can't believe it's happened. Sophie said Dad had left, is that right? Really gone for good? Is that right?'

'I'm afraid so, dear.'

'And with that woman? I can't believe it of Dad.'

'It's been a shock, yes.'

'Mum, why didn't you call me? I would have come straight away, you know that.'

Oh, dear.

'I know you would have. I just . . . well, it was the shock.'

'But you were alone. You shouldn't have been alone. What actually happened? When did you know?'

'He asked for a divorce, that's all. He said he wanted to marry her – Louise.'

While he was tying his tie.

'And then he left? Like that?'

'I asked him to go. It seemed the best thing.'

'You must have needed support. I wish you could have turned to me.'

Ella, who never wished to hurt Caroline's feelings, managed it too often without trying.

'I suppose I just wasn't thinking, not acting normally.'

'She said you were out with your student.'

'That took my mind off things, I suppose. I realise I should have rung you, dear, but I knew how upset you'd be, and somehow . . .'

'It wasn't very nice, hearing it from Sophie.'

'Well, we'll talk it all over on Sunday. We'll talk about it then.'

'Yes.'

Saddened by the tone of that last word, Ella wished as she put down the phone that poor Carrie didn't take things so much to heart. She had a just grievance; Ella hadn't thought of her at all on that terrible first day – she hadn't thought of anyone, or perhaps not thought at all, but there had been time since to acknowledge Carrie's rights as the eldest child, married woman and mother. She might well resent getting the news from Sophie.

Ella hadn't been much of a success as a mother, either, as far as poor Carrie was concerned.

Pam arrived at 10 o'clock. Thin, dark and strongly featured, deprived for the moment of her usual alert and cheerful air, she looked forbidding, but put her arms round Ella and hugged her.

'That's that, then,' she said.

'Yes, that's that.'

Pam drew a deep sigh.

'What a mess.'

'Yes. Would you like a cup of coffee?'

'Unless you'd rather get slightly drunk. Nothing vulgar, of course. Enid's minding the shop and I brought a bottle.'

No wonder deserted wives turned alcoholic. People seemed to expect it of them.

'I tried that the first day. It didn't work.'

This was the third day.

'He was standing at the dressingtable tying his tie and he asked me for a divorce.'

Her voice quivered with rage and remembered astonishment.

'Just like that?'

'Well, very nearly just like that. Not much notice, I can tell you.'

'And it's for good?'

'Yes.'

Pam got up to fill the kettle and switch it on.

'You didn't ever have an inkling? No suspicions?'

'You mean, how did I manage to fool myself so long? I've been asking myself that. I knew there was something wrong; we never seemed to have anything to say to each other any more. I tried to ask questions about the research and he just passed them off, but I thought they were probably silly questions.' She winced, realising just how silly they must have been. (Have you made a breakthrough? Do you like working with Louise?) 'You know, when there's a noise breaking into your sleep and you don't want to wake up, you can dream a long, complicated dream that explains the noise away. When you do wake up, you're astonished that it was only a minute. You don't follow me?'

Pam was looking troubled.

'I follow you, but you don't sound like yourself. I never heard you talk like this before.'

'I was never in this situation before. I hated it, the time he spent with her, but I had the situation wrong. I was jealous for the children's sake. Seeing she'd been his student and the brilliant great success, I thought she was the brilliant child he'd never had. I thought she made up for his disappointment over David. Mind you,' she spoke with an excess of energy, 'if he hadn't driven David from the age of two with number games and mind-stretching exercises . . . well, that's past history. I hated it, but in a way I thought I had it coming.'

'Oh, how could you? Don't talk such rubbish.'

Pam spoke from the workbench where she was pouring coffee.

'Something I had on my conscience. There's cake in the blue tin. What I did . . . It's worried me for years. You remember when David got the selection to go to Sri Lanka with the under-nineteens?'

'Of course I do.'

'And he was so happy. Didn't say anything, but so happy. You know what it's like to see someone so happy that you're frightened for them?'

Pam nodded.

'Like they're juggling with the heirloom china. I feel like that when a girl comes into the shop to buy a dress for her wedding, even if I don't know her. I'm thinking, Oh, God, make it last, while I'm bringing things for her to try on.'

'Well, that's how I felt about Sri Lanka. I didn't think I'd feel safe till he was on the plane. Then I got a call from the school, the headmaster wanted to have a chat with me about David. I went up there in a panic, and there were the headmaster, Mr Crowe the head maths teacher and Mr Wellings the sportsmaster. It's such a relief to get this off my chest. I've never told anyone about it before. David hadn't been in any trouble, but he'd put in his choices for Year 11 and he'd taken two unit Maths instead of four unit. I suppose it did have something to do with Sri Lanka, in a way. The story was, too much cricket, not enough study. The headmaster said that David was an underachiever with a brilliant mind. A genius IQ, he said. They didn't believe in pressuring but they were hoping he would mature and begin to work to his ability. He had a special aptitude for mathematics and their hope was that as the work became more challenging he would involve himself further. That was the maths teacher talking. I didn't like the look of him. I didn't like the look of that man at all. They were very disappointed with David's choice of history as a major. They'd got poor old Wellings there to say how uncertain the life of a professional cricketer was. He said David was pretty certain to make it to State level but after that it was dedication and a lot of luck. I hated that, too – getting poor old Wellings there, like an awful example of what was going to happen to David if he didn't do his maths. I suppose they were right about that. Well, they said, "Talk it over with the Professor and let us know what he thinks." And I didn't. I should have told him and I didn't. I don't know why. He wouldn't have stopped David going to Sri Lanka.'

'You can't be sure, can you? You didn't really trust him.'

'It was that maths master. I don't know. I didn't like the look of him. I didn't say anything to anyone. I thought it over and I wrote them a letter, very pious, nothing like a bit of religion if you want to shut people up. I said that if David had been blessed with special gifts, their purpose would no doubt be revealed to him in . . . I don't think I actually said in God's own time, but that was the idea.'

Pam was grinning.

'Fear of thunderbolts? I like that "blessed with". That's a nice touch.'

'I felt guilty the whole time, but I did it.'

'Religion aside, it was plain commonsense. They were

David's gifts and he was the only one who could dispose of them.'

'We haven't seen much sign of them yet.' Ella sighed. 'I look back now at poor old Wellings and I think, is that David in thirty years or so? Not much of a future for a genius IQ.'

'Too much ambition in this world. If David was mine I wouldn't want him different.'

'How did I get on to that? Oh, yes. Thinking she was . . . you'll believe anything before you can take it in. Rejection, I mean. I keep forgetting you've been through this. But that was different. You left him.'

'Oh, yes. I left him. So he got married and lived happily ever after with a very nice wife and two lovely kiddies. Two children. Three. When Thomas said he wanted to go and live with them, it murdered me. I've never got over it. Do you know, I've wondered ever since what I really feel about Thomas? He comes with presents at Christmas and my birthday and Mother's Day – I wish Mother's Day had never been thought of. Such suitable presents, I'm sure she picks them. I feel like saying, "Don't bother." I just give him money. I know, if he was ill or in trouble, I would care. Of course I would. But I have to keep asking myself, like digging at a sore tooth.'

She lit a cigarette and as usual looked round for an ashtray. Ella as usual got up and fetched one from a cupboard.

'Why Pam, I never knew you were so unhappy.' She was shocked at the sight of a stranger's face, the alert, cheerful expression pinned on and held by an act of will.

'I'm not unhappy all the time. It just comes over me now and then. I trained him for her – that's what galls me, mostly. It was the divorce that woke him up to himself. But then, she's the little homemaker and I'm not. I don't give a damn for him and I'm happier in the shop. And I know in my heart that it's better for Thomas. So there you are.' Suddenly, she shouted with rage, 'But this makes me burn. Oh, this makes me burn all right. That man never waited for a meal nor wanted for a clean shirt. You've done all the working years, brought up those kids alone, for all the help you got from him, and now!'

'He worked such long hours at the hospital and then there was so much study when he took the university job,' said Ella and wondered why she was defending a dead marriage. Out of habit, no doubt.

'I was hoping for too much from that trip to England to the conference, because we'd been so happy in London. Cold and poor, but young and happy.'

'I'm a tactless beast. Now I've made you cry.'

Ella hadn't been aware till then that she was crying. Clearly, there were subjects not to be dwelt on. That other would be going with him to London to the conference. Perhaps that was what had brought him to the crisis, the moment of confession.

She wiped her eyes.

'No use in crying, is there?'

'Sometimes it helps.'

Pam picked up the cups and took them to the sink.

'Leave them. You'd better be getting back to work.'

'I don't like leaving you alone. Though I don't seem to be doing much of a job of cheering you up.'

'Well, at least you've given me a good example. I never could have guessed that you were carrying a load of misery.'

'But I'm not. Not always. It just hits me now and then. It doesn't last, believe me. Most of the time, I'm quite happy. To tell you the shameful truth, the thing that's hard to bear is that someone else is happier.'

The face bloomed in Ella's mind, bloomed, died and vanished.

'That really is – pardon me – salvation, being able to accept the others' happiness.' She added in embarrassment, 'And that is the sermon for today.'

Ella did not think she could ever reach that salvation.

'Give yourself time. If you're sure . . . I'd better be getting back.'

She saw Pam off with the promise to ring her if she was needed.

Meanwhile, there were lamingtons to be made for Saturday's fete. If she were to produce the promised six dozen, she must start the sponge today. She got out the ingredients and the mixing bowl, but while her hands were busy with the sponge, her thoughts were revisiting the past.

There had been two crises of conscience: David's mathematics and Caroline's illness. Think of one and along came the other.

Could she really have been responsible for Caroline's mysterious, psychosomatic illness?

No, no. Not possible. It was overwork and worry about the public exams. Poring over her books with that strained, bleak look, poor girl. Why was everything so difficult for Caroline, so easy for the other two?

It was a coincidence, that was all. A little thing like that . . .

Nevertheless, she examined the evidence, as she had

done so often before, with the familiar sympathy for poor Carrie squeezing her heart. Outshone in all things by David, Caroline had turned to virtue for compensation. It had not rewarded her much. In spite of constant praise from teachers, for diligence, neatness, punctuality, trustworthiness, she had not been made a school prefect. Ella, who spent much time wishing intently for some small triumph for poor Carrie, had hardly been able to contain her disappointment. Who could blame the girl if virtue toppled over now and then into self-righteousness and a bit of mischief-making?

Caroline must have hurried home from school that day. She had come earlier than usual, looking for Ella in the kitchen.

'Mum. I'm worried about David. He's taken up smoking.'

Ella had said sharply, 'Are you sure? How do you know?'

'One of the girls told me. He's been seen smoking in the playground at lunchtime.'

'What are the teachers doing? Why don't they stop it?'

'Oh, Mum. Teachers can't be everywhere at once. The boys go into the bush near the bottom fence. Not very nice boys, either. Now David's started going with them.'

There was nothing to be seen in her face but genuine concern. That was one point on which Ella was still uneasy, that Caroline had appeared so convincing.

'Don't you think you should tell Dad? You know how he is about smoking?'

'I'll think about it,' Ella had said, meaning that she would think about Caroline.

She had had no intention of involving Bernard – quite the last thing to do if one wanted David to give up smoking, the sort of thing Martha would call counter-productive. She thought only of extricating Caroline from the situation without hurting her feelings.

When she was alone with Caroline again, the next day, she had said, 'About that business – it's no use telling Dad, you know, if we want David to give it up. That might just make things worse. Why don't you have a word with Mr Wellings? He has a lot of influence with David. He could tell him it would be bad for his cricket, that's an argument that would impress David.'

'I can't talk to Mr Wellings. School doesn't work like that.'

'You're David's sister. You have a legitimate interest.'

Caroline was shaking her head.

'He'd just think I was talebearing.'

Had she really read something in Ella's eyes to cause the terrible disintegration? the dreadful look of panic terror coming as slow as a dawn? then the rage that had twisted her whole body, bending it forward as if she were going to vomit?

Ella found it hard to face even the memory of it, though she had faced it often enough.

Caroline had run away and Ella had been glad of it. At dinner she had been quite her usual self.

Yet Ella had been shocked and mortified, for she had expected Caroline to be appeased by the suggestion. Being sent to consult with Mr Wellings should have increased her self-confidence, surely? And if it had been a mistake, what a little thing . . . the symptoms had appeared soon after: headache, fever, joint pains, then the mysterious red, raised blotches for which no explanation could be found.

She had been overworking. That was all there was to

it. She asked too much of herself – so Ella told the doctor, who had been explaining that psychosomatic did not mean imaginary. There was certainly nothing imaginary about large red raised blotches.

'An unhappy love affair?' the young man had asked, as if Ella with her talk of overwork had been hiding something.

'Good heavens, no!'

The look he had given her was not sympathetic.

'It's not out of the question. She is a very beautiful girl.'

'She doesn't seem to be very interested in that sort of thing.'

Confusion had made her sound prudish, though she would have been delighted to see Caroline find an object for her affections.

The quick, closed look and the 'I thought as much' nod had been for Ella, not for Caroline.

Until then, Ella had not questioned her performance as a mother, nor the quality of her marriage, which was certainly not cosy, but, like a large, imposing house, impressive, though a little draughty. Caroline's illness had been an accusation. When the doctor had suggested a change of climate, she had taken his meaning, painfully.

'She'll have to repeat the year. That would put her in the same year with her younger brother, who doesn't have so much trouble with schoolwork. Perhaps if she went away to school?'

What guilt will do for you. She had positively been playing for the young man's approval with her air of concern, though the concern was real, and playing quite in vain. He must have had serious trouble with his mother.

'So long as she doesn't see it as rejection,' he agreed.

Giving up, Ella had snapped, 'She'd have no reason to.'

The alternative was to dispose of David, who must be allowed to have some right to live.

In spite of the daunting expense, she had urged the move to the boarding school at Moss Vale, concealing the real reason as if it were a guilty secret and using the doctor's advice as a pretext. Bernard had agreed. His conferences with the doctor had taken a different tone, no doubt, since the young man had been deferential and perhaps had not had trouble with his father. Ella had wished those conferences more frequent, but Bernard had objected that medical etiquette forbade his interference and there was nothing he could do. He might have been as troubled as she was, for he gave in fairly readily over the ruinous school fees.

We weren't communicating even then, about our child's illness, and I didn't protest. I seemed to take it for granted, though I felt the lack. Well, he had paid the fees – to do him credit, he did care for the children's welfare, in his own way, and the move had been a success, Caroline coming home for holidays healthy and cheerful. Repeating the year had helped, too – she had passed the exam very comfortably and qualified for entry to her course in physiotherapy.

It was all to the good, thought Ella. She must have been very unhappy, the trouble would have come some time, even if that was the last straw, it was only a straw.

But how she wished she had not been the one to place it on the camel's back – if indeed she had. Such a thing – it didn't seem possible, yet she could never forget it nor absolve herself. Poor Carrie.

One failure after another and now the last and the worst.

As she slid the second tray of raw sponge into the oven, she said to it grimly, 'You had better rise, that's all.'

The day the cakes stopped rising, she would give up.

• V •

Next morning she made the last batch of sponge while she contemplated the small ordeal of ringing Ursula Rodd and the large one of sacking Mrs Barlow. Mrs Barlow must certainly go; her cleaning services had been a luxury since the elder children left home, and Ella knew she could no longer justify the expense of sentiment. She rehearsed the phone call, not having the heart for the interview:

'Rather better, thank you. Just one of those twenty-four-hour things. I'm making the cakes but I don't think I'll be up to coming to the fete. Could you get someone to pick them up on Saturday morning? Bernard (watch your voice) isn't here at the moment . . .'

'Yoohoo,' said Mrs Barlow at the back door. 'Sorry I'm late, dear.' She came in, stepped out of her shoes and groped in her large bag for her slippers, saying, 'The old lady's very bad with her arthritis, couldn't raise herself out of bed, I had to do the lot for her. Still the comedian, mind you. "Ivy," she said to me, "old age is a bigger bummer than love, and that's saying something." ' Inserting a bunioned foot into a black felt slipper which had taken the shape of the bunion, she confided to it, 'She'd be a whole lot better if she kept right off the grog, but it'd be a shame to deny her a bit of pleasure.' Slippers adjusted, she stood up and faced Ella. 'For God's sake, Mrs Ferguson, what's the matter?'

'Mrs Barlow, I'm very sorry, but I'm afraid I won't be able to have you here again.'

Mrs Barlow's lively face was still, first from shock, then from offended dignity.

'I hope you've been satisfied with my work?'

She had dropped what David called her comedy act. ('Mrs Barlow talks like that because she thinks that's how charladies are supposed to talk.')

'Of course I have. You've been wonderful, always. It's nothing like that – it's a change, a change of circumstances. I won't be able to afford help in the house in future.'

After a pause Mrs Barlow said with conviction, 'Him.'

She nodded to herself in agreement.

'I'll just sit down for a minute if you don't mind, dear.' She sat and sagged. 'In fact, no offence, but I don't think I can stay. It's a shock.' She rallied. 'No, that's no good. There you are up to your eyes in cooking and you need the help. I'll get to it. Anything special you want done?'

Ella shook her head.

'The usual, then. I'll start upstairs.'

Two hours of silence from Mrs Barlow made a solemn and eerie experience. Waiting, while she made the chocolate icing, for the face and a burst of chatter at the inner door, Ella told herself that the phone call would be easy after this. She was relieved when Mrs Barlow made her farewell appearance in the kitchen.

'Not much I can do here. You've spread yourself properly.'

'No, I'll clean up when I've finished.'

'Lamingtons for a cake stall, is it?'

'That's right. The Sunshine Home for Retarded Children. It's one of our charities.'

'Always someone worse off than yourself.'

Ella fetched the housekeeping purse from a drawer and counted out thirty dollars, feeling paltry.

'I'm sorry,' she said miserably.

'Understood, dear.'

'Will you have a drink with me?'

Mrs Barlow looked more cheerful.

'I wouldn't say no to a glass of port. We go back a long way, you and I.'

Alcohol to the rescue again. Ella fetched the bottle of port from the living room and poured two glasses.

As Mrs Barlow accepted her glass, she said, 'Gone off, has he?'

Ella was startled. She hadn't meant the glass of port as an invitation to intimacy, but, as it had cost Mrs Barlow her job, no doubt she was entitled to hear the truth of the matter.

'Yes.'

'Found somebody younger.' Mrs Barlow nodded, looking grim.

That face again. Gone. It goes, it dies and goes.

'Mind you, though it isn't my place to say, as soon as I set eyes on that one, I said to myself, "You're too handsome for your own good, you are." The old lady told me early. "Never trust a handsome man," she said to me.' She added reflectively, 'Not that I got much good of the plain ones. But then, I never met one who didn't think he was handsome. The others just get away with more. Well, here's to better days.'

Ella drank to that in silence, without conviction.

'I'll tell you one who won't see better days. He'll live to rue it. There's never been a better wife and mother than you and he won't find your like again. And there you are after all you've done, like they say, traded in, traded in on a later model.'

The anger in her voice took the offence from her words. Harsh and commonplace as they were, they were set to Nina's grieving music, comforting in one way, in another frightening.

Mrs Barlow emptied her glass and left it available. Ella refilled it and from courtesy topped up her own.

'Will you be looking for another place? If I hear of anything . . .'

'I've a waiting list. A friend of Mrs Ramsden wants the first vacancy. I never thought it would be you.' She girded herself to humour. 'You're never short of a job if you vacuum under the bed and clean down the S-bend in the toilet. Mind you, what some of those people get away with is a disgrace. They should have more pride. Oh, well, I'll be off then. If you're ever in a spot where you need a friend with a mop and a broom, dear, you let me know. In the way of kindness, I owe you plenty.'

'Thank you.'

Port and true charity were bringing Ella to tears. Mrs

Barlow saw this and added to her charity by hurrying away.

A searing smell and a gush of black smoke came from the stove, where a neglected pan of chocolate icing had reached burning point. She seized it and thrust it into the sink, wrenched the cold tap violently open to drown the contents, then sat down to a bout of serious weeping.

On Sunday afternoon the two elder children came, twenty-six-year-old David with his wife Martha, twenty-seven-year-old Caroline with her husband Max and three-year-old daughter Becky, to hold a family conference.

When the young Fergusons were assembled, they gave the daunting impression that extreme physical beauty was a family estate. 'What a pair of heartbreakers,' people had said to Ella of the elder two. 'You must have had a time of it when they were teenagers.' However, they had broken no hearts. David had settled early with Martha, who had some charm but little beauty – her overlarge bespectacled black eyes, set in the small delicate face, gave her the look of an appealing insect. Caroline, in spite of her blonde beauty (which was perhaps too ethereal, a little too saintly to rouse carnal desire) had never formed a serious relationship before she met Max, who was a little too old, a little too fat and slightly foreign, a physics lecturer with a brilliant brain and indeed a splendid family man. Ella hoped Becky would not inherit that broad, flat nose.

As they sat, David and Martha side by side in the rosewood chairs, Caroline and Max together on the sofa, they appeared mismatched, yet David and Caroline were winners. In the words of the proverb, they were the ones who extended the cheek while the others kissed. From her new status as loser, Ella knew this and resented it, even in her children. She remembered Pam's words about accepting other people's happiness. She was right there. That was one thing learnt and, no doubt, a lot more to go.

She looked to Becky for comfort. Becky and Sophie were sitting on the rose rug, Sophie sorting out from the old toybox the animals which belonged to the Noah's ark standing in the centre of the rug. As Sophie handed her the animals, Becky arranged them along the central wreath of roses.

'The two horses have to go together, Becky.'

'Why?'

'They are like Mr and Mrs Noah. Mr and Mrs Horse, Mr and Mrs Cow.'

The Noah's ark had belonged to David, who was watching with amusement.

'Mr and Mrs Bull, I think.'

Sophie said earnestly to Becky, 'Uncle David is a rotten old sexist. Don't pay any attention to him.'

David looked startled, recovered and grinned at her.

'My apologies. Ms Cow and Mr Bull.'

'Don't confuse Becky, please,' said Ella.

She feared that her pain could be heard in her voice. Such a gust had come to her from the past, from Sophie's babyhood when so many things had been different, the house brightened by David's delight in her, and a more discreet tenderness in another face, so like his. Against this anguish there was no shield.

'She'll have to sort it out sometime, Mum.'

'Early days yet,' said Martha.

Becky had heard enough nonsense from her elders.

'Where's Mrs Sheep, then?'

Max beamed at this indication of intelligence, while Sophie returned to her task.

Max got up to take a third slice of strawberry cream sponge. With the air of one bringing the meeting tactfully to order, he said, 'He's certainly going to miss Mother's cooking.'

Ella hid rage. Eyes, nose, cheeks, hair, chin, throat, piano wire, violence, release. She was calm again.

'He's searching for youth, of course,' said Martha.

'Well, he seems to have found it.'

'No, Ella. It doesn't work like that. It's the illusion of his own youth he's seeking, not the reality of someone else's. That's just the thing to make the situation worse and that's why these relationships can't last.'

No fool like an old fool, as one used to put it. Max with his 'Mother' made her feel ancient, while Martha seemed to think Ella had come down in the last shower. Both good people, who made her children happy.

'Whether it lasts or not is their affair,' she said.

This comment had some impact on the listeners. Caroline said, 'I hope you wouldn't be unforgiving, Mother.'

'Nobody's asked me yet,' she answered, and regretted the sharpness of her tone as Caroline flinched.

The movement had been brief, almost subliminal, but Max had observed it, too, and closed his hand on hers for a moment.

In spite of appearances, that had been the best of marriages for Caroline, who needed just such a warm, constant, uncritical love as Max provided.

David asked soberly, 'What are we going to do now?

What's the next step? Somebody tell me what I'm supposed to do and I'll do it. There are some things – money, I suppose.' Having pronounced the ugly word, he added defensively, 'Mum has to know how she stands about money. And what is Dad doing? Where is he?'

'He is lecturing as usual,' said Max. 'I saw him in the common room on Friday. I nodded but I didn't speak. Not my place, I thought.'

Max was inclined to speak with pride of his rare excursions into tactful behaviour.

David nodded.

'I'll ring him at the Medical School and arrange a meeting, get a few things sorted out . . .'

The prospect of handing over responsibility to the men of the party, which lifted Ella's spirits, made Martha twitch with annoyance.

'What about yourself, Ella? Do you have any plans? Any idea what you want to do with your life?'

She put some emphasis on the words 'you' and 'your'.

Ella, who wanted to go on doing what she was doing now, said perversely, 'I could be a cook, I suppose.'

'Oh, something more ego-positive than cooking! What about your teaching? You're so good at it, and you like it.'

So even Martha didn't think it was her life.

'Teaching 2B English? That's ego-positive? Ego-negative, I'd call that,' said David.

'I go on trying. They are improving slowly. I try to build up an atmosphere of trust and acceptance.'

'This is all about nothing,' said David. 'Mum will get support. Dad wouldn't want her to work.'

'What Mother needs,' said Max, 'is a really good divorce

lawyer, someone to watch her interests from the start.'

Sophie had looked up sharply from the Noah's ark play and sat staring, unmoving. The other Ferguson children wore the same startled look.

Mum and Dad, that house made of flesh – the thought of its being demolished and carved up by lawyers shocked them all. Now they know, thought Ella, with some revengeful feelings. Until that moment they had not taken in what was happening.

'Can't we leave the lawyers out of it?' asked Martha.

'How can you leave the lawyers out of it? Divorce is a matter for the law, is it not? And the law is a matter for lawyers, I think. If you want to watch Mother's interests, you will go to a lawyer who specialises in divorce.'

To be Max's mother, Ella would have to have given birth at the age of thirteen. It was the European background, of course. It made him a wonderful family man, but sometimes strange in his manners. It was a pity Caroline had picked up the habit. From her it was a little chilling, though she was only copying Max and meant no harm.

'You hear such terrible stories of all the money going in lawyers' fees. It's much better if you can avoid confrontation and handle things yourself.'

The debate was between Max and Martha. The Ferguson children were still tasting and trying to swallow the word 'divorce'.

'Where money and property are concerned, there is always confrontation. Your father is not the only one involved, remember.'

He never called the other one Father. Christian names in the common room, no doubt.

As if she had seen a bad vision, Caroline cried out, 'This house will have to go.'

What a ridiculous idea. How could Ella be put out of her house? Anyone would think that she was the guilty one.

She had to make allowances for Caroline, who was obviously distressed, but the idea was unthinkable in this room, where everything spoke of permanence, where the wreath of roses in the hooked rug shaded from the crimson of David's school blazer through the rosepink of Caroline's winter dressing-gown to the paler pink of Sophie's skirt, and pictures, vases and ornaments seemed to be rooted like plants in their accustomed places.

She waited for someone to protest at the absurdity. Since nobody spoke, she was sorry she hadn't protested herself.

'Wait till I've talked to Dad. We don't have to assume that there's going to be confrontation, as you call it. We can wait and see.'

Max shrugged.

'As you like.'

His body language announced that this neglect of his advice would be regretted.

It was clear that Sophie had received a blow. When it was time for the others to leave, she packed away toys in silence and allowed David to take possession of Becky and carry her out to the car.

David kissed Ella on the cheek and said, 'I'll be in touch, Mum,' while Becky climbed out of his embrace to put her arms round Ella's neck.

Hugging Becky to her, Ella thought how much she loved her and how different this love was from her feeling for her children – a joyful extravagance, an accidental, unexpected source of happiness.

If only David and Martha . . .

Sophie was in the kitchen washing the used china.

When Ella picked up the teatowel she spoke.

'We wouldn't have to leave here, would we, Mum?'

'No, of course not. Caroline didn't mean it. She was upset.'

Sophie nodded, relieved.

'I couldn't imagine living anywhere else.'

Ella felt guilty, since she had expected Sophie to leave, though the other two had stayed at home in an oldfashioned manner till they married. Sophie had seemed different, a lover of groups, happy, one would suppose, sharing a flat with other young people. Ella had even spoken to Bernard about the need to settle Sophie in a new home before they left for England in September. His response, now she came to think of it, had been vague.

After all, Sophie was not ready to leave home. She made bold excursions into adulthood, from which she needed sometimes to retreat.

There was another problem now. Ella thought of the mother-and-daughter pairs one read about so often in novels, the querulous, possessive mother and the trapped, resentful daughter. Could she ever turn into such a person? There was no telling what one might not become.

'You'll be wanting to leave home some day, Sophie.'

'Oh! Some day!'

She took the plug out of its hole and watched the water run away, but it was only Ella who saw time running as it disappeared.

• VI •

On Monday, David took a day's leave from his school and went to see his father. He called for Martha at the end of her school day and drove to the house. They found Ella in the dining room, cutting out a jumper dress for Becky. Martha, pale and strained from the effort of creating atmospheres of mutual trust and acceptance, nevertheless smiled brightly. It was not her fault that in these circumstances the smile appeared mask-like.

'I brought dinner, Ella. Salmon steaks and salad. I hope that is all right.'

'Of course, dear. Very good of you,' said Ella, though she resented having her kitchen invaded. It was well meant, and they would one day stop treating her like an invalid.

'It's all I can cook up to your standard. I thought you might want to talk to David while I get the dinner.'

Oh, thought Ella remorsefully, she is a dear, well-meaning girl and at least she doesn't call me Mother.

David had brought a bottle of sherry.

'Do you want a drink, Marf?'

'After I've made the salads.'

David poured two glasses of sherry, sat down at the table and produced an envelope from his pocket.

'Dad sent this, Mum. Financial arrangements, for the time being, until things are settled. If it doesn't suit . . .'

He had fixed on a neutral and businesslike tone, which deserted him. He shook his head, shaking off the awkwardness of the situation.

'But I'm sure it will. It will be quite all right.'

They were both slightly deranged by embarrassment. She looked for a place to stow the envelope, decided on the side table under the little Buddha which had always pinned down the incoming mail, and saw at once that it was a mistake. Too late to do anything about it.

They had worked their way through a conversation in which David asked permission to go upstairs to pack a few things for . . . Dad. Ella had in a voice thin with strain offered to help him. He had answered that it was just a few things as . . . Dad was living in a motel for the moment and didn't have room for much.

Ella was giving instructions for finding the large blue suitcase when Sophie came in from the hall, saying, 'Hullo. What are you doing here?'

David shouted, 'I'm bloody well not going through all that again!' and fled for the stairs.

Ella laughed the first laugh of the new season.

'He's packing a few things for your father, that's all.'

'It's such a minefield.'

Sophie was in her mature mood.

Martha came in from the kitchen, asked no questions and said 'Hi!' to Sophie.

'I'd like my drink now, please.'

'Martha, if this is going to worry David, acting as go-between, perhaps he shouldn't be doing it.'

'It would worry him more in the long run if he didn't. He can't turn his back on his father. It must have been a deadly lunch, though. He'll live, Ella.' She yawned. 'Oh, dear. I am so sorry. It's just . . .'

'We all feel like that,' said Sophie. 'I feel as if I'm carrying something heavy and I don't remember what it is. And then I remember.'

'I've made the salads. The steaks won't take long. Ten minutes. We can eat as soon as David's ready.'

Conversation was made over dinner.

Ella pronounced the salmon steaks delicious. Martha thought they could have been improved by parsley butter and asked how Sophie was enjoying her job.

'Wonderful.'

She spoke with enthusiasm but did not enlarge on the topic, asking instead, 'How's teaching?'

It was not the moment for Martha to enthuse about teaching.

David said, 'I've been taking a maths class. Filling in for Dombey while he's on sick leave. A bit of a change of pace. I'm enjoying it. I've just about got the kids convinced that I can function outside the gym and the sports ground and we're going well. I had to show off at first though, go through my paces.'

'They don't like it when you step outside your role,' said Martha.

How could Ella get the information she so much wanted without betraying her juvenile and deceitful behaviour?

Go carefully, play down that visit to the school.

'Are you ever sorry you didn't specialise in maths? Instead of cricket?'

David looked at her, bewildered.

'What has maths got to do with cricket?'

'The headmaster thought you were wasting your gifts, not taking four unit maths. He seemed to think you were sacrificing maths to sport.'

'When did all this come up? I didn't hear about this.'

'You were just about to set off for Sri Lanka. We thought you should make your own decisions.'

'I'm glad you've got your priorities right, Mum. And Dad thought that? Good for him.' He smiled, softened by surprise and pleasure, then cried, 'Oh, hell. I'm sorry, Mum.'

'I don't want you to hate your father, or think you can't mention him. Things are bad enough without that.'

She was now deeper in deceit.

'I'd have taken four unit maths like a shot, if Svenson had been taking it. And I am sorry I didn't.'

'I bet it was Crowe behind that, stirring the boss,' said Martha. 'Carrion Crowe.'

She shuddered with genuine horror.

From Martha the idealist, the reaction was shocking.

'I shouldn't have let Crowe put me off. It was my best subject and I enjoyed it. It would have taken less time than history, more effort but less time. I've always been annoyed with myself that I didn't do it.'

'Annoyed' was a mild word for the feeling in his voice.

'He was gone before my time,' said Sophie. 'What was up with him? Was he a flogger?'

'That sort of thing doesn't go on in schools any more, does it?' asked Ella, dismayed by the hideous word and its uglier meaning.

'Well, it's harder to get away with. I think it's worse in private schools – not the College. It's banned there. I checked before I took the job, of course. Though Pritchett has thought out a few penalties that seem remarkably like corporal punishment and the head lets him get away with it.'

'With Crowe it was mental torture,' said Martha. 'He'd pick your weakness and work on it to torment you. I was in his class for a year once and I've never forgotten it. There was a boy with a stammer.' She looked bleak. 'I still feel sick when I think of it. Guilty because I was just glad it wasn't me. I was safe, I was average. Besides. I was a girl. Mr Crowe,' she added with contempt and clear meaning, 'wasn't interested in girls. Saying to that poor wretched boy, "Control yourself. You must master your weakness. You are keeping us waiting. Do not waste our time with this mangling of the language, please." And all of us with our heads down, pretending it wasn't happening. I've been ashamed ever since, whenever I think of it.'

I'm the one who's joined the younger generation, thought Ella wryly. They've never talked like this in front of me before. She didn't find any great advantage in it. It was a loss of status and led to some very unpleasant revelations.

'I still should have faced up to it.'

'You were meat for Crowe. He was waiting for you. And

it wouldn't have worked. You'd have wasted so much energy in keeping your cool and not letting him get to you that your maths would have suffered in the long run. Crowe was malevolent. He meant harm. People who mean harm have it over the rest of us. They always win. The only thing to do is to keep away from them.'

So, according to Martha's view of the world, Ella had done the right thing for David. She was still not prepared to give up her own world view so easily.

'How do such people get away with it? That boy who stammered – why didn't his parents complain?'

Martha looked at her sadly.

'Where would he get the words to tell them?' She began to stack plates. 'Who wants apple pie? From the cake shop. Apple pie for everyone?'

'I'll help serve up,' said Sophie.

'Ice-cream in the top of the fridge, dear.'

They were all subdued by the ghost of the stammering boy, and ate dessert in silence.

Later, while David finished the packing upstairs and the women washed up, Martha said, 'It was David's looks. A very sore point, not to be spoken of. Crowe was known for bullying the goodlooking boys. Being the maths master he could always get at David; he'd been tormenting him for years, going over his papers, giving him punitive assignments whenever he lost five marks. It was all supposed to be for David's good, but the maths was just a pretext.'

Sophie said, 'Was he gay?'

'I don't know how much he knew about himself but he certainly had a special interest, like wanting an intimacy of hatred, if that was the best he could do.'

She hung up the teatowel, saying, 'Crowe was poison. Not to be taken.'

Ella observed how greatly the feelings she condemned as negative sharpened Martha's wits.

When the young people had left, Ella opened the envelope to which her thoughts had frequently returned during the evening. It contained a brief financial statement:

I shall make no further withdrawals from the current account and shall deposit . . . no, he couldn't mean three hundred dollars a fortnight, he must mean three hundred dollars a week . . . no, there it was . . . three hundred dollars a fortnight . . . *As you see from the enclosed statement, this is the sum which remains after deduction of* . . . well, he wasn't stinting himself in the matter of motels, certainly that was no fleahouse, meals and incidental expenses likewise. *This sum will be deposited for your exclusive use each fortnight, until a permanent settlement is reached.*

The tone was lordly, the offer was not.

What had she been expecting? Some sort of bonus for innocence? Some admission of guilt and penitence?

It won't be for ever, she thought. I can't fight him for money. He'll find some cheaper way of living than motels and restaurants, then things will be better.

That night was the worst one yet. She was a small boat spinning on a wild black sea; she clung to her pillow for safety, buried her face in it to muffle the whimpering of terror. What would become of her? She built up the face and destroyed it again and again without feeling either rage or relief, not even the fatigue which might have brought sleep.

At half-past 3 she got up, went downstairs and poured a large glass of port, took it back to the bedroom and set the alarm for 7. She must get up, shower, dress, make Sophie's breakfast and preserve a calm exterior, since the surface of things was all that was left. Then she drank the alcohol in one long, quick draught.

• VII •

At breakfast Sophie asked, 'Was that letter about money, Mum?'

Simple things like suitcases and socks had become almost unmentionable, while topics domestic convention had buried in silence were surfacing now. Sex was the main one, of course. What a barrier young people set up always against the thought of their parents as sexual beings. ('I can prove they did it twice.' 'Tried it once and didn't like it.') Though they didn't speak of it, how the children must be suffering from the picture of their father as a lover. Money, too, had belonged in the domain of silence. While she nodded at Sophie, she felt the awkwardness of the moment.

'How do we stand, then?'

She wished Sophie didn't say 'we' and she wished she didn't take comfort from it.

'We'll get by. It's just temporary. Dad's living in a motel and that's expensive.'

The word 'Dad' came with difficulty. She had felt she owed it to Sophie.

'I've been thinking I should pay real board. Twenty-five dollars a week is nothing.'

'It's what the others paid. We banked it for them and gave it to them when they married.'

Should she have told Sophie that? Would it add to her burden of bitterness? Perhaps she remembered the gift, so that to be silent would be worse. The fatigue of making decisions, regret for the world of birthday parties, engagement parties and shower teas which she had somehow allowed to slip away defeated her.

That face was sliding through her mind of its own accord. She had not called it up.

'Times have changed, Mum.' She added, 'Rob says to keep in mind that you can't see the final outcome of anything. What looks bad now might be in hindsight a good thing.'

'Yes.'

Her tone, however, was not affirmative.

When Sophie had left for work and the early morning tasks were done, she sat down at the kitchen table and began to write. It was lucky that he had set the tone. If he had written 'Dear Ella' she would have had to force her pen to a corresponding lie.

You will remember that when Caroline and David lived at home, they paid twenty-five dollars a week in board. By agreement I paid this money into a savings account which was handed over to them when they left home. I had begun a savings account for Sophie and I think it is important to continue the arrangement (considering that you haven't sent a word to her and seem to have forgotten her existence.) *but I cannot manage this on the fortnightly sum which you suggest.* ('Suggest' was a good touch.) *Will you give this matter your consideration, please, and let me know what you mean to do?*

She read the letter over, changed 'please' to 'Would you kindly', and copied it out with care. She was addressing the envelope to the Medical School when Pam came in.

'Money,' she said as she closed the envelope, and got up to start the coffee-making routine.

'More important than feelings, in the long run. Do you know how you'll stand? That is, if you feel like talking about it.'

'This is just a temporary arrangement, thank goodness. It isn't much. We'll eat and that's all. He's living in a motel and that's terribly expensive. It's Sophie.'

She shared the problem of Sophie.

'It's terrible, the way she talks about him. So hard-hearted, as if she despises him and has done for years. I don't want her stuck with a burden of hatred. If he'd just show a bit of concern for her – I can't tell him, I can only remind him what he did for the others.'

'Living in a motel. He'd better move out of there quick smart and find something cheaper. Wouldn't be a bit of spite in that, would there? Because you'd turned him out?'

'What was I expected to do?' she asked. 'Move over?'

As she drank her coffee, she reflected that there were different kinds of anger. That little flash was a good kind, blasting the disgusting, blossoming face out of her head.

'Oh, I sympathise, never fear. Ella, after all those years

as a surgeon, he must have money. He has to pay you proper maintenance.'

'There isn't as much money as you'd think. He took a big drop in income when he took the University job and he had to pay an enormous superannuation, joining the fund so late. He took out the maximum because it was security for the future and we'd paid off the house and didn't have many expenses. The investment account went down and he had some bad investments and lost money during the crash, but we were building it up again. I don't know exactly, but it's no fortune. His fortnightly salary is paid into a joint account and I draw on that for housekeeping. Money just didn't seem to be important. You don't expect a thing like this.'

'Well, the house should fetch a good price. Don't move too far away. I'd be devastated.'

Ella gaped with shock.

'Sell this house? I couldn't. I couldn't live anywhere else.'

(Why should I lose my house? I haven't done anything wrong.)

'What are you going to do, then? Get a job? Join the workforce? There's a lot to be said for that, not just for the money.'

Ella considered.

'If it came to that, yes, though I don't know what I could do.'

'I'd take you in with me but I couldn't let Enid go after all this time, apart from her being such a mainstay. There are plenty of things you could do. You have presence, intelligence, education – they're all marketable skills. I can see you as a saleswoman in a boutique, or better, a receptionist for a professional – '

'I must ask him to recommend me.'

Not a good anger, that one, a flick of spite, punishing Pam for her absurd idea about the house. Pam had flinched at it.

Ella said firmly, 'That was positively bitchy. I'm sorry.'

'Forgiven. I do think it would be the right sort of job for you. If I hear of anything, I'll let you know. I'll be off, then.'

'I do appreciate you, you know.'

Pam acknowledged the apology with a hand raised in blessing from the doorway.

The answer to her letter arrived promptly, three days later.

It was assumed that the original sum proposed would be adequate for Sophie's maintenance as well as your own. You are welcome to draw on the current account for your needs.

Ella wrote:

I enclose a statement of my daily expenses, which I hope will convince you that the sum offered is inadequate. I also enclose the electricity account, which arrived yesterday.

Sophie came home on payday and offered one hundred and fifty dollars for a fortnight's board.

'Seventy-five dollars is the going rate, they say.'

'I don't want to take it, Sophie. You should have the same advantages as the others.'

'I will not take his bloody money.'

'Sophie, don't talk like that. Don't swear. You mustn't hate your father, it's wrong.'

'Don't you be so bloody saintly, either.'

'I can hate as much as I please,' said Ella. 'That's different.'

She had made Sophie laugh, which was a relief. She accepted the money, with the private resolve to add it to Sophie's account.

The next communication read:

I have settled the electricity account and am prepared to take responsibility for gas, electricity, rates and all major expenses incidental to the maintenance of the house, except, of course, the telephone.

In your statement of weekly expenses, I note the inclusion of a dry-cleaning bill. Is this a normal household expense?

In rage, Ella wrote:

The sum you have offered is pitifully inadequate and a disgrace to your position and any shred of human dignity your recent behaviour may have left you.

You may be in a better position to meet your commitments when you find a less self-indulgent and less expensive way of living.

(How about getting that creature to cook your dinner instead of lording it in restaurants?)

She read this over with great satisfaction, then tore it up. It was beneath her dignity and, as Martha would say, counter-productive.

• VIII •

Routine was a frail net stretched over emptiness, ensuring survival, if nothing more.

Pam came in for coffee on Monday morning. Ella changed the day for Nina's lesson to Tuesday, to shorten the gap which stretched to Thursday evening, when David and Martha came to dinner, bringing fish and chips and cheerful conversation. On Sunday afternoons Max and Caroline came bringing Becky. Sophie seemed to bear her burden of hatred lightly, joking with David, playing with Becky, and spending Friday nights absorbed in working on the film script with Rob. .

After two meals from the Small Palace Garden, Ella began to make dinner for the film-makers. She could tolerate fish and chips once a week, but would go no further along that path. Besides, cooking filled in time, of which there was an excess. She did not admit to herself how much she wanted Rob's approval.

The script had now left the spider-keeping daughter for

the mother, who was obsessed by an album full of photographs, images of a divinely happy past. Mother was manipulative, brooding over the album, involving the daughter in an illusion of lost happiness (so leading to hatred and funnelwebs).

The photographs came to life as she talked. (This was called a voice-over.) They were supposed to have all the gloss and the false authority of a soft drink commercial.

Ella, who listened intently, measuring herself against the mother, looking for clues to her own failure, asked, 'How will the audience know it isn't true?'

'Ella, my love, you have reached the nub. I sometimes wish I was William and could just tell people what I want them to know.'

'William doesn't find it so easy,' objected Sophie.

'I suppose not. The other media always seem so much easier than one's own. Well, people get things on different levels. I'm aiming at an audience which despises soft drink commercials, I suppose.'

So much detail, thought Ella, like working away at some enormous jigsaw, but Sophie remained enthralled. Ella listened for the next nasty revelation of Mother's character, the next evidence of her own innocence.

Rob read dialogue onto tape:

'Darling, here we are with Daddy on the beach at Ulladulla. What a lovely holiday that was. You wouldn't remember it, you were only three. You dropped the ice-cream, I remember, just after I took the photo. You started to cry, but Daddy took you back to the kiosk to buy another.'

Rob abandoned her plaintive dreamtone to ask, 'How fast does a three-year-old walk?'

'I'll time Becky. She's three. She'll be here on Sunday.'

'Can you get me a video?'

'I think so. Max won't mind. He's crazy about photography.'

'Great. Leave it this week, then. I'll bring a tape next week.' She paused, embarrassed but amused, being after all sure of her welcome. 'That is, if you'll put up with me next week again, Ella.'

'Of course.'

'Say from your garden gate to the next corner, then pick her up and mime getting the icecream.'

'There won't be any miming about it, if I know Becky.'

'One icecream, to incidental expenses. Note it down.'

'I'll contribute the icecream,' said Ella, feeling quite ridiculously proud of the contribution.

'Right. That's it for tonight, then. I'll be off.'

She's a bright spot, thought Ella, watching her depart. I'm going to be really sorry when the script is finished.

• IX •

After their dinner of fish and chips on Thursday night, Martha and Sophie withdrew tactfully to the kitchen sink, leaving Ella alone with David, on the pretext of an extra cup of coffee, to give them the chance to talk privately.

Ella hadn't as yet taken advantage of the privacy to talk about the subject in her mind, but since the bank account was sinking dangerously, she was forced to mention money.

'David.'

He came to attention.

'Mum?' He smiled at her. 'Come on, spit it out.'

'It isn't easy, talking about money, but I have to. It's about Sophie. She's been paying full board since he left. She insisted, it's just a couple of fortnights, of course, and I accepted it, though I didn't want to. I didn't want to make a fuss, but I haven't spent it, I've gone on banking it for her. We did that for you and Caroline, remember, and gave it to you when you married. But it's got to the point – I can't really keep the house on what he's putting in the account unless I do use Sophie's money and I don't think it's right. I hate worrying you about this, but if he'd offer maintenance for Sophie, it would show he cared about her. I don't want her to hate her father. It isn't right. It's terrible to hear the way she talks about him.'

'She sounds bright enough.'

Sobered as he was, he smiled over Sophie's brightness.

'That makes it worse, that she can hate him and not worry about it. It seems so hard-hearted. But he isn't helping.'

'Have you written to him about it?'

'Yes, but he answered that he'd made allowance for that already. He doesn't understand how much it costs to keep a house. I suppose it's expensive, living in a motel and eating in restaurants and that's all he has to spare, but even if he cut into capital . . . he can't want her to despise him.'

'Dad isn't living in a motel. He hasn't been since that first week. He moved in with her but of course that wouldn't do. It was just a bachelor pad. Now she's managed to sublet it and they've moved into a bigger unit. I had dinner there last week. Alone. Martha isn't in to doordarkening yet. We're debating the issue. I think Martha has to support me. Why am I blathering on like this? Shock. Shock. I never expected this of Dad.'

'You never know, do you?'

She was terrified by her anger. It was like a tall, black wave rearing, threatening her . . . she could lose her footing, drown in it, and she never knew where it might be waiting to rise.

'Well, Max is right, after all,' David was saying. 'He

keeps on about getting a solicitor. There's a woman he knows who's good and isn't expensive. Mary Duckworth. What do you say, Mum? Shall I make an appointment with her?'

'It would take some of the weight off you.'

'I'll talk to Dad about Sophie, too. He must want to do the same for her as he did for us.'

'He always cared for your welfare. He never grudged you anything you needed.'

That orthodoncy had cost hundreds of dollars.

'You're a Trojan, Mum.'

You wouldn't say that if you could see into my mind. You wouldn't want to know me – that disgusting face coming and going like an advertising sign and not even doing its job – no discharge of rage any longer. If I found myself in the same room with that lying bastard I'd take an axe to him.

'Credit where it's due,' she said briefly. 'It's Sophie I'm worried about, not your father.'

'Some women would be trying to turn Sophie against him.' He added bitterly, 'This business of the money – it's not him, it's her. I'd swear to that. She's got him hypnotised. Oh, I'm never going to understand it.'

Remembering the tone of that one's communications, Ella doubted that he was under hypnosis, but if thinking so made it easier for David, he was welcome to the idea.

'I don't like asking you to do this.'

'Who else?'

Caroline, she thought. She would have expected Caroline to show responsibility, David to slide away with an amiable, apologetic grin.

No doubt, Max's relationship with that one . . . being

a colleague, made it difficult for Caroline, but she had never let personal considerations stand in the way of duty till now.

And Max was clearly sympathetic to her cause.

People were mysterious, even one's own children.

• X •

Pam knocked at the open door and walked into the kitchen, where Ella was carving fine slices from a piece of raw beef.

She looked up astonished and said, 'Friday?'

'It's slow at the moment. Enid's going to ring if she needs me.'

'Time for coffee, then? I could do with a break.'

'Thanks.'

Pam sat in her accustomed chair at the kitchen table while Ella set down the knife and filled the kettle.

'I thought I'd better warn you. The news is out. Official. Ursula Rodd was in last night looking for a semi-formal for one of her charity dinners. Sometimes I wonder about charity. She asked after you and I thought it was time . . . six weeks, isn't it? It must be.'

To Ella's changed expression she answered, 'Well, time flies, as they say.'

No, it doesn't. Time's a great heavy wheel that doesn't

move at all unless you turn it by hand, with effort.

Her change of expression had been caused by a different, ugly thought.

'I told her there'd been a marriage breakup. "Oh, they've separated, you know," I said, as if it was tired old news. I was crouching at the time, pinning up the hem of a midnight-blue crepe. She said, sharply, mind you, "I hope this doesn't mean she'll be giving up her charity work," then on and on about the difficulty of finding reliable workers and the burden falling on the few. I was trying to play it down, but I needn't have bothered. I felt like sticking a pin into her fat ankle.'

Six weeks. Six weeks and a couple of days. That was right.

Pam said angrily, 'Not a thought for your feelings.'

'I don't want her to think about my feelings. I'd rather she didn't know I had any.'

Anyone who went about for six weeks with a face – a hideous face like a great pink and purple orchid with two bulging eyes – blossoming and fading, blossoming and fading, like an advertising sign running in her head – such a person was mad.

'Are you going to?'

'Do what?'

'Give up on the charity work?'

I should have made a wax image. Then I could have thrown it away. Like giving a baby a dummy. Mum saying, when David was a baby, 'You can't throw a thumb away, you know.'

'It's lady-of-the-manor stuff, love, and you're not the lady of the manor any more.'

Ella set down a cup of coffee with unnecessary force,

so that the liquid slopped into the saucer. 'Sorry.' She set down an ashtray with controlled gentleness.

Pam said, in a subdued tone, 'You've never seen yourself as the lady of the manor. Not for a minute. Nobody could think it. You think too little of yourself, if anything. I only meant, you have yourself to think of now, can't go devoting yourself to noble causes.'

She couldn't tell Pam, to whom she could confide most things. You could say, 'I have a bit of a headache,' but you couldn't say, 'I have a touch of madness.' Perhaps there were other people walking about with madness in their heads, just as much alone with it as she was.

She set down her coffee. Pam had lit a cigarette and was smoking in silence. She looked for refuge at the pile of sliced beef.

'Kids coming tonight?'

'Sophie and her boss. This is a regular thing now till they finish their film script. I'm minding Becky this afternoon, so I'm getting dinner ready early.'

'Truly,' said Pam, 'I meant no offence. It was Ursula Rodd put the words into my head. There I was crouching at her feet like a labouring peasant while she talked about the burden of noblesse oblige. You aren't in the least like her. I never thought so for a minute.'

Ella was suddenly aware of Pam's distress.

'Oh, that's all right. I was thinking about something else, sorry. Maybe you'd better give up crouching.'

They both laughed, then Ella smiled at Pam's cigarette.

'I used to go about emptying the ashtray and squirting air-freshener and opening windows after you'd been here. I don't have to do that any more.'

'Pompous old killjoy. You're well rid of him.'

In the hall, the phone chirped.

'That'll be for me. Enid yelling for help.'

Ella went to answer it and called backwards, 'Yes, it's Enid.'

She had tested Enid's voice for any officious show of sympathy but heard only casual friendliness. That was a relief.

Pam called out 'Goodbye' and Ella came back to the empty kitchen, which looked all the emptier for its antiseptic air, being mainly white with touches of black, stainless steel and clear glass. Black and white tiles on the floor, white Venetians at the windows, no colour except in the covers of the cookery books ranged on a shelf above the white louvred door of the food cupboard and in the slices of beef which glowed like stage rubies on the cutting board.

They had modernised the kitchen in the hospital days and it looked like a hospital kitchen, but she had only herself to blame for the chill colour scheme, which now made her feel like a specimen under observation.

She rinsed the coffee cups and put them in the dishwasher.

I am never alone, she thought. I have my monster.

Now that was a mad thought. It seemed that, having admitted to madness, she was now prepared to indulge it.

Instead, she must fight it.

'It isn't always there,' she told herself as she picked up the knife and began to slice the beef again, acting carefully because of the troublesome nature of her thoughts.

What were the good times?

Things went better when the children were here, but

she couldn't say they banished the madness. There were always bad moments, chance remarks which threatened sanity or caused pain – but pain didn't matter, in this context. It was better than rage. Safer, at least.

Teaching Nina. The face never showed when she was teaching Nina, concentrating on a point of grammar or drilling a difficult sound. That brought a peace which outlasted the lesson, so that she came home serene, smiling over some advance in Nina's English.

It's because I'm in control, I'm running the show. Just as if I was driving the car. I'd be thinking about the traffic, not about . . . Oh, go away!

She put a slice of beef between two sheets of waxed paper and began to beat it flat with the heavy meat mallet, wishing she could reach the hideous face and beat it to pieces – not the real one, of course, but the advertising sign, so ugly and all her own work.

Her mother used to say, when Ella made a crab face, 'The wind will change and you'll stay like that.' And so it had and so she had, though it was her mind that was afflicted, not her face. She was astonished indeed at her own face and its power of concealment, though glad of it.

She hadn't had a car to drive since the event. He had driven off in it and that was that.

There must be other things.

This was a new kind of housekeeping – a dark cupboard without walls and cleaning equipment she had to find for herself.

The film.

The film was not a good thing. There it was. She enjoyed Friday evenings so much it was hard to admit it.

Friday evenings were good, Friday nights racked with the fury of outraged innocence as she compared herself with that cold, selfish, manipulative mother, entirely to the other's disadvantage. She would not, however, give up on the film, so there was no point in thinking about it.

Scenery?

If she had the car, she would drive to the shore and sit beside the sea. Even to evoke the rhythmic collapse of the waves and the salt breeze from the water promised healing.

Yes, she would try for the car.

At half-past 2, Caroline arrived with Becky. Seeing them together, Ella felt her usual pang at the contrast, Caroline the tall, perfectly formed classic beauty, exquisite in a short, white tennis dress, her fair hair smooth and shining, Becky dark, ruddy, rough-haired and short-legged. 'Doesn't take after her mother, does she?' was a frequent comment. 'Quite a different style of beauty,' was Ella's unvarying firm reply. But people must say that when Ella was not there, and would be saying it still when Becky was old enough to hear the unspoken 'What a pity!'

When Caroline was Becky's age, passers-by had stopped to say, 'Hullo, angel!' 'Where are your wings, angel?' And to Ella, 'That's a little angel you have there.'

It would have been better for Caroline, perhaps, if they had held their tongues. Indeed, her beauty had not brought Caroline much good. That did not prevent Ella from wishing the same gift for Becky.

Becky was so far quite delighted with herself.

'I brought my Textas, Grandma. I'm going to make you an enormous picture.'

'Now you be a good girl and don't tire Grandma. Are you going to kiss Mummy goodbye?'

If she grows up to call you Mother, you won't like it either.

That was an ungrateful thought, seeing that Caroline had undertaken a long drive to bring Becky, though she could have taken her to the tennis club, where other mothers brought their young children to play together.

'We'll come out to wave goodbye,' Ella said remorsefully.

She and Becky stood hand-in-hand watching as Caroline bent forward to turn the key in the ignition and looked towards them, raising her hand in farewell. Her beauty stabbed at Ella. It might be a dangerous gift, but who would ever refuse it?

'I'd better find you a very big piece of paper for your very big picture.'

'As big as the table?'

'As big as Sophie's baby table. We'll put it in the kitchen. I have to do some cooking.'

According to Max, it was a sign of artistic talent that Becky wanted to organise large spaces, though Ella wasn't sure what she organised them into. To Max, the placing of round-headed stick figures and wobbling box-like houses was the beginning of composition.

Installed on Sophie's nursery chair in front of the low table covered with butchers' paper, she set earnestly to work, looking like an enchanting miniature of a serious artist. Ella looked away from her cookery book to watch her tenderly.

'Grandma.'

'Yes, love?'

'What's divorce?'

In a sickening moment, the face came to life. The eyes stared at Ella, the tongue which was protruding helplessly under the attentions of the noose expressed conscious insolence.

No, no. It wasn't alive. Just a coincidence that it seemed like a comment, just an effect of the light.

She was saying, 'Married people getting unmarried.'

'What do they do that for?'

'Perhaps they don't like each other any more.'

Or one of them likes someone else.

The thought that there were further reaches of madness, that things might get worse and the repulsive monster she had created might come alive to torment her was terrifying.

And in front of Becky. In front of Becky.

'You're very fond of Grandpa, aren't you, Grandma?'

'Mmm. Would you like to make gingerbread men?'

'Like in the story? Can you make them?'

'You can eat them, too. That's why the gingerbread man was running away.'

'Suppose they run away and we catch them? We won't eat them then, will we?'

'They won't run away. That's only a story.'

Becky thought deeply, then opted for the real world.

'I can finish my picture later.'

Introducing Becky to golden syrup and other ingredients of disorder was either a cure for madness or a test of sanity. By the time the cakes were cooling, Becky unpinned from a tabard of teatowels and washed, the benches and the floor cleaned of cake dough and Ella with the icing gun was adding a wide smile and a waistcoat to a gingerbread boy with currant eyes and an almond nose, she did not notice whether or not she had an advertising sign running in her head.

Becky had found her compromise between reality and imagination.

'I shall take this one home and if he runs I'll chase him but I won't eat him.'

When she heard the car stop in the driveway Ella said, 'Here's Mummy coming,' with relief, but it was Sophie who came in with Rob, Rob sniffing the air and saying 'This house always smells delicious,' while Sophie ran to pick Becky up and hug her.

'I made a gingerbread man all by myself. I put on his eyes and his nose. Grandma just helped a little bit with his mouth.'

'It'll have to be your dessert. I was going to make pineapple upsidedown cake but we got involved.'

'Is that our standin?'

'I made a gingerbread man all by myself.'

Caroline came in before Rob got her answer. Becky struggled out of Sophie's arms to run to her. 'Mummy, I made a gingerbread man all by myself. Come and look.'

'In a minute, Becky.'

'Oh, this is my sister, Caroline Vorschak. Rob Tressider.'

Ella fetched the tray of beef olives and put it in the oven, thankful the oven was still hot.

'Vorschak? Does your husband lecture in Physics at Sydney? I think we have a friend in common. Tom Harrison?'

'Mummy!'

'Yes, Tom is a friend of my husband. Are you an artist, too?'

'Rob is my boss. She is making a film. Rob, don't forget to ask about the video.'

'Mummy, will you please come and see my gingerbread man?'

'In a minute, Becky.'

'In a minute. In a minute. In a minute. I mean now.'

Ella was muttering in the same tone, as she tried to plan vegetables for dinner, 'This is a three-ring circus.'

Sophie came laughing to pull Becky away from Caroline's skirt. 'Show me the gingerbread man. I haven't seen him yet. I haven't heard about that three-ring circus in years, Mum.'

Ella opened the oven door unnecessarily, to hide her face. Some thoughts were so sharp that they pierced flesh and became visible. It hadn't occurred to her till now that the three-ring circus had been happiness. Pain is good, pain is better than rage.

'A very good gingerbread man.'

Rob had rallied to the cause of the cooks while Sophie explained the purpose of the video.

'Grandma did the mouth. I'm going to take it home.'

'Well worth the trouble,' Rob smiled. Over her shoulder she said, 'It's not for display, you understand. I want to use it to pace a piece of dialogue.'

'Max won't mind at all.'

'Not he. Any excuse to play with the camera.'

'Good. I'll leave the tape here then, shall I?'

'Yes. I'll be off, Mother. Put your pens back in their box, please, Becky and say goodbye.'

Sophie was packing the artist's materials, with token help from Becky.

'I'll bring her out to the car.'

'Tough work, running a three-ring circus,' Rob said when they were alone.

She was tempted to unburden herself to Rob – *unburden* was a good word, unload her griefs, look for comfort, expose her misery. If *unburden* was a tempting word, *expose* was its corrective. Once she began confiding – and to Rob, whom after all she hardly knew, she might not be able to stop. She had to preserve that outer envelope which was her only defence.

'A bit tiring,' she agreed.

'I feel guilty for my part in it.'

'Please don't.' Ella spoke earnestly. 'I'm sure you're helping Sophie and I enjoy it, too.'

'I hope you're not being merely polite – though I don't think you would be. Polite but not merely polite.'

When Sophie came in and sagged into a chair, Rob added, 'I am about to make the unforgivable comment. You have a very beautiful sister.'

Unperturbed, Sophie answered, 'Yes, Carrie's not bad.'

'You have a son, too, Ella?'

Sophie answered the unasked question. 'That's David. He's the goodlooking one.'

'That's a relief. I thought on the law of averages he must be a misshapen gnome.'

Sophie accepted the implied compliment with calm.

It was Ella who felt uneasy, a feeling which reached Rob and silenced her.

'Dinner's late. I'm afraid.'

'We'll have time to do a bit before dinner, then. Come along, Rob.'

Alone in the kitchen, Ella poured herself a glass of sherry and sat down to face that frightening memory.

The face was blooming in her head still – fatigue made it tolerable, almost unnoticeable, but if there was worse to come . . . it hadn't really come to life, it had been coincidence that the face seemed to mock at the word 'divorce' – there was no comfort in that. She had no control over the thing. It could come to life to torment her and she would be helpless.

These were mad thoughts.

I could try to paint it. If I painted it and looked at it in the open, that might be the cure.

She was taken by a wild giggle, thinking of telling the face to hold still and pose for its portrait.

The giggle was madness again and madness in the outer world. Suppose Sophie came in and caught her giggling for no reason?

The painting would be externally visible, too, and would look like madness. Odd how therapy did often look like madness.

She would have to buy a box of paints. She would have to work in secret.

The thought of facing that hideous object made her feel queasy.

But I would be in control of the painting, that's the thing. If I can paint it and burn it, maybe . . .

The shrilling of the oven timer interrupted her thoughts, which left her with some hope of release.

Over dinner, disposing of beef olives and mashed potato with her usual speed and neatness, Rob said, 'About the softdrink commercial aspect, Ella – this is delicious. It certainly leaves Chinese takeaway far behind – about the colours of illusion, you know – there's the contrast, the final delirium is in the colours of reality, whatever they are. I suppose I'll have to take to black and white, though it's a bit of a cliché. What I want – replaying that beach scene, a grey man plodding beside a grey sea with tears on his face.' She chewed with relish while she contemplated this picture of misery. Right now I'm looking for a visual symbol of obsession.'

Well, thought Ella, I could give you one. Obsession. That was it.

'I've been thinking about white mice. They tie in with childishness and loneliness and the caged feeling. I'm fancying a white mouse on a treadmill. I see her sitting staring at a mouse on a wheel, running and running, getting nowhere.'

This, Ella understood, was the girl, not the mother. She had not identified with the girl before. She found the age gap embarrassing.

'Could you train a mouse to push a treadmill?' Sophie asked with the affectation of innocence which did not annoy Rob as much as one would expect.

'You mean an exercise wheel. They're still about. Thomas used to keep white mice and they had an exercise wheel.'

Obsession. She wasn't astonished at the coincidence. It was like hearing about a rare illness – you were bound to hear about two more cases in the next fortnight.

'The mice loved it. It wasn't like a treadmill.'

She did not think of mentioning how much she had disliked the mice.

'People have to love their obsessions, I suppose. Cherish them, at least.'

Much you all know about it, thought Ella, the expert.

'Do you want me to find out about exercise wheels? The pet shops will be open tomorrow. Morning at least. I could ring around,' said Sophie.

Except of course the telephone.

Rob had seen the shadow cross Ella's face.

'Keep a list of the calls then, so that I can pay you back.'

If only Sophie could meet a man like Rob, if such a man existed.

'If I find one, do you want me to buy it?'

Rob reflected and adopted the white mice.

'Yes. Okay. How's the property money holding?'

'It's all right.'

Silently, Ella made a sacrifice to friendship. She would endure the mice, so long as they were kept out of her sight.

Since the day had been tiring, the mother was not on the agenda and she had private thoughts to entertain, Ella decided to withdraw to the living room and watch television. She found an old English comedy starring Alec Guinness which provided competition for the face.

Though fatigue was no cure, it made it easier to co-exist with it in peace. She felt better, too, for the word 'obsession', as if being able to name the thing gave her some hold on it.

The film took over. She was absorbed in it when Rob and Sophie came in. They sat down quietly and watched it to the end.

'Not working late tonight?'

'It's turned into an absolute dog's breakfast. We're leaving it to settle. Sophie wants to ask you something. I'm not a party to it.'

'It's about William, Mum. You know, he's writing a

novel. It's all but finished but he's on a grant and the money's run out. Can he come and stay here? He could have my room. Anyhow, I've been thinking of moving upstairs, to be closer to you.'

'Why. Why, Sophie I don't know. I'd have to think about it.'

Sophie said to Rob, 'You're the one who's worrying about him. You know there isn't anywhere else. It wouldn't be for long, Mum. A month, maybe.'

'You can't be sure of that. He may get another brilliant idea and decide to rewrite the last five chapters. It's a shame. It isn't as if he's been roistering, too much the other way, if anything. He's been sticking too close to it.' Rob rubbed fingers through her hair and sighed. 'I've persuaded him to take a break. A friend of mine has lent him his beach house but he wants it for the school holidays and that's the week after next. He promised to leave the book alone and walk on the beach. If he does that he might be able to let it go. I'm pretty sure it's finished if he could just accept the fact.'

It was interesting to hear about the making of books, like going backstage at the theatre.

'They won't carry him at the place where he's living. It's hard, because he'd pay the back rent. He always pays his debts. Poor old William, he's clean, quiet and harmless. You'd think they'd give him a break. But there it is.'

Ella asked respectfully, 'Is he a close friend?'

'No. He's a poor sap but he might be an important writer. On the other hand, he might not. It's always a chance.'

'Mum, it would be good. I'll move up to Caroline's room and he can sleep downstairs and scare off burglars.'

Ella did not wish to think about intruders. It would be a score to the enemy if she allowed herself to be nervous. Nevertheless, the house, though it stood at the junction of two suburban streets, was screened by trees and isolated by the sloping terrain. The thought of having a man in the house was attractive.

Rob was laughing.

'Him? He'd interview them.' She took on an attentive expression and said, 'Have you been long in this line of work? Does it become routine? Are you satisfied with the financial return?' She added, thoughtfully, 'Perhaps his size would put them off. Like owning a big, mild dog.'

'I could go and spend a weekend with Laura. I don't feel like leaving you alone.'

Since it was Ella who urged Sophie not to lose her school friends, she saw that she was being manipulated. She liked the whiff of parental power.

'I suppose it will be all right.'

'Ella.' Rob endured an awkward pause. 'I don't want to intrude on your private affairs, but you are divorcing, aren't you? There's a property settlement in the offing?'

Ella nodded.

'Are you sure this is a good thing? There won't be any repercussions? Things can get very delicate, I know.'

'It will be quite all right,' said Ella, her mind now firmly made up.

'Well, at least you can't be expected to feed him. I'll lend him eating money.'

The mention of food had set Ella's mind to work.

'You don't want to be wasting money on fast food. Let me have sixty dollars and I'll see how far I can make it go. I'll clear a shelf in the freezer for him and cook some casseroles. Bulk chicken is the cheapest, but you can't expect a man to live on chicken.'

The silence was so deep that the two young women might have stopped breathing.

Rob said carefully, 'Could one specify male chickens?'

'They're still supposed to fight burglars,' Ella said drily.

Rob uttered a shout of astonished laughter.

'Touché! Touché!'

'And mince. Chili con carne is a cheap dish, if you use the dried beans.'

This was like being poor in London, when Bernard was doing his surgery exams – *The Pauper's Cookbook*, looking for bargains in the market. How happy she had been in the days when she had owned the future.

Sadness was all right – a salt wave washing the mind clean.

That was a strange thought, a strange image. It must be the company she was keeping.

'Pasta sauce. Does he like pasta?'

'He likes eating. I truly appreciate this, Ella. So will William. I can see that it makes sense, if you really don't mind. I'll send the money by Sophie.'

'I'll help. Mum. We can do a cookup at the weekend.'

'I'll be off. You look exhausted.'

'It's been a long day,' she agreed.

Planning cookery was such a simple thing, one wouldn't have thought of it as therapy, but it worked. If she could only find enough things that worked . . .

Revising recipes in her memory, she went peacefully to sleep.

• XI •

On Saturday it rained.

Sophie made telephone calls to pet shops and discovered that white mice were not popular in the district.

'They cause a population explosion,' one proprietor explained.

Ella thought of drowning baby mice and shuddered with revulsion.

That I will not do, she promised herself, and hoped the mice would be transients.

At last Sophie learnt of a pair of mice with cage and exercise wheel in a pet shop at Hornsby. She came into the kitchen disconsolate and stared through the window at the rain, which she had denounced already, since it threatened her plans for the video of Becky.

'If we had the car we could go to Hornsby and fetch them. Why should they have the car? She has her own car, I suppose. So they have two cars and you have none. Very self-righteous, too, about people using cars when they needn't.'

'Sophie, please don't talk like that. You know your father always practised what he preached. He took the train and the bus and I had the car all the week. There's nothing wrong with caring for the environment. We all should.'

But it's the grandparents who do that, she thought. Since Becky was born, she had shared his fears for the world in which the new generation would grow up.

'Mum, I wish that just once,' – Sophie was speaking through clenched teeth – 'you would stop being balanced and sensible. Why can't you get mad and throw something?'

Ella, who would not wish to get any madder, found it too difficult to explain that rage was her privilege, not Sophie's.

'David's seeing about the car. I think we'll get it back. I wish you wouldn't prowl, love. What do you want for lunch?'

'Is there any soup? It's a soup day.'

'David might run you to Hornsby. I suppose sport is off.'

Tipping a block of frozen pumpkin soup into a saucepan, she added, 'You watch the soup while I go and ring David.'

She did not like the errand, not only because of her dislike of mice. She had thoughts of Sophie sitting in front of the cage staring as the wheel went round. It would suit her present mood.

'I was about to ring you,' said David. 'I've got us an appointment with the solicitor. Wednesday at 2. Is that all right with you?'

'You're not taking too much time off work, are you, dear?'

'They're pretty good about that. I get credit for the out-of-hours stuff. It'll be all right.'

He was amused at Sophie's errand but willing to assist.

'She surely is wrapped in that job of hers, isn't she?'

Ella lowered her voice.

'A little too much, I think.'

David answered in a tone which shocked her with its bitterness, 'Half her luck!'

Was David unhappy? Could no appearance be trusted?

'About the car, Mum. It's in dock. It should be ready in a week or so. Dad's quite agreeable to your having it. I'll collect it for you as soon as it's ready.'

What sort of interview had they had about the money? It had at least been effective; though nothing had been said, the cheque account had received a substantial increase.

'Oh, that's wonderful, dear. It will make a difference.'

'See you in an hour, then.'

The rainy day was brighter for the arrival of David and Martha, though Ella had only a brief sight of them in the car, tooting the horn to call Sophie, who ran through the rain with her waterproof jacket over her head. Umbrellas were not part of Sophie's world.

When the young people had left, Ella took down cookbooks from the shelf and began to plan menus for the unknown William. How fortunate that she would have the car. She could buy in bulk. She made lists and calculated quantities, then strayed to luxury recipes, desserts that she had made and since forgotten, which she might make again. For whom? Herself and Sophie? Firmly, she closed the page and the topic and went back to the study of economy dishes.

She heard the young people laughing and talking on the garden path and opened the front door to them before they reached the bell. The rain had stopped; a late ray of sunlight had struck the garden, making raindrops glitter on the bushes.

Sophie looked happy enough now, walking with Martha behind David, who was carrying a cage shrouded in an old teeshirt. Sophie was carrying a carton, Martha two pizza boxes.

'The mice.'

David bowed, offering the cage to Ella, smiling widely at the absurdity of the errand.

Ella stepped back in haste.

'I suppose I should be thankful they're not funnelweb spiders.'

'This film is getting curiouser and curiouser. Where do you want them, young Soph? I think Mum wants them stowed out of sight. We brought pizzas, Mum. Is it all right to stay to dinner?'

'Of course.'

It was difficult in the light of his cheerful manner to take in the bitterness of his remark on the telephone, but she decided to open a bottle of the good claret, in case her ears had not deceived her.

When he and Sophie were upstairs installing the mice in the bedroom to which Sophie was migrating, and Martha was helping her to prepare salad in the kitchen, she said, 'David isn't happy in his job?'

'Oh, Ella!' Martha put down the carrot she was scraping and sighed deeply. 'That beastly sportsmaster! All the work David put in at College on remedial exercises, and it was really scientific, measured and tested. You know the wonderful results he got with the group he took through with his master teacher.' She said angrily to the absent sportsmaster, 'He graduated top of the year and they thought enough of his thesis to publish it in their journal. First of all, he said he wasn't going to have any clowning in his department and when David explained that the clowning was serious, he took the thesis to show him and the beastly man said, "Laughter therapy for the awkward squad. The awkward squad can smarten itself up quick smart and they'd better not try any clowning round here." He wouldn't even look at the thesis. He just humiliated David. He took that job because the school was supposed to be so progressive and he'd have a chance to do what he wanted, real physical education. He thinks everyone has the right to be at ease in his body, but all that lot think about is cups and trophies. They sneer at Speech Days and academic prizes and they can't see the inconsistency. Such intellects!' She picked up the knife and began to abuse the carrot. 'He doesn't mind coaching the teams, of course, and he likes to win, but he isn't allowed to do his real work.' She paused to listen. Talk and laughter were still sounding from upstairs.

'Couldn't he try another school?'

'He's very discouraged. He has this idea, you know, that he can't cope with people. Says he can handle kids all right but not adults. So he thinks it would be the same everywhere. I tell him it's all rubbish.' She tapped one finger. 'A, I don't think Pritchett qualifies as an adult.

He's not more mature than David, he's sillier. B, ' – she tapped a second finger – 'he's David's superior in an organisation where he has all the power, so nothing David did would make any difference. So it's commonsense to walk away, not weakness. I think he'll see it in the end and maybe go to a smaller school where he can run the department himself. What do you suppose they are doing up there?'

'Teaching a mouse to use an exercise wheel. Don't worry about them.'

'David's a real idealist, you know.'

Martha had given up preparing salad and was watching Ella slice tomatoes.

'About me, I'm not so sure. We seem to have gone wrong somehow. Everything seemed so straightforward, like adopting a Third World child instead of adding to overpopulation – it seemed like a responsibility, really. But now, I'm so jealous of Caroline, when I see her with Becky . . .' She shook her head. 'I'm wondering whether I was rejecting my own children because my father dumped me on my aunt. And never seeking money or power – but I burn when David is pushed around. Other people seek power all the time.'

'Do you think you'll have children then?' Ella kept her voice neutral as she bent to check the pizzas in the oven.

'I'm going to be a mean, vicious old woman if I don't. Ideals!' Martha said glumly. 'You have to know where they come from and what they cost and whether you're the type who can afford them. I'm afraid I'm not.'

This was cheering news for Ella.

'Well, that's the salad made. We'd better call them.'

'I haven't been much help.'

'I was interested. I'm glad you told me.'

David and Sophie came downstairs arguing about names for the mice.

'Mickey and Minnie! How corny can you get?'

'Don't get too attached to them, Sophie. You are going to have to give them up, you know.'

David raised his eyebrows.

'Are you making fun of us, Mother dear? Taking the mickey?'

'I wouldn't dream of it.'

Their eyes met, unsmiling.

How much I love him. I can't stand it if he's unhappy.

He was cheerful enough at the dinner table, ready to tease Sophie about the film.

'I never heard of a film that had a star part for a funnelweb spider. Are they going to audition?'

'Ass. It's a symbol, a visual expression of hatred. She keeps it in a jar and calls it Hannah. That's the father's girlfriend.'

A ghost visited the table. They gave it a moment's silence.

David said, 'Isn't this going to be dangerous? Playing about with funnelwebs.'

'I've been wondering that myself,' said Ella.

'It won't be a real one. There'll be a closed jar with a real one crawling but outside it'll be a fake.'

Seeing her so much in earnest, David had given up teasing.

'What about the mice? Are they a symbol, too?'

'It's the exercise wheel that's a symbol of obsession.'

That word again.

'I think that's good,' said Martha. 'The mouse running

and running, getting nowhere. Over and over again.'

Oh, Martha, please. But nobody can see inside my head. I can handle this, even when people talk about obsession. My face shows nothing. Nobody can see behind my face.

'I hope somebody explains it to the mice. More wine, Mum?' He refilled the glasses. 'What did we do to deserve the good claret?'

Ella shrugged. 'We might as well drink it.'

Pity again, damn it. Lowered eyes and pity. She couldn't learn to avoid such moments. She had to remember they were well meant.

Meanwhile, David must be rescued from embarrassment.

'If I'd had some old cooking wine, I'd have offered it.'

The idea of David as a lame duck was new but plausible. His amiable and flippant manner, which seemed to announce to the world that all things came easily and nothing was worth a stir, might well be a cover for disappointment and self-doubt. Do we all wear masks and send out deceiving messages?

It was becoming more and more difficult to trust in any appearance.

When she had got into bed, she considered her day with the monster. Had she made any progress? There were three stages: short spells of quiescence, even moments of peace in which it disappeared altogether, long spells where they co-existed reasonably well, and moments of crisis, when somebody mentioned obsession or some other cause of pain – nothing so bad again as that moment when the thing seemed to be conscious and mocking her. It had been coincidence, a trick of the light.

I am making progress. Things are getting better.

She was practising Pam's exercise against insomnia: five forward and two back, if you make a mistake, begin again at the beginning. One, six, four, nine, seven, twelve - five sheep jump forward, two jump back . . .

Sunday was fine, a day of mild autumn sunlight washed clean by the rain, a perfect day for photography.

They made the video. It was a more complicated affair than they had expected. Sophie and Caroline had to work hard to persuade Becky into the little walk with Aunt Sophie. Max, proud behind his fine camera, spent so long planning angles that Becky complained 'This is getting very boring,' and was threatening to walk off the set.

'For Pete's sake, Max, it isn't an artwork. We're only trying to time a three-year-old's walking pace,' said Sophie, but the artist in the photographer could not be denied.

It was done at last, Becky adding a note of realism by roaring for the icecream which had been for the moment forgotten. Ella ran to the refrigerator to fetch it, Becky accepted it with the abashed smile that followed tears, and Max insisted on filming that, too.

'It isn't as if we were going to keep it,' said Caroline, but Ella kept it for ever, though she never saw the tape. The picture of the two walking together, Sophie in yellow sweater and jeans, stooping towards stout, serious Becky in her best Sunday red and white, fluffy white Bunny bonnet, white jacket, red skirt and red tights, staring at her mysteriously important feet with unchildlike earnestness, the world glowing in the benign light of autumn - all this had a finished beauty which made it seem already filmed and stored away.

An ordinary day, but offering a promise of permanence.

Since the evening was cool, Ella had lit the gas fire in the living room, where she and Sophie were watching television, Sophie intently, Ella with some attention for the sweater she was knitting for Becky.

The doorbell chimed.

'I'll go, Mum,' said Sophie without stirring, her eyes fixed on Geraldine Doogue and the visiting feminist she was interviewing.

'That's all right, dear.'

Ella put down her knitting and went to open the door to a stranger with a strangely familiar face.

She said, 'You've changed your hairstyle.'

Louise stared at her, so taken aback that she forgot her script and had to pause to recover it.

'I have come to collect some papers for Bernard. Since he seems to be barred from entering his own house.'

'Oh.' Ella stood back from the doorway. 'Come in, then.'

She was considering with interest the news that that person thought himself ill-used.

'While I am here, I think I should collect all the documents from the file in his study. Then I shall not need to intrude further.'

There was no guide to conduct in this situation, no book of manners to refer to.

Sophie had come to the living room door and was gazing at Louise with a malevolence that made her face hideous. Ella looked at her in horror, thinking, 'Rob should have – shouldn't have – ' It had all been a mistake. Sophie looked well able to put a funnelweb spider into a shoe. She went back into the living room and shut the door.

Louise, too, had been gazing at Sophie. She said shakily, 'Do you think it right to teach somebody to hate?'

Ella examined this outrageous remark and selected one of many answers.

'I don't discuss you with Sophie. I don't discuss you at all.'

Louise reddened and made for the stairs. Ella moved fast to intercept her, got to the stairs ahead of her, climbed backward up three steps and stood guarding the approach to the upper floor. Memories of Hollywood films, visions of costumed heroes brandishing rapiers did not deter her. They did not even embarrass her.

'There's nothing upstairs.'

Louise stood disconcerted.

'Bernard told me that all his papers were in the small room on the right at the head of the stairs.'

It was clear that she hadn't expected to be dependent on Ella for information.

'Everything has been moved into this room.'

Ella opened the door of the small study and stood back.

'There are empty cartons in the laundry if you need them. That is the last door on the right.'

Louise cried out, 'Civilised people don't behave like this. They . . . they communicate. They have rational discussions. Turning a man out of his own house . . . it's not civilised.'

'What is there to discuss?' asked Ella.

Well, that must be right. That must be the thing to say. She could remember it from at least half-a-dozen films.

An astonishing thing was happening. She was feeling

a growing elation. Absurd. How could she be happy? Where did this lightness come from, this relief?

The face was gone. Gone for good.

Louise walked down the hall to the spare room, Ella went back to the living room where Sophie was glaring sullenly at the admired Geraldine.

'It's all right. It's all right. She's only fetching some papers.'

She uttered this nonsense in a soothing tone.

'I didn't imagine she was moving in.'

Ella murmured, 'Darling, don't hate. Don't hate. You'll damage yourself, not them.'

'I'd damage them if I could.'

Ella wished she could communicate her own joy to Sophie.

'It makes it worse for me if you suffer for this.'

'That's emotional blackmail.'

Her face softened, however, and she looked with friendlier eyes at the screen.

'You're being saintly again, Mum. It's too much.'

'I don't feel saintly. I'm glad you moved that stuff downstairs.'

Sophie nodded.

'She was all set to go upstairs, was she?'

'I think I looked like Douglas Fairbanks Junior daring her to advance one step.'

Effort rewarded. Sophie began to grin at the image.

Ella had left the door of the living room open. They watched the screen in silence till they heard the front door open and close.

'Lovely manners,' said Sophie. 'Could have put her head in and said goodbye.'

'Thanks for having me.'

'It's been a pleasure.'

They laughed at the little exchange, Ella on such a joyful note that Sophie looked at her in astonishment.

She sobered then but remained joyful.

No more obsession. Her mind her own again. Never to be mad again.

• XII •

The prospect of having David as escort made Ella look in the glass and decide to have her hair done.

This was unexpectedly difficult.

She had slept deep and peacefully and woken with relief to an uncluttered mind, but found now that she had expected too much of sanity; it had brought with it a lassitude which made picking up the telephone and fixing an appointment with the hairdresser a formidable task.

Come on. She had only to check the number in the phone index, lift the handset, press seven numbers, wait, say, 'Ella Ferguson here. Can Lilian give me half an hour today or tomorrow morning? I know it's short notice . . .'

She mastered the task, one step at a time, found that Lilian could fit her in at 3 o'clock, and was remarkably cheered to find that people were still getting their hair done in a world where things went on as usual.

The next call was easier.

'Pam, I need a new outfit. Do you have anything that would be suitable for a visit to a solicitor?'

'Oh.' From the heartfelt tone it was clear that Pam had been waiting for this moment. 'I have the very thing. It's been hanging in the stockroom since the new season's stock came in. I wouldn't put it out on the rack. I'll be down with it in ten minutes. If it won't do, you can come back to the shop with me and try on a few things, but I'm pretty sure you'll like it.'

Pam arrived twenty minutes later with the promised outfit sheathed in a drycleaner's bag and draped over her arm.

'It's a two-piece, cardigan top and straight skirt, medium weight, but you could put a skivvy under it for winter. Just your shade of blue. When I unpacked it, I saw you in it straight away. Don't you love that braid?'

Meanwhile, she was unsheathing the prized object and holding it up to view.

'It's beautiful,' Ella agreed. 'How much?'

'Eighty-five.'

'Don't lie to me.'

'Cost. Oh, come on. Let me do it just for once.'

'Well, thank you. Just this once, mind.'

Watching as Ella tried on the new outfit, Pam said, 'I'm sorry for the occasion, but there's a lot to be said for a new dress when you're down.'

'I don't want to shame David. He's taking time off work to go with me.'

'You may be unlucky in other ways,' Pam said with a note of sadness, 'but you're certainly lucky in that son of yours.'

'Your turn will come,' said Ella. 'Wait till you're a grandmother. It's sheer joy.'

'You look very nice, Mum,' said David as she stepped into the car. 'Is that new?'

'Yes. So do you look nice.'

'I was sent home to change into my gent's suiting. The head approves of dutiful sons.'

There was an undertone there.

'So do I,' said Ella, with a different undertone.

Starting the car, David gave her a sidelong look and a meaningless wink which she took as an expression of embarrassment. He would have to put up with that. There were things that must be said when the chance came.

When he had stopped for the first red light, he spoke with his eyes still fixed on the road ahead.

'Mum. About the car. Dad crashed it. I don't think it was so very bad, nobody was hurt.'

Ella was thinking, furiously, If it was that day, don't tell me. I don't want to know.

David was not eager to tell anything.

'I don't know the details because I don't like to ask. I couldn't understand at first why Dad was being so cagey about the car. It was always yours, to use at least. I couldn't believe that he meant to keep it. Then she . . . Louise told me not to go on about it.'

It was that day and she blames me, thought Ella without pain.

'I should have told you before but it's all too embarrassing. It shouldn't be long now. We should have it back next week.'

'A lot of things are embarrassing.'

'You're not wrong, you're right,' he answered, as they travelled on in a shared silence.

There was nothing wrong with Mary Duckworth. It was not her fault that the interview proved so depressing.

She was a tall, blonde woman with a small waist and a handsome, bony face which bore marks of honourable wear and so appeared pleasantly shabby, like her office. She had, too, a look of sympathy felt and withheld which set Ella, after the first moments of wretched exposure, almost at ease. She accepted without surprise Ella'a ignorance of financial affairs, saying only, 'I'll have the necessary searches made and get back to you.'

It was David who appeared to be diminished by the situation.

'I'm the one who wants the information. I'm . . . I want to represent Mum in the negotiations. I can let her know what's going on. You understand . . .'

But what Mary was supposed to undersand, he could not say. He seemed to be searching for words in a way that was quite unlike him.

'Does the other party have legal representation?'

'No. Not so far. Dad and I . . .'

Should he be saying 'Dad' or 'My father'?

The question was plain on his face. Ella suffered for his embarrassment.

'We think we can work it out together, but I have to know what Mum's legal rights are and how much we can expect.'

'I see.'

One could not guess what Mary Duckworth saw when she looked at him. It was the moment when he should be showing confidence and authority, but they were not visible.

'So I get back to you and you report to Mrs Ferguson.'

'That's right.'

She said to Ella, who seemed to be the other half of an odd pair, 'I'll get you to sign a fees agreement and I'll be in touch.'

When Ella had signed her name to the document, the interview was over.

David drove her home wearing an expressionless calm which indicated deep depression. Was he humiliated by his appearance as mother's boy? Dutiful son?

But I couldn't be expected to face those creatures myself, she thought.

Martha had said, 'He would feel worse if he didn't do it.'

It came down to right and wrong again. If doing the right thing made him look rather silly, tied to his mother's apron strings, that discomfort would pass.

There were so many causes for depression that his silence required no comment.

• XIII •

Caroline rang on Tuesday morning to say that she wouldn't be bringing Becky next Friday.

'You looked so tired last week, Mother. I don't think it's being fair to you. It's no trouble to take her with me. She enjoys playing with the other children.'

'But I really like having her.'

Ella knew there was little use in arguing with Caroline when she was acting for one's good.

'It really is too much for you,' she said firmly. 'You should think of yourself more.'

Ella mastered disappointment and said brightly, 'See you Sunday, then.'

There was a pause in which she grew nervous.

'I'm sorry. We really can't make it on Sunday. There's a family party for the Vorschaks, for their golden wedding. You do understand, don't you? We have been neglecting them. I feel quite guilty about it.'

'Of course, dear.'

As she put down the phone, she thought sadly, I am no longer interesting.

It was bound to happen sometime. They had their own lives to lead, after all. Twelve whole days without Becky – Sophie wasn't going to like that either.

David brought the car on Wednesday afternoon. He parked in the driveway and tooted the horn, while Martha, who had followed in the old Holden, stopped in front of the house and came to join him. Ella hurried out beaming, greeted the car with love and refrained from stroking the bonnet.

'We're here too, Mum.'

Ella reached up to kiss his cheek.

'I'm glad to see you. I want to talk to you about Sophie.'

David and Martha stared at each other.

'So do we. I'll put the car away, you go and start the coffee, eh?'

Martha came with Ella to the kitchen and got down cups and saucers in unusual silence. There was no conversation until David came in and they had cups of coffee in front of them.

'You first, Mum.'

'I was hoping you'd talk to your father about Sophie. Ask him to make some sort of gesture, take her to lunch or write to her, tell her he misses her – something. You've no idea how bitter and hostile she is. He has increased the maintenance. That's all right now. But she says she doesn't want to take his money. He just has to make an approach, show her he loves her . . .'

'I don't quite see Dad doing that, Mum.'

Martha said, 'Men of your father's generation were

discouraged from showing emotion. That was one of the evils of sexism. Women weren't supposed to think and men weren't supposed to feel.'

'He seems to have picked up the knack.'

David, too, sounded bitter and hostile.

'You don't understand how bad this is. If you'd seen how she looked at Louise . . .'

'When did she see Louise?'

'Oh, that's nothing. She called in to get some papers.'

She noted with surprise that indeed it was nothing.

Martha muttered, 'What nerve!'

'It was the way Sophie acted, the way she looked at her. I didn't think Sophie could look like that. I don't care how hard he finds it, it's his responsibility and he has to face up to it.'

'Yes, Mum.'

David's thoughtful expression reminded her that she had never been so bold when the man was in residence.

He added, 'I'll talk to him about it,' in a tone which promised nothing.

'I think it's one reason she's so obsessed with this film. She's neglecting all her school friends. She isn't acting her age at all.'

Again, there was an exchange of glances.

Martha's eyes said 'Now' and David's 'Yes'.

'That's what we wanted to talk to you about. Sophie's boss – that's Roberta Tressider, the film woman?'

'Yes?'

'Mum. She's a dyke.'

'I thought that was a sea wall in Holland. There was a story about it in the school reader, the little boy who put his finger in the hole in the dyke.'

David answered in a controlled voice, 'Not little boys, Mum. Little girls.'

Martha said angrily, 'Don't make fun of your mother. You shouldn't have used that awful word. If you mean lesbian, say lesbian.'

'All right. Calm down. I'm embarrassed, talking to Mum about sexual perversion. But we thought you ought to know.'

Ella could no longer refuse the message.

'I knew, whatever it was, it wasn't a sea wall in Holland. I just didn't want to know.' She added sadly, 'She's so nice.'

'There's nothing against a lesbian being nice,' said Martha.

'Are you sure?'

'Yes. Max knows a friend of hers and he told Max. There's no secret about it. She lives with this woman poet, they're quite open about it.'

'I don't know what I can do about it.'

David was shocked.

'But do you think you should have her here around Sophie?'

Ella paused, as if for reflection, then said, 'I'm sure she'd never harm Sophie.'

'She wouldn't think it was harming her.'

Moral decisions. She had thought she was done with them. You did your best and then wondered for the rest of your life if you'd done the right thing.

No help for it. Here she went again.

'If I'd known in the first place, I suppose I wouldn't have encouraged her to come here, but it's too late now. I can't do anything about it now.'

And Rob wouldn't do anything to hurt me.

'But Sophie's at risk!'

'I don't suppose it's catching.'

'I don't think this is a matter for joking, Mum.'

'If it was a man . . . say a married man, I'd have questioned it, bringing him here. If it was her boss and a married man, yes, I'd have objected. But I'd have asked. That's it. I'd have seen to it that she knew the situation, if he was hiding a wife – I can see, I did take her on trust and I suppose that was a mistake. However.'

Martha was changing position.

'They see each other at work, David. If Ella says she can't come here, it's the old story of forbidden fruit, isn't it? Ella will be worrying whenever she comes home late.'

David looked sulky.

'This isn't a debate. All I know is, Sophie's at risk. The woman's her boss, it's a power position. Having her here is like giving approval, condoning it. Mum,' he said with anguish, 'how would you feel if Sophie went that way?'

'It's Sophie's risk,' she answered wearily. Moral decisions were a tiring business. 'I can't face it for her.'

Martha had been following the same train of thought. Did Sophie love that job so much that she could . . .? It was up to Sophie.

'Plenty of women have to leave their jobs because the boss is a chaser. And probably men have trouble with women bosses, too. It's not a matter of being male, female or homosexual, it's a matter of being a chaser. And if she is, I don't think she'd be coming to this house,' said Martha.

'She's a bit young to be alone with it.'

'She'll be nineteen next month. You wouldn't have

thanked me to be choosing your friends for you at nineteen.'

'That's different.'

The two women started at him and said in unison, 'In what way?'

David looked from one to the other and retired into dignified silence.

'All I can do is make sure she knows the situation. I'll ask her about it when she comes home.'

David looked at his watch.

'I suppose that won't be long. We'd better be off. No point in our being here and mixing in.'

'She'll have to know where the information came from.'

'Yes.' said Martha. 'Tom Harrison to Max, to Caroline, who rang me yesterday.'

There was something in Martha's tone as she spoke Caroline's name which made Ella uneasy. But Martha had confessed she was jealous of Caroline.

'I'm with you, Ella,' Martha said as they were leaving. 'I think you are taking it the right way.'

'Thank you, dear, and thanks for bringing the car.'

She could not thank them for the information.

Ella was checking the casserole in the oven when Sophie came in by the kitchen door and dumped her shoulderbag on to a chair, saying, 'What's for dinner, Mum?'

'Chicken and mushroom. Sophie, did you know Rob was a lesbian?'

Sophie stood for a moment absolutely still, then relaxed and said, 'Yes. I know she is and she knows I'm not. Okay?'

Ella nodded.

'So long as you know.'

'It's no secret.' Sophie relaxed further, moved her bag to the floor and sat down. 'She lives with this woman poet who gives her a pretty bad time, I think. Not that she'd talk to me about it, of course.'

This was the awkward moment.

'You don't think . . . you don't ever get the idea that she might have designs on you?'

Ella was embarrassed. Sophie shouted with laughter.

'Good Lord, no.' Then she sobered. 'I just did feel a bit uneasy about the shirt and the necklace from Hong Kong. And she must have seen it, for she said, "I'm not courting, dear. It's just a thank you for all the overtime." I felt very silly, I can tell you.'

'No need to feel silly. You were quite right to be uneasy and to show it.'

'Well, she put me straight on that and I don't think she took it wrong.'

A less personal present might have been a more suitable thank you for overtime.

'Don't leave your bag and your boots there, dear.'

Sophie pushed the objects under her chair.

'I'll take them up when I check on the mice. I'm glad you know, Mum. I didn't like to tell you because it seemed like making too much of it. But I'm pretty sure she likes to come here to work because it's such a bad situation. They say this Liz is so jealous she makes Rob's life a misery. She comes here to work in peace.'

'Don't be too trusting, Sophie.'

'Look, she's a wonderful boss and brilliant and I'm learning so much from her. And I don't think about the other thing. It's messy and tragic and I'm sorry about it. Apart from that it isn't my business.'

How odd that lesbians could torment each other just like normal married people.

Sophie picked up her bag and her boots.

'Don't be too long. Dinner's about ready.'

'Ten minutes.'

At the table, Sophie said, 'Speaking of Rob, she gave me the sixty dollars for William's food. Many thanks and let her know if it isn't enough. William will be here next week, maybe next Wednesday. I'll get the room ready at the weekend.'

'I forgot to tell you the car's back. David brought it this afternoon.'

'Great. And the information about Rob? I thought it was probably Caroline.'

'She rang David.'

'How very odd.'

'They can't help being worried about it, you know. David is most upset.'

Sophie frowned over this and chewed in silence.

'You can tell him it isn't catching.'

Ella looked back at the argument and said with astonishment, 'As a matter of a fact, I did.'

Sophie smiled broadly.

'Good for you, Mum. I'd like to have seen his face. Getting very narrow-minded, the old David.'

Her smile became a private chuckle.

'What are you laughing at?'

'Mum, if Rob was prospecting, it wouldn't be for me, it'd be for you.'

'Sophie!' Ella gaped and blushed, not finding words to comment on that insanity.

'Fact. She thinks you're marvellous. She said Dad must have a head full of sawdust to give up someone like you. Which is the utter truth, of course.'

'That's very kind of her, but it doesn't mean what you're making of it.'

'Watch your step, that's all,' said Sophie with an air of deep solemnity.

'You are being absurd.'

She smiled, however, with pleasure at Rob's praise, while Sophie giggled at her own daring.

Ella woke sharply at 3 in the morning to a voice saying, 'You can't go by the look of things. You can't take anything on trust. You thought David was happy. You thought that one was faithful. You were fooled. The way Sophie acts with her, sunning herself . . .'

Another voice spoke, reasonable and calming, 'She's just proud of being part of something important.'

'How much does she have to do with the script? She's the messenger, the property girl and the listening post.'

Her dislike of the mice surfaced as a small, live grievance.

'Perhaps a listening post is important. She may be listening and learning. You've always wanted her to show more ambition. She isn't fooling herself. She says Rob comes here to work in peace.'

'Doing research. Working in peace. That's the sort of thing you fall for every time. You've encouraged her, cooking special dinners, taking in mice – you couldn't have stopped it but you didn't have to encourage her.'

Summoning up faces was a dangerous pastime, but when Rob's face came to her mind, all doubts vanished, until the voice began again, 'You can't go by appearances . . .'

There was no reason for this debate ever to finish.

She looked at the clock radio: twenty to 5. She had remarked before how quickly the time passed when one lay awake and worried. One would have expected the opposite.

'I'll talk it over with Pam. I'll go and have lunch with Pam.'

She had the car. A helpless woman worrying about her daughter, a woman with a car worrying about anything – the difference was subtle but immense.

She went back to sleep.

• XIV •

Over salad at Dino's, Pam listened attentively and endorsed Ella's daytime judgment, which was what Ella required of her.

She asked, 'What does she look like?'

Ella was startled.

'She doesn't have a moustache!'

'You're fond of her, aren't you? Yes, that was a funny thing to ask. It's just that I don't think I've ever . . . well, there were two teachers at school . . . when I look back, I realise. We thought they were weird, but we didn't know why. Miss Roach did look weird. Now I think about her nickname – children are cruel little beasts. I know I'm lining up with Queen Victoria, but I've never really known what they do.'

'I don't want to know what anyone does, not in detail.'

Like going through the motions with your stupid wife once a fortnight, all the time thinking about someone else. That was respectable?

Remembering what a disagreeable experience madness had been, she averted her thoughts with haste.

'I wonder how it would be, if one of one's children – an only child would be worse – how would I feel if Thomas turned out homosexual?' She added thoughtfully, 'If he is, he's putting up a marvellous front.'

Ella's night thoughts were surfacing.

'Don't think I haven't thought of that. She's nearly nineteen and where are the young men? Not one in sight.'

'I used to wonder that myself, at nineteen.'

'But she doesn't even seem to be wondering. Suppose this business with her father has put her off men? One minute I think, she never played with dolls, she imitated David in everything, the next I think, she's so fond of Becky and so good with her. Then I ask myself what that proves. Last night, 3 in the morning was not a good time, I can tell you.'

'Oh, 3 in the morning. You never want to believe what you think at 3 in the morning.'

Ella was aggrieved.

'I never expected any trouble with Sophie. She was so cheerful and so uncomplicated, loved the Girl Guides, always had good reports – the only worry she ever seemed to have was getting into the hockey team. "An excellent team member in every sense." That was the principal's comment on her final report and I thought it really summed her up.'

'Shouldn't have got those bands off her teeth.' Sensing that she was not showing enough sympathy, Pam added, 'Look, if this woman, whom you like, had designs on Sophie, she wouldn't be coming to your house. That's a good sign.'

'She's so proud of that job, like a boy with his first long trousers.' Ella sighed. 'Things were simpler once.'

'Simpler but not better,' said Pam with bitter reminiscence. 'You like her. I trust your instincts. You don't often make mistakes about people.'

'I might have thought so once. I never will again.'

'Adultery is a special case. For all that, you are looking better. More like yourself.'

How could she express the joy of being sane again, after being mad? She was conscious of peace at every moment. No matter what worries came, even at 3 in the morning, they came to a sane person. You can't know what sanity is till you lose it, she thought, knowing that she would be changed for ever by the experience, thinking how little sympathy she had felt for people who suffered all their lives from things much worse than the nagging little misery of a haunting face.

'It's good to have the car again. I tried not to fuss, but I hated being without it. Now I can shop where I like and come out to lunch with you now and then.'

She would drive out to the markets, looking for mushrooms and cooking tomatoes for William.

'I'd hate to be without a car. I'd feel as if my wheels had fallen off. Frightening, isn't it?'

'I'm not worrying about the environment at the moment. I'm having enough trouble with my own.'

The weight of trouble had lifted, however. She looked forward to the afternoon. Four wheels and a shopping list – it didn't take much to make her happy.

It was disappointing not to be seeing Becky on Friday and to miss the Sunday visit, too, but she and Sophie would fill the time with cooking.

I never really worried about Sophie, she admitted in her daylight mood. I was going through the motions, doing my duty as a mother.

Life was liveable. Liveable, at least.

Setting the table for Thursday dinner and listening idly for Sophie's arrival home, Ella heard her voice in the hall. She must have come in by the front door. That was unusual.

Sophie was standing with the receiver in her hand, saying into the mouthpiece, 'If you want a good look at a pervert, go and look at yourself in the glass.'

She put the phone back in its cradle and turned away to see Ella at the door of the dining room.

'What was that, dear?'

Whatever it was, it had made Sophie very angry.

'Just a nuisance call from a freak, Mum. Nasty.'

'I didn't hear the phone.'

'I'd just come in. It had hardly begun to ring when I picked it up.'

Ella understood that Sophie was lying, and no doubt Sophie knew that Ella knew it, but she was serving notice that she didn't intend to explain further.

'Oh, I see.'

She played her part dutifully, thinking, whatever the trouble had been, Sophie had handled it with admirable firmness.

The fish and chips dinner was not as lively as usual. After ten minutes or so, David said irritably, 'Cat got your tongue, young Soph?'

Sophie set down her knife and fork, gulped and spoke.

'That was Caroline on the phone, Mum. She rang me at work and I couldn't take the call, so she left a message for me to ring her back. I knew she meant me to ring from work but I wasn't going to let her pick her own time. I had a fair idea of what she was going to say. She can't bring Becky to a house where she might be exposed to meeting perverts. Meaning Rob. So unless you tell Rob she's not to come here again,' Sophie's voice shook, 'goodbye Becky.'

Into the silence Martha said quietly, 'The sterilised needle.'

Sophie had swallowed her tears.

'Of course it's up to you, Mum, and I shouldn't have said what I did. I was too mad to hold my tongue.'

Ella, too, had stopped eating. She was thinking how shortlived her expectation of happiness had been.

Martha said, 'This is incredible. What possible harm could Roberta Tressider do to Becky? She's a lesbian, not a paedophile.'

Though stupid with shock, Ella still had room for the passing thought that she could never have expected to hear such a remark at her dinner table.

'I don't suppose Caroline knows the difference,' said Sophie with easy contempt. 'What do you want me to do, Mum? Do I tell Rob she's not to come again?'

Ella had thought before that once you say goodbye to convention, all you have left are right and wrong, a very slippery pair. The three were watching her. She could see what importance they were placing on her decision.

She said with difficulty, 'No' and repeated, 'No.'

'Oh, good for you, Ella,' said Martha.

'You understand, Mum,' said Sophie with forced

humour, 'that if I join the sisterhood, your name will be mud forever.'

This drew a shamefaced grin from David.

'She can't mean it,' said Martha. 'She can't be serious. She won't carry it through.'

'Oh, yes she will,' said Sophie bleakly, and to Ella's horror David nodded agreement.

'But Becky.' Sophie's poise didn't hold. She said wretchedly, 'How can we live without Becky?'

Ella thought, you are doing this to me, Carrie. How can you do this to me?

'Things are never so clearcut,' said Martha. 'There's Max. He's too civilised to go along with this. And what about Becky? Think how she'd fret for Ella.'

'Oh, yes. And that will make Caroline very, very unhappy, but it won't change her mind. She'll never give in.' Sophie spoke calmly, from experience. 'And Max does everything that Caroline wants.'

The thought of Becky's fretting had cut like a knife.

'She is probably thinking of Becky, you know.'

'Oh, yes, Mum,' said Sophie piously.

'You must stop this, Sophie. You mustn't talk like this about your sister.'

However, she could not check her own thoughts. She went on contemplating with horror the cold and settled dislike that had lain under the calm surface of the household. The children had never quarrelled, at least in her hearing.

If she had heard them, she would have stopped them, of course. It was only now that she had lost authority and become a victim that all this emerged.

They hadn't been close – well, Sophie had hero-worshipped David but that hadn't been friendship, because of the gap in age – they had gone their own way, had their own friends and so far as she had known had co-existed in peace.

Their parents hadn't quarrelled either.

'Eat up, Mum. Your dinner's getting cold,' said David.

Ella ate a mouthful of fish.

'How long,' he asked Sophie, 'does it take to write a film script?'

'I don't think that's the point,' said Ella, painfully. 'David, did you ever take up smoking?'

David began to laugh.

'What on earth brought that on?'

'I just want to know.'

He quoted, 'I tried it once but I didn't inhale.'

'Oh, yes,' said Martha. 'The big smoking crisis.'

'Peer pressure entirely. I don't know why I gave in to it.' From the safe distance of the years he looked back with wonder. 'How could I have been such an ass? Some of the A grade team were caught smoking and a big anti-smoking drive started. The word went forth that anyone found smoking, in school grounds or elsewhere, would be expelled from all sporting teams. It was the 'or elsewhere' that got the hackles up. It was a bit dramatic.'

'Draconian,' said Martha.

'Well, somehow they got me convinced I had to join the smokers and strike a blow for freedom. Test of manhood, like. So there I was, down in the bush with the wild boys, puffing away. It was a test of manhood, all right. I thought I was going to lose my lunch. Oh, Gawd, but I was sick. And I knew that if I threw up, I'd be a joke for ever. Being thrown out of the first eleven would be nothing to it. So there I was with the cold sweat on my brow, hoping for someone to come along and catch me in the act before I disgraced myself.'

'I was gnawing my fingernails in the distance, of course.'

'I didn't think we'd started going together then,' he said, examining Martha's remark with surprise.

She concealed embarrassment.

'My fingernails were mine to gnaw, I suppose.'

David looked quickly to his plate and ate in silence.

The account had cheered Sophie, at least. She was smiling over David's nervous antics with an imaginary cigarette.

'Did many people know about this?' asked Ella, trying for a casual tone.

'Everyone knew,' said Martha. 'It was the great freedom debate. Down with the tyrants, and so on. Looking back,' she said to David, 'I think the teachers probably knew what was going on. They took good care not to catch anyone smoking.'

They were still at school, that pair, still the cricket hero and the star of the debating team - though Martha showed signs of moving on.

'They thought Wellings wouldn't have dropped me at any price, but they were mistaken.'

'He'd have been shattered,' said Martha.

'Yes. Well, it didn't happen.'

Poor Carrie. She had told her to go and talk to Mr Wellings. The tactful solution. Poor Carrie.

'It was Mr Wellings who came to see you play for New South Wales, wasn't it?' she asked.

It was a pity she had to strengthen the impression that she had never been face to face with Mr Wellings, but it was necessary to introduce this absorbing topic before David could ask again what had made her think about smoking.

'My fingernails again,' said Martha. 'I wouldn't want to go through that again.'

'I just didn't want to disgrace myself.'

'I remember.'

Ella interposed, 'Well, you didn't disgrace yourself, did you?'

'It was worth it.' David's face glowed. 'It's great, going to your own limit, seeing the best you can do, and getting close to the greats, playing on the same team. But I wouldn't want to be one of them. A game's a game, after all. It's terrible when it gets to be life and death.'

No sigh of disappointment there; only the light of remembered glory.

In spite of their efforts, the conversation died of sadness. Ella was remembering the easy contempt of that 'Caroline wouldn't know the difference'. No wonder she hated them. There should be room for hate, somehow. One shouldn't have to dress it as virtue. Poor Carrie. She couldn't give in to her; she loved and pitied her, but she had to oppose her.

Martha gathered the plates and took them to the kitchen. David went to help her with the washing up. Sophie sat on at the table and began to cry, or rather to whimper with rage.

'I'm sorry, Mum.'

'It can't be helped. She's thinking of Becky, I suppose, but Becky's in no danger and I can't have Caroline deciding who comes to the house.'

'I can't stand the thought of not seeing Becky again.'

'Do you think I like the idea? It won't come to that. Something has to happen. She'll come to see . . .'

She won't do this to me. She might do it to you but she surely won't do it to me.

'She didn't mean it for you, Mum. She rang me at work. She thought I'd give in. She never thought it would get as far as you.'

Ella listened from a distance. She was suffering black grief for the infant Caroline, who had grasped, stared and chuckled as candidly as any other baby.

I did everything right, she thought with bitter indignation. I thought of her more, I felt for her more than the other two. I know what it's like to feel inferior.

Sophie was saying, 'She must have thought in the first place it would be enough to tell you about Rob. Couldn't even do that herself, had to get at you through David. She wouldn't have expected you to be so broadminded.'

There was a querulous note in Sophie's voice. Life would perhaps be simpler if Ella were more rigid.

One of Ella's firmest rules was being broken. It seemed important to hold to such rules as were left.

'I can't talk about it, Sophie. Perhaps I can talk to her about it myself.'

Sophie raised her eyebrows in disbelief and Ella was forced to admit that the silent comment was justified.

'I'll start on your friend's food tonight. I'll trim the stewing steak and put the trimmings into the slow cooker for stock.'

'Good. I'll help. And we'd better bring something for dinner tomorrow night. We'll stop at the Palace on the way home.'

Bury the topic and bring on the future. On that they were agreed.

• XV •

Rob brought William to the house on Tuesday evening after dinner. As she followed Sophie into the living room, a glance at her face reassured Ella that her intentions were virtuous. No villain could afford to look so villainous.

She stepped aside and said abruptly, 'Here's the new lodger.'

The large shape behind her stepped into the light. No threat to Sophie's virtue there, either. He was indeed large, but with areas of smallness which made his size absurd: bulky rounded shoulders, thin torso, large hands and bony wrists, thin neck and narrow, gingery head, a small, nervous smile which he directed apologetically at Ella. The silky reddish hair, worn long and tied back, was the final absurdity.

He was older than she had expected, too old for the jeans and teeshirt he was wearing.

Feeling protective, Ella welcomed him firmly, earning a warm gust of approval from Sophie.

'I'll show William his room.'

Rob conceded, 'I'll bring the stuff from the van.'

When the stuff – a dufflebag, a carton of books, a carton of papers and an old portable typewriter – had been carried to the downstairs bedroom, Ella offered coffee and they gathered in the kitchen.

'Get this straight, William,' said Rob. 'Anything I say in this house is copyright. If it's worth remembering, I'm going to use it myself.'

William frowned, thinking it over.

'I would have thought the spoken word was in the public domain.'

'Not my spoken word, so watch it.'

'I could give provenance in a footnote.'

Ella smiled inwardly, thinking Rob was well served by this sarcasm. She was being simply naughty – one might almost think jealous, if that were not absurd.

After a silent moment, she began to wonder if William had been joking.

'We have to tell him about the food, Mum.'

Ella was eager to show her achievements there, yet wary, suspecting that the young people found her interest in food ridiculous, though they took a keen interest in the result of it.

'Rob said you'd like to eat at odd hours, so I've done some cooking for you. All this shelf in the freezer is yours. Rob bought the ingredients.'

He was looking with reverence at the stacks of plastic boxes. He nodded to Rob, acknowledging the debt.

'You owe me sixty dollars.'

'You got all that for sixty dollars?'

'I made a lucky buy on chicken pieces. Not much

variety, I'm afraid. I spent the last few dollars on dried peas and lentils - real poverty filling. I hope you like pease pudding and lentil soup. Those foil packets are sandwiches - all roast beef. I couldn't think of any other filling that froze well.'

'I made the sandwiches,' said Sophie.

'I think it's amazing, and very kind of you.'

'This is sauce for pasta. The pasta is in this cupboard,' she added, shutting the freezer door and speaking dismissively, in case she was skirting ridicule.

'Thank you. Thanks for the coffee.'

His voice was more impressive than his appearance. Ella had expected a squeak.

'I must go and unpack.'

'I put towels for you in the downstairs bathroom.'

After his departure, Rob shook her head, grinning.

'What luxury. The downstairs bathroom. Anywhere I've been before, the bathroom was always the bathroom. He'll become accustomed to luxury and you'll never get rid of him.'

'Downstairs study, too,' said Sophie, pleased to astonish.

Having made her impression, she added, 'Just a box-room, really, next to my room. We called it the computer room.'

'My God.'

'No expense spared on our education.'

Answering the tone of the remark, Rob said mildly, 'I don't think that quite amounts to child abuse.'

Sophie thought that over in silence.

Ella wondered if they knew she was there.

'There's the guilt of not measuring up,' said Sophie. 'Not justifying the expense.'

'I don't know that anyone ever pressured you, Sophie.'

'David felt it, Mum. He knew he was a disappointment to Dad. And what David felt, I felt. Goodness,' – she looked back indulgently at her childish self – 'I surely thought the sun shone out of David.'

'Your father hadn't had an easy time getting his education. He wanted you all to have the advantages he had missed.'

'That's an attitude which can lead to overkill, quite apart from the rule that everything a parent does is wrong, by definition.' Rob added, 'Not a trouble I'm likely to meet.'

'Mum didn't pressure. Mum was a buffer state.'

'An excellent thing in a parent.'

Rob gave Ella a smile which salved her wounded feelings.

'Well, the computer's going to come in handy now,' said Sophie. 'William can finish his manuscript on the word processor.'

'He seems very nice, to me,' said Ella. And so reassuringly homely. Such an uncertain life, poor fellow.

To punish Rob for her ungracious behaviour, she added, 'Don't you think we should ask him to dinner on Friday night? It seems so unfriendly not to.'

Rob scowled.

'We couldn't talk film at the table and I like talking film. I like answering your questions. It helps me to organise my thoughts.'

Ella forgave Rob all offences.

'He doesn't really steal things, does he?' asked Sophie.

'Well, to do him justice, he doesn't mean to. He sits there and sucks everything up, like a vacuum cleaner.

Your talk and your face and your clothes and every fact he can pick up.'

'Is that how people write books?' asked Ella, who was fascinated by this mystery.

'All gathered in from the outside? Now that's an interesting one. No. Sometimes it's all from the inside and it stays there, as far as I'm concerned. I suppose if you have the right proportion, outside to inside, then you're good.'

'Is William good?'

Rob frowned and shrugged.

'Some people think very good. Not my style. No sense of humour. No sense of humour at all. You might have thought he was having a go at me about the footnote and if he had been I'd really like him. But he wasn't. He was dead serious. Sometimes it takes you a long time to realise that he isn't being funny. He was praised by the critics for delicious comic scenes in his first book and he was quite annoyed. He had no idea he was being funny.'

'There has to be some selection somewhere,' said Sophie, 'between what goes in and what comes out.'

'Yes. Perhaps he has something more important than a sense of humour, but I don't know what it is. He's somewhere between a genius and a crashing bore.'

Imagine, living so poorly, working so earnestly to be perhaps a failure, a crashing bore. Rob, however, had paid for his food. There must be some hope for him.

Ella was sorry now that she had asked the question which had begun the conversation. There was no danger of being overheard – the knowledge that the subject was in the house had kept their voices subdued. There was no malice intended, either – well, she had intended none, but she could not really answer for Rob.

In my house. Under my roof. There it was. Genius or bore, William now had the status of a guest.

Rob had sensed disapproval.

'Well, I'd better be going.' Standing up, she smiled directly at Ella. 'May I still come on Friday, even though I'm a sullen bitch?'

Ella was taken and shaken by a powerful attraction, a longing even to touch her hand.

So that's how it feels, she thought. That's how it comes about.

In a moment she was herself again, saying, 'Of course you may,' in a tone that reproved folly.

She hadn't changed her nature, but she had changed her thinking. It had been a beautiful moment. She could never be sorry she had experienced it.

• XVI •

Later, Ella decided that what she had got from William's stay in the house was the illusion of permanence, the same illusion that had made the afternoon of the video so enchanting.

William kept odd hours. His program was simple but impressive. He slept when he was tired and ate when he was hungry, coming into the kitchen wearing the sweet abstracted smile with which he warded off conversation. If Ella was working there, he asked politely, 'Am I in your way?' and she answered, just as formally, 'Not at all.' Then he emptied the contents of one of his plastic boxes into a saucepan without noticing whether he had taken beef or chicken - an omission which annoyed Ella so much that she found it wiser to look away - heated the food, scooped it onto a plate and washed the saucepan before he carried the meal away to his room.

He was, as Rob had said, as neat as a cat.

She had left cleaning materials in the bathroom cupboard with little hope that they would be used, but when in the course of housecleaning she looked in the room, she found all surfaces shining and the harsh, virtuous smell of cleaning powder and disinfectant rising from tiles and lavatory bowl.

She was still in the kitchen one day when he brought back his plate and his knife and fork and put them in the sink.

'Don't bother to wash those,' she said. 'Put them in the dishwasher.'

He looked with distress, not at her but at the objects in the sink. Clearly, it caused him pain to leave anything unwashed. Dirt and disorder fretted his soul – a fine quality in a lodger, but one wouldn't care for it in a husband. How like poor William to have such a maddening virtue.

His presence was most comforting when it was unseen. Coming downstairs at one in the morning to make a sleeping draught of rum and milk, she would see the light under William's door, know that he was awake and working, and feel that it was good to have a man in the house again.

Sophie took over the computer in the study next to William's room and began to make a clean copy of his manuscript. That was an odd way for a young girl to spend her leisure, but Sophie seemed to be happy, working alone and now and then going next door to consult William about a difficulty. Ella, too, took pleasure in the growing stack of clean, typed sheets and the thought that something important was being produced in the house. How could she express this satisfaction? It was like hearing running water, having a fountain playing in the garden, a small pleasure which offset her continuing sadness over the defection of Caroline and the loss of Becky.

William avoided society. He vanished at the sound of voices. In a short time he had gained the status of a mild, harmless domestic animal, so unobtrusive that a fortnight passed before David and Martha knew of his existence.

This is ridiculous, thought Ella, on the third Thursday of his presence in the house. She caught William on his way out for one of his solitary walks and said firmly, 'My son and his wife are coming to dinner. I want you to stay and meet them.'

Sophie said, 'Yes. You're not the Phantom of the Opera, you know.'

Sophie's attempt at humour did not make him smile. He sat down obediently and watched Ella make salad.

'That food,' he said.

Ella was startled. Was he going to make a complaint?

'Will you show me how to do it? Tell me what the cheapest foods are and how you cook them?'

'Yes. I'd be delighted.'

'And that's no lie,' Sophie commented.

'Which dishes do you like best?'

William looked puzzled.

'They're all economical. We might as well start with the things you like.'

It was useless trying to extract praise of her cooking from William, who did not seem to know that one food could be preferred to another. Pique gave way to pity as she understood what bleakness of life lay behind that indifference. She hoped urgently that his book was good and would bring him success and a little ease.

David and Martha came in to an awkward silence and made it no better, looking at the stranger with an astonishment which was perceptible, though quickly suppressed.

Sophie ignored formal manners to claim territory.

'William, this is my brother David. Oh, sorry, wrong way round. Martha, meet William. My sister-in-law Martha, my brother David.'

Oh dear. William really did look out of place, large, ungainly, uncertain, too large for the kitchen chair he was perched on and looking quite alarmingly large as he stood up, towering over slight Martha, wearing a guilty look which made it plain that he had no right to be there and making Ella feel positively shifty.

'William is a friend of Sophie's. He is staying with us while he finishes a novel.'

'Is it your first novel?' asked Martha.

William nodded to the introduction, shook his head at the question and plunged away through the back door.

When they had heard it close, David said, 'You're taking up with some odd characters, Mum.'

Sophie directed a ferocious but affectionate grimace at the back of her brother's head.

Ella said, 'He just writes books, dear. I don't know anything about his sex life.'

She was herself astonished at this remark while David took on a pinched and peevish air quite devoid of the glamour of youth. A good young man, Ella reminded herself, yet she felt sadly that there should be something more between the school prefect and this.

Martha was unwrapping fish and chips and distributing them onto plates.

'Tell Ella about your lovely letter.'

David smiled and youth was restored.

'I got a letter from a Phys. Ed. teacher who'd read my thesis in the Journal and tried out the exercises. He says he's had great results with them. You know, I thought it was great when they published that thesis but I never thought about anyone reading it and using the stuff.'

'I suppose,' said Martha, 'that is what publication is all about.'

'That just hadn't sunk in.'

'That's wonderful, dear. You don't know how many other people have used them and didn't bother to write.'

Martha said, 'This man – this Harry – he's very serious about them. There's one problem class he has where he says behaviour has improved in other subjects, too. He says it's an increase in self-respect and general physical control. He's coming to see us this vacation to show David some ideas of his own. So you didn't waste your time over it, in spite of Pritchett.'

David nodded, silently happy.

'Harry wants to write a book. He wants David to do it with him.'

David shrugged.

'I don't think I could go as far as that. I wouldn't mind helping but I've said all I want to say about it.'

Ella and Martha both looked disappointed. That was David always – so far and no further.

At dinner Martha introduced the topic of William.

'I said the wrong thing to your friend, didn't I? I gather it isn't his first novel.'

'He won a prize with his first book. His second didn't do so well. There's a lot hanging on this one.'

'Oh, dear. One needs to be briefed before one talks to writers. I hope I didn't give offence.'

Martha, no longer the enthusiastic girl sure of her ability to change the world, had become the tactful domestic manager, selling David the idea of William.

'All I said was William. Could have been William Smith. He's deadly shy with strangers.'

'That was tactful of you.'

'Oh, I'm cunning all right,' said Sophie complacently.

'A proper barrel of monkeys,' David grumbled.

Martha was, after all, a teacher of English.

What is his surname, then?'

'Anstey. William Anstey.'

'William Anstey.'

As Martha pronounced the name, William's looks improved mysteriously. At least he ceased to be 'poor William' and acquired some dignity.

'Now I am offended, Sophie. You could have trusted me. I've read both his books. I'm one of the few who really admired the second one.'

'Sorry.'

In the silence which followed, it became clear that Sophie had been protecting William from intrusive conversation. Sophie owned William and did not intend to share him.

Martha, who now had real cause for offence, decided instead on indulgent understanding. She ended the pause by saying, 'I wish he'd collect his short stories. You might suggest that to him.'

Sophie smiled, her territory restored intact.

David said, 'How's the *Curse of the Funnelweb* going?'

'It is progressing,' said Sophie with dignity. 'You are an author yourself, now. You should speak with more respect.'

'Strictly utilitarian,' said David, but he glowed a little.

To Ella, the film script had become boring. The main themes were set; there was little pleasure in listening to the details which now occupied them.

'How hard they all work,' she thought. 'I wonder they have the courage to begin.'

She was contemplating a major work herself. She had decided to make a hooked rug for Becky. The work would dull the pain of Becky's absence, which must surely be temporary. If it were not, the gift would be a message, a permanent one. She will know how much I cared for her. That will be something.

With a film script proceeding in the dining room and a novel (perhaps famous) being produced in the downstairs study, she began to take the infection, feeling the stirring of creativity.

When Rob and Sophie came in to suggest coffee, she was busy with a sketch pad and felt-tipped pens, studying a print in a book of Chinese scrolls.

'Hullo,' said Rob. 'I always suspected this. You're an artist.'

'Heavens, no. I'm working out a design for a hooked rug, that's all.'

'Hang on to your clothes,' said Sophie.

'Sophie,' said Ella patiently, 'you had outgrown that pink skirt long before I cut it up.'

'You didn't ask me.'

'I didn't think it was necessary. You were ten years old at the time.'

'A very old grievance,' said Rob with amusement.

'Well, there it is in front of me. See the pink rosebuds in the wreath? A constant reminder of Mum's perfidy.'

Sophie was kneeling on the floor by the rose rug, pointing to the remains of her pink skirt.

'Did you make that, Ella?'

Rob's tone was awed.

'Mum's an expert. She made us each one. Martha's carried off the one she made for David. Caroline took hers, too. I suppose it's in Becky's room.'

'I mean this for Becky.'

Pause for pity. She did not look up.

'I didn't imagine this was handmade.'

Rob had joined Sophie on the floor and was examining Ella's work.

'The cutting is the worst thing. That's the finest I've made.' Ella was talking quickly, blushing over Rob's admiration. 'I started making them in London because it was a cheap hobby and it kept me warm, then I got interested and kept it up. The ones I made for the children aren't so fine.'

'You live creatively,' said Rob with enthusiasm. 'You make beautiful rugs, cook beautiful meals, teach English – give people a voice – '

'Ask useful questions,' Sophie finished helpfully.

'Too good to walk on,' said Rob, getting up and coming to look at the print Ella was studying.

'They're very hardwearing. It's what they are meant for.'

'I don't know how people could bear to walk on them. Why don't you make wallhangings?'

'Not so useful.'

'Are you going to translate this picture into a rug?'

'No. I'm just getting help with the proportions. Once I have my design and my colour scheme, I go looking for secondhand woollen clothes in the opportunity shops. I always enjoy that.'

'The pleasures of the hunt. I understand that.' Rob studied the painting and Ella's sketch. 'Are you making out that something beautiful to hang on a wall and make people feel good isn't useful? That's a shocking thought.'

'You'd have to be sure it was beautiful.'

Rob sighed.

'Oh, yes. That's the risk we all have to take. And think of the fun of hunting for the materials, breaking up old junk jewellery for the river stones, silver gauze for your little cascade . . .'

'Pale brown silk,' Ella contradicted her, then wondered why she had found the moment so satisfactory.

The risk that made Rob rueful and furrowed William's brow was certainly not for her.

• XVII •

It was Max who brought Becky to visit on a Saturday morning.

Ella heard Becky's voice calling 'Grandma!' at the back door and came joyfully, ready to help Caroline over an awkward moment, but the awkward moment was her own as she tried to hide shock and disappointment. She picked Becky up and hid her face for a moment against the firm, round belly, holding her so tightly that she wriggled for freedom and slid to the ground.

'You got any of those little cakes with the pink icing?'

'I didn't know you were coming. I'll give you a slice of big cake later with your milk. Will that do?'

'Oh, well. Next time, then. Where's Aunt Sophie?'

'Up in her room. You can go up and look for her. She has two little mice in a cage. You'll like them.'

Becky departed. Ella and Max were left to look at each other in silence.

Since all she knew of Max was his protective, uncritical

love for Caroline, she knew what this visit must be costing him. It was a gift she didn't know how to accept.

Max spoke.

'She said to me, "When people get very old, they die, don't they?" I said, "Yes. When people get very old, they get very tired and just go to sleep." I didn't know where this was heading, you understand. She didn't say anything for quite some time, then she said in a very casual voice, "Grandma's pretty old, I suppose." You know Becky. If she is very frightened about something she will pretend that it is of no importance at all. I thought we must come and see for ourselves that you are in good health.'

'Thank you for bringing her.'

Did Caroline know that he was here? Yes, surely. Max would never risk his dignity on a surreptitious expedition.

Poor Becky, poor Max, poor Caroline.

'You understand that where Becky is concerned, Caroline can be overanxious.'

His voice was strained. He was not convinced by his own attempt at justification.

'Caroline should have more confidence in me.'

Max nodded unhappily.

'This film script cannot go on for ever.'

'Rob will always be welcome in my house.'

Max looked bleak.

I love her as much as you do, thought Ella angrily. I can't give in. You'll find out. There isn't any easy way.

At length Max nodded agreement.

'Roberta Tressider is a very fine person.'

Sophie came in hand in hand with Becky, saying easily, 'Hi, Max.'

'Aunt Sophie has two mice. They have a big wheel

and they run on it sometimes but they won't run on it for me. The man mouse is called Oscar and his wife is called Emmy. Pretty silly names, I think. Daddy, will you please come upstairs and make them run on the wheel?'

'I don't think they will listen to me, Becky.'

'We are going to have coffee now. You can have your piece of cake and a drink of milk.'

'Then we must go home but we will come again if we may.'

'Of course,' said Ella, though she doubted that he would make use of the invitation.

Sophie cast an interested glance while she carried on her conversation with Becky.

'No, I don't let them out. They like it in the cage. No, I can't take them for walks, they'd run away and get lost. Yes, I could put them in my pocket but they wouldn't see much. They really are better off at home.'

'I suppose they have each other to talk to.'

'Mice can't talk.'

'How do you know?'

'I would have heard them.'

'Perhaps they talk to each other when you're not there.'

Sophie reflected and gave in.

'I can't disprove it.'

Max said, 'I think they talk to each other a little, you know. In a kind of a mousetalk.'

'That's right. I suppose they do.'

Becky beamed with satisfaction. Max smiled towards her, gentle and regretful.

Max loved Caroline, but he loved Becky more.

When they had left, Sophie looked with raised eyebrows at Ella.

'How about that?'

'He thought Becky was fretting,' Ella said in the tone which forbade further discussion.

'He didn't say anything else, then?'

'Nothing that mattered.'

Sophie said, 'Poor Mum,' and came to give her a comforting hug.

'Light at the end of the tunnel, Mum.'

Ella nodded, strangled by tears.

I can't give in. I can't give in. I can't give in.

• XVIII •

Nina told Ella, with a proud smile, that she now had job.

'You have a job. A job.'

Ella corrected the sentence automatically before she took in its meaning.

'I have a job in hot bread shop. In a hot bread shop. I think I have enough English for the hot bread shop. You think?'

Ella was more disappointed than was reasonable. Her ambitions for Nina had been vague, but they had involved more glory than was offered by a hot bread shop.

'Yes. You don't need any more lessons.'

'I am very thankful to you, always.'

She paused, looking expectantly at Ella.

I should invite her home.

She saw at that moment how uncertain the future was, how little she could promise.

'You come to buy bread in my shop. I am sad if I don't see you again.'

'I'd be sad, too,' Ella said truthfully.

She was sad at this moment. She could find another student, but there would never be another Nina.

Nina wrote an address on a page of her English folder and handed the tornout page to Ella.

'One moment. One moment.'

She had a gift for Ella, a tiny perfume bottle of enamelware suspended from a neck chain.

'It's beautiful, Nina. I haven't anything to give you.'

Nina leaned forward to kiss Ella's cheek, while she smiled at the absurdity of her remark.

'What you give me is very big present.' She smiled the old mischievous smile. 'A very big present.'

Well, that was something to take home with her, but she went sadly, for all that.

• XIX •

Permanence was threatened everywhere.

David had begun to talk of selling the house.

'No. I couldn't do that. No.'

'But Mum – '

'I can't talk about it. No.'

In spite of her obstinate mental silence, the conversation edged forward week by week.

'That is where all the money is, Mum. There really isn't much cash. I don't know. We always lived as if we had rich parents. I feel guilty at what you both spent on us.'

'It didn't seem to matter. Your father put so much money into superannuation when he took the University job.'

David brightened.

'You have a strong claim on that, I think. And it's indexed, safe from inflation. If you take a lump sum you'll have to live on investments and you could be vulnerable.'

They could not understand the bottomless terror she felt at the thought of losing her house.

Why should I? Did I do anything wrong? She thought, but she did not ask the question aloud. They talked about the nice little unit she would buy as if it were a charming friend they wanted her to meet.

'At least we have to have the house valued,' said David. 'There can't be any sort of settlement until we can put a figure on the house.'

He took silence for consent and brought in the valuer.

Ella escaped into the garden and weeded in the rockery while he walked through the house, measuring, prodding and tapping.

He startled William out of his burrow into the air.

'What's going on?' he asked Ella.

She straightened up and looked towards the house. The man had emerged now and was examining the outer walls and the foundations.

'He's valuing the house. Deciding what it would fetch on the market.'

He looked startled and questioning, then remained standing beside her, watching the invader with earnest attention.

She hadn't expected any companionship from William - not even any communication, except about food. They had a serial conversation about food, which did make the association a little easier.

She concentrated on her impressions of William to keep her mind off the valuer.

William didn't take advantage, that was certain.

When Sophie spent a fine weekend at the computer, bringing the clean copy up to date, Ella thought sadly of other young people out bushwalking, playing tennis, courting, or at least engaged in activities that could lead to courtship, but she couldn't blame William for that. There was even some grace in his acceptance of her help. He might take it for granted, but he took it seriously, ready to respond when she knocked at his door with a question about the interpretation of his tiny script.

Sophie was doing the favour, yet somehow it was William who was showing kindness.

But in some ways, how difficult! One would think a man could help himself to instant coffee without being asked. It had taken her a week to find out why he didn't drink tea or coffee with his meals, and then of course she had felt guilty about it.

Then there was the dirty washing. Her tactlessness there. Not his fault if his underwear was in rags. No wonder he had been washing his clothes out at night and hanging them in the laundry. 'Leave those,' she had said. 'It's no trouble to put them through the machine with the rest of the wash.' He had complied with a look of dumb suffering. If she had been more observant, she would have left him alone. She had hung the garments on an inner line of the hoist, concealed by the sheets, ironed them and waited till he was out of his room to leave them on his bed.

Sparing William's feelings was work for two women.

It was over cooking that they communicated. He carried a small notebook and a ballpoint pen to record her recipes and her observations. Such a small notebook, such a large man – he did look absurd, poor fellow, making notes in the tiny script which one connected with the all-important novel, and asking questions with the earnest air one connected with matters of great importance.

Well, she took food seriously, too, so that was a real meeting of minds.

'Pea soup. How much water? How many stock cubes to that weight of peas? How long should I soak them? Would this recipe do for lentils?'

'It's a good idea, when you do have money, to build up your store of spices and flavourings.'

He made a list: curry powder, chili powder (mild), paprika, dried onion flakes, stock cubes (chicken and beef) . . .

If only he showed some enthusiasm. Clearly, food was survival only.

He said unexpectedly, 'Were you ever poor?'

'Yes, in London, when my husband was studying. That's when we learnt to live on lentils.'

'Ah.'

It seemed that he knew enough of the matter to leave that subject at once.

Drifts of sadness did come with some of the recipes. Pease pudding – she hadn't made that since those days in London, in the cold little bedsitter where Bernard studied and she cooked their meals on a gas ring, living, as her mother would have said, on the smell of an oily rag.

Sadness was all right – painful but not dangerous. Rage was the enemy.

David had come out of the house. He raised his hand in greeting and came to join them.

'How's the novel going?'

'I'm nearly there. Perhaps ten days more.'

Ella was astonished at her own dismay.

• XX •

Rob fetched three long envelopes out of her shoulderbag.

'Mail for William. I suppose he's in his room.'

'Yes.'

Rob thumped on his door, calling out, 'Hoy! William!' with little respect for the mental processes of genius.

William emerged.

'Mail for you. Nigel dropped it into the office.'

They reached the kitchen as she was saying, 'Looks as if the drought's broken.'

'If I'm lucky.'

William opened envelopes with more obvious emotion than Ella had yet seen in him.

He frowned over the contents of one and put it away in his pocket, detached a cheque from another with a look of satisfaction and looked at the next cheque with delight and astonishment.

'*Mirror* has taken off in the States.'

'Oh, great.'

He handed her the cheque. She read the amount with raised eyebrows and real pleasure.

Money was indeed the topic which brought them close.

'I can leave now,' he said with awful simplicity, then recollected himself and said formally to Ella, 'I need not trespass any longer on your kindness.'

Ella found herself smiling over this but Sophie, she saw, was wounded.

'There's no hurry, William.'

Rob, who, like Ella, had been smiling over William's gaucherie, asked, 'Are you going back to that fleahouse? I think it's getting too much even for Nigel. He says nobody's touched a broom since you left. Doesn't occur to him of course that he might pick up a broom himself.'

'Until I find something else. I can't be bothered about it just now.'

'Why can't you stay till the book's finished?' asked Sophie. 'Who's going to do your typing?'

William's gaze for Sophie was unreadable. Kind, certainly, but what else did it convey?

'You have better things to do with your young life than type manuscripts for me.'

Sadness. William knew the distance that stretched between him and any such representative of the joys of life. Ella was conscious of a dignity which checked her smiling.

'I'll certainly miss it. You've been doing an expert job.'

Sophie was mollified.

'When are you leaving?' asked Ella. 'You aren't going off into the night, are you?'

'Tomorrow.'

'Come and have dinner with us tonight then.' And try to show a bit of social nous.

'I need to finish what I'm doing, get it in order before I go.'

He nodded and escaped with the liberating mail.

'Not one for pretty speeches,' said Rob as she heard his door close.

For Ella he had made one very pretty speech. She hoped it had reached Sophie.

'He hasn't left yet.'

'Oh, hell. I detect reproach. Deserved. I don't mean that he isn't grateful, I'm sure he is. Only that he isn't articulate, doesn't unpack the heart. Why do I bitch at William? Why do I seem to be bitching at William even when I'm not? Envy. The protean passion.'

Ella had no idea what a protean passion was. She was relieved that Rob had identified it.

'You don't have to be envious. You have your film.'

'I envy him his singlemindedness.'

Sophie nodded agreement.

'He certainly is singleminded,' said Ella. 'I think it could be quite difficult to live with in the long run.'

She remembered with a start that William was still in the house, with guest status, not a subject for discussion. No human being should be so unobtrusive. It was like living with a ghost.

However, she admitted to herself that she might miss the familiar haunting.

On Saturday morning Sophie slept late and came down to the kitchen flushed and yawning, wearing the customary teeshirt and jeans, and barefoot. Ella, allowing herself only the briefest of glances at Sophie's feet, reminded herself that she was seeing some return for a lifetime of expensive, expertly fitted shoes. The high-arched feet were at least without blemish.

'Do you want a cup of coffee, Mum? I think I'll just have toast.'

Ella accepted the offer and was drinking the coffee when William came in and stood, awkward and silent, but prepared to be sociable.

He had got up early, had stripped his bed and taken the linen to the laundry, had cleaned the downstairs bathroom (every inch of the downstairs bathroom, thought Ella, who had from the kitchen been following his movements with some irritation), and had packed his belongings and set them outside the back door. Now it was time to tackle the pretty speech.

'Hi,' said Sophie. 'Sit down and have a cup of coffee. Accept a small slice of toast. Just to show there's no ill feeling.'

'Why should there be ill feeling? You have been very kind. I'm grateful to you both.'

Well, there was a pretty speech. Ella regretted her irritation over the remorseless cleaning and scrubbing in the downstairs bathroom. It had been well meant.

'Just a turn of phrase,' said Sophie. 'Do sit down and have some breakfast.'

William sat and said unexpectedly to Ella, 'Do you live in this room? I always see you here.'

'It's the sunniest room.'

'This is how I'll see you in my mind. The woman in the kitchen.'

Sophie was amused.

'Not very flattering.'

Ella, however, was flattered to appear in any guise in William's mind.

'And that door. I was thinking when I put my stuff out there, this is where they all come in, expecting to find you.' He smiled and she experienced a moment of real affection for him.

'Thanks for the cooking lessons and the meals. That was great.'

'There are some packs left, you know. Can't you take them with you? They'd last a few days in a fridge.'

She had been discreetly replenishing the stock for some time – in every casserole an extra helping for William. He had not appeared to notice and that suited her.

'I don't think I can carry them.'

'Oh, the pair of you,' said Sophie. 'Food. Serious subject. Deadly earnest.'

'Why shouldn't food be a serious subject?' William asked with interest.

Ella said sharply, 'It's serious enough when it's hard to come by. And what is your first question when you come in the door?'

Sophie grinned.

'Sorry. Sorry. You'll never carry your stuff by yourself anyhow, William. You'd need three arms. Wait till I get my boots on and I'll come with you.'

At Sophie's age Ella would never have offered her company to a man in any circumstances. That would have been thought forward. Was Sophie being unwise?

If it had been anyone but William . . .

He said, 'That would be a help,' showing no emotion

but slight relief, and Sophie went to survey the stack at the back door.

Coming back, she said, 'I'll borrow the airline bag, Mum. That should take the manuscript and some of the books – under the manuscript,' she added hastily to William. 'If you can get the rest of them into the dufflebag, we can take the food. I'll just go get my boots on.'

Ella went to fetch the airline bag from the laundry cupboard, feeling depression settle its cloak on her.

She didn't want Sophie to go. She didn't want to be alone.

Clinging to Sophie, becoming possessive and demanding, was the danger to be avoided, with resolution.

If only Caroline would come back.

She will come back when she can do it without losing face. Now, of course, it would mean giving in to Max. Ella felt some sympathy for her situation. It didn't do to give in to one's husband, particularly when he was in the right.

This was the day to lace the hessian onto the frame, she thought, as she saw off the pair with an appearance of cheerfulness.

She had begun the cutting for Becky's rug but she had left the tedious job of lacing the hessian to the frame for a rainy day. Mum had always said, When you feel life isn't worth living, that's the day to clean the stove. You're going to feel bad anyhow, you might as well make use of it.

Ella hadn't thought before to question her mother's happiness – but how many of her mottoes and devices had been antidotes to despair.

Dad had been happy all right, a real party man,

everybody's friend. Perhaps his happiness hadn't spilled over onto Mum.

Well, she had done right to teach us antidotes, thought Ella, as she fetched frame, hessian and twine into the kitchen and set to work.

• XXI •

Sophie's nineteenth birthday, which should have been a family celebration, a dinner with the menu chosen by Sophie, presents in bright wrappings and a cake with nineteen candles, had now become a matter for diplomacy.

Martha, the emerging diplomat, rang Ella and suggested that she and David should take Sophie out to dinner and to the theatre.

'That's a wonderful idea,' Ella said gratefully.

Martha asked carefully, 'What do you think about coming with us?'

'Make it a young people's evening.'

They agreed silently that half a family party was much worse than none.

'Fine. Wait a minute. David's saying something.' She reported. 'He says to tell her no jeans. She has to wear a dress. He says, no dress, no dinner.'

Good, thought Ella. Now I don't have to tell her myself.

Sophie smiled at the invitation and frowned at the condition.

'Won't it do if I wear my good shirt?'

'They're going to a lot of trouble and expense for you. I think you should consider their feelings.'

'Oh, all right. Have a look around the op shops for a size twelve, will you, Mum, when you're looking for your colours?'

Ella said, 'I got my first good outfit for my eighteenth birthday. Ice blue tailored linen. I thought I was made.'

'I bet you looked lovely, Mum, but times have changed. I'm not going to spend my good money on dresses.'

'I could make you a skirt. A black skirt always comes in handy.'

'Oh, not black. Nobody wears black.'

How odd, that Sophie's reprehensible outfits should be governed by fashion.

'It goes with everything.'

'Yes.'

That was clearly not a point in its favour.

Sophie, however, had begun to interest herself in the project.

'What about a sort of mucky green, not very full but kind of swirly round the ankles?'

There was hope for Sophie yet.

'You buy the pattern and I'll get the material. You had better get the pattern tomorrow. There isn't much time.'

'I'll get it at lunchtime. Do you want the telly tonight? There's a film on SBS Rob wants me to watch.'

'No, I don't want to watch anything in particular,' said Ella, but with an inward sigh.

Must Sophie always be hitching her wagon to one star or the other?

On the birthday, Ella waited in such anxiety for the sound of the postman's motorbike that at last she went out to the gate to wait for him and take the mail from his hand.

It was there: a card at least from her father, with three more cards and a parcel from dear, faithful Laura (and I hope she takes that to heart).

There was a letter for herself, too, addressed in his hand.

She carried in the mail and opened her letter. It was a note pinned to the latest electricity account.

Please explain the abnormal increase in this account.

Without involving herself too much in the process, she added the words: *Normal domestic use,* transferred the note and the account to a fresh envelope and addressed it.

'So long as you have something better to say to Sophie,' she said grimly to the name she had written.

She picked up the olive green swirly skirt and went on hemming it with small shallow stitches, turning it now and then to make sure that none of the olive green thread showed on the right side. The work required care and was taking longer than she had expected. She had hardly cut the last thread and was heating the iron when Sophie came in, carrying a sheaf of yellow roses.

'I asked for an early mark because of the birthday dinner and they gave me the afternoon off and the roses. Wasn't that nice?'

How lovely she was – and whoever had chosen roses of that colour was well aware of it.

'What's the matter, Mum?'

'Nothing at all. I was just thinking how nice you look. There's some mail for you in the dining room.'

'Oh, great.'

With a return of childish exuberance she ran into the dining room and came back with the letters gripped in her armpit while she opened Laura's parcel and discovered a white mohair scarf.

'Isn't that terrific? She's made it herself. I'll ring her up tomorrow. I've been wanting to and I left it too long and got embarrassed. Now I will. Isn't she a dear?'

She draped the scarf round her neck while she opened three of the envelopes and read the messages on the birthday cards, still wearing the smile of joy Laura's present had brought.

The last one lay unopened on the table. The smile faded as she looked at it without favour and slit it open.

A card and a cheque. She let the card drop to the table while she read the cheque.

'That's one that goes straight back where it came from.'

Ella set the iron carefully on its rest and spoke.

'You have accepted so much from your father already that a little more won't hurt.'

Sophie gaped.

'If your father hadn't paid all that money to Dr Scobie, you would be walking about with crooked teeth.'

Remembering her strange disquiet over the yellow roses, she added mentally, And that might have been just as well. But no. Wealth and beauty – whatever dangers they brought, one never wished them away.

'He didn't have to do that, you know. Plenty of parents wouldn't have wanted to spend the money. You have had eighteen years and more of first-class care and you owe your father some gratitude, so you'll accept the cheque and write him a nice letter of thanks, please.'

'Yes, Mum.'

Sophie was too stunned to argue.

A moment later she said, 'Will it do if I send a card? That's all right, isn't it? I mean, he sent me one.'

'Yes, a card will do. With a nice message.'

Sophie nodded.

'Here's your skirt.' Ella shook out the swirl of olive green crepe. 'I pressed your shirt this morning. It's on your bed.'

'Thanks, Mum.'

Still too astonished to utter unnecessary words, she took the skirt and went to shower and dress for the evening.

She came downstairs in high spirits to greet David and Martha, resplendent in the new outfit, with Laura's scarf round her shoulders and swinging the shoulderbag Ella had given her that morning.

David uttered a low whistle.

'Satisfied?' She spun about so that the skirt flared. 'Prepared to be seen with me? Mum made the skirt and look at the bag she gave me. Isn't it terrific?'

It was of Italian leather and had cost too much – an expensive substitute for the cake with nineteen candles.

'I'm the one who shouldn't want to be seen with you,' said Martha. 'I think I'm rendered invisible, and just as well.'

David seized the lobe of her ear and pulled it gently to reprimand such stupidity.

Martha had little cause to lament her lack of beauty.

She was carrying a gift-wrapped book which she offered, saying, 'You don't have to open it. It's the new biography of Orson Welles. I can take it back if you've read it.'

'Oh, terrific. No, I haven't and I want to. I am having a good birthday.'

Ella's reprimand hadn't depressed her. Ella hoped it might even have lightened that load of hate.

'You're a bit early, aren't you?'

'I want a word with Mum before we go.'

Ella felt dread. David was wearing his money face.

It was Martha who had first drawn attention to this. 'You look like a different person when you're talking about money. You look like a hunter stalking his prey.'

'I just want to do my best for Mum.'

'You don't have to relish it.'

David had uttered a grunt which expressed surprise and willingness to give the matter further thought, but he continued to wear that keen, alert expression whenever he reported the progress of the settlement.

What expression Ella wore she did not know – certainly it did not convey her determination to remain in the house, whatever happened.

Her mistake, she reflected, had been to let that valuer into the house – but what could she have done, lain down in front of him barring the way like a greenie in front of a bulldozer? Ever since the house had been valued it seemed to be converted in other minds into a quite terrifying sum of money, and she was in danger of losing her hold on it.

It shouldn't have been translated into money at all. She didn't mean to give in, she would give up everything else, if it came to that, but they must understand that this wasn't a matter of money.

Any statement she made on the subject instead of conveying meaning roused pity. After one prolonged discussion she had said irritably, irrationally, 'I wish you'd get those mice out of the house, Sophie,' and Sophie had looked at her with the same pitying look.

'All right, Mum. I'll get Rob to take them on Friday.'

And what a stupid thing to say that had been – as if the mice were the invaders.

Now David had sat at the table and was unfolding figure-laden papers.

'I think we have to give way on the units of super, Mum. They've offered surrender value of three and I think that's the best we can do. Perhaps it's better, anyhow, to take a lump sum and make a clean break. That brings us up to seventy per cent of the valuation and Mary thinks that's the best we can do. What do you say?'

Ella could not speak.

'If we pressure any more, they'll fight it in court. That's what Mary thinks. That's when the money starts to run away in lawyers' fees and everyone is worse off.'

'Whatever you say. Settle and be done with it.'

What she had said meant more than she had intended. She could tell that by the degree of relief with which David had greeted it.

'Great. Mary will let them know it's acceptable and they can take it from there.'

Too tired, she thought, everyone is too tired. I'll think it all out later.

Ella had invited Pam to dinner.

She arrived soon after the departure of the young people, bringing a present for Sophie.

'And I only hope it's a success. It's so hard to know what they like at her age. They're like Martians to me. I thought I couldn't go wrong with a shirt.'

'She'll be collecting quite a wardrobe. Does it go with olive green?'

She related the story of Sophie's outfit, then found herself telling Pam about the disagreement over the cheque from her father.

'After all,' she said, 'there has to be a bottom line. When we look back to where the money went – well, a lot of it went on the children. They weren't spoiled, but they always got anything they really needed, like that year at boarding school for Caroline, and the orthodontist for Sophie, and David had to have the best possible equipment, always. David's beginning to see that now that he's looking into the finances and he's a bit shocked by it. Whatever Sophie thinks about his . . . well, I suppose she hates it, but she ought to remember that he worked hard for the money that fed and clothed and educated them. There doesn't seem to be much reward for that.'

Pam dropped a bombshell.

'Doesn't that go for the house, too, Ella? His daily work went into buying that, too. I know it isn't his house entirely, but it isn't yours, either, not entirely.'

Like Sophie, Ella gaped. Like Sophie, she was too subdued to answer.

Pam said, 'Don't forget that Sophie probably realised what was going on, so she's been a long time building up this resentment. And her age, too. Just when she wanted a reason to rebel against authority.'

She was speaking quickly, avoiding Ella's eyes.

'But the house. That isn't a matter of money. It's different.'

Though she could not explain what this difference was, she felt that it needed no explanation. Everybody should see it at once.

'Sorry, love. Somebody had to say it sometime. If that's where most of the money is, then it's as much his as yours.'

Ella shook her head.

'He was the one . . . he was the one who broke it up. I have to keep things together. I have to.'

'Don't be so upset, love. You're putting me off my lovely dinner. Drink up. Have another glass of wine.'

As she poured the wine, she promised, 'We won't talk about it any more.'

Since no other topic of conversation presented itself, they ate and drank in silence, until Pam, after all, burst into speech again.

'A house is only bricks and mortar. And think of the future. Sophie is bound to leave and you'll be rattling around in this great house like a pea in a bottle.

'Even if you manage to hold on to it, what about the expense? How could you keep it up? What about rates? And maintenance? What about repairs? It wouldn't be you owning a house, it would be a house owning you.'

In a minute, it would be that nice little unit again.

'I could work. Get a job.'

'Well, yes. And if you'd been really bent on keeping the house, that's what you should have done, straightaway. Pronto. Shown you could be independent. But you didn't, you see.'

What had she been doing?

Fighting madness. That was a fulltime job.

'Ella. It wouldn't be right. And in the long run, you would never be happy doing what wasn't right. End of sermon. And now perhaps, I'd better be going.'

'Don't be ridiculous. There's dessert and coffee to come. And you'd better wait till that wine goes down a bit. I wouldn't be surprised if you were over the limit.'

'Dutch courage.' Pam breathed deeply and smiled in relief. 'Though that's supposed to be schnapps or something, isn't it? Ella, trust my friendship, will you? Please?'

Ella nodded.

'Yes. I do that. But no more just now, please. Don't say any more just now. Give me time.'

Pam had served her a mouthful difficult to chew and impossible perhaps to swallow.

She was still up and working on Becky's rug when Sophie came home.

'How was the evening?'

'Oh, great.'

At the restaurant, the waiter had brought in a cake with candles and had led the singing of 'Happy Birthday to You'. A bit embarrassing and yet nice, and they had wrapped a piece of cake for Ella. The play had been, well, cheerful, but not challenging, real birthday stuff, but she had enjoyed it.

The evening's enjoyment was shining still in her face.

How could Ella talk to her about it? Sophie was at the age when things went on for ever. No doubt that belief had been harshly tested lately, but it was of her age, too, to recover quickly from the blows of fate.

'That's taking shape, Mum. What is it, some sort of aerial view, like a map?'

'Yes, a kind of picture map. I hope it comes off. It's supposed to be cultivated land either side of the little stream. I haven't found anything right for the stream, yet.'

'Back to the op shops,' said Sophie. 'Half the fun. I'm dead beat. They said I could be late tomorrow. Isn't everybody nice?'

'I have to make a home for her.' Mentally Ella argued with Pam. 'At least until she is ready to go.'

• XXII •

At half-past 3 on Wednesday afternoon the slam of the front door and the sound of running feet announced disaster.

That must be Sophie, avoiding her and running upstairs as if the devil were after her.

Thinking with anguish, 'Oh, my darling, what is it?', Ella put down her scissors and hurried after her.

Sophie was in her room, pulling open a drawer of her bureau. She straightened up and turned her rigid pale face towards Ella.

'I've lost my job. Been sacked. Got the push. Made redundant. Okay?'

Last week she had been everybody's darling. Rob had been here as usual on Friday, deep in calculation and discussion about the precious film. Ella sat on the bed.

'But how? How could they do it? Couldn't Rob stop it?'

'It's Rob who's doing it.'

'No.'

'Oh, it's that woman.' Rage gave way to contempt. 'Tried to kill herself. Well, that's the story. Took an overdose. She knows just how much to take, she's done it before.' She stopped for breath and went on more calmly. 'When Rob got home, she found this Liz in a coma. She'd found that video. You remember when we made the video of Becky? She's mad jealous, always snooping. Well, she played the video and she got the idea into her head that I . . . ugh!' The disgust in her voice was as real as her rage. 'Sick. That's what she is, sick. As if I cared for any of them, dirty, rotten perverts. The very thought makes me sick.'

You flirted with Rob, thought Ella. You had me worried.

'It was the film I cared about, doing something real for once in my life. And they'd started shooting and I was going on location with Rob.'

The dirty, rotten pervert.

'Damn that creature. I wish she'd died. Too smart for that, of course. Rob got into work late, she'd been at the hospital all night, and she told me I had to go. That very day. She'd promised, sworn it. So I went. Walked out and here I am.'

Surely, when she got over the shock, she would feel some pity.

Sophie had turned back to the drawer and had begun to sort out underwear.

'Rob can't be very happy.'

'Makes her own fun, doesn't she? Letting that creature rule her life. If she called her bluff just once – could have called it this time.'

'What are you doing with those clothes, Sophie?'

'Oh, that. I can't stay. I'm going to William. That book – it's not the film, but it's better than nothing.'

He's not a book, he's a human being. And so, thought Ella bitterly, am I. And Rob, and that poor neurotic in the hospital. Didn't Sophie know the difference?

Suddenly, Sophie was the only stranger in the world.

'Does William know about this? Does he expect you?'

She remembered David saying, 'Have you explained to the mice?'

Oh, David, come and help me with this. Say, 'Come off it, young Soph. Calm down. There are other jobs, even other films.'

The stranger had paused in her packing, studying the extraordinary notion that she might not be welcome.

She shrugged,

'Well, he can say so, I suppose.'

She had finished her hasty packing and was pulling tight the drawstring of the dufflebag Ella had given her for Christmas.

To throw yourself at a man and be refused – how could you survive such a humiliation? Ella could hope only that William would behave with tact, find some way of letting her down lightly.

She could trust in William's good intentions, but not in his diplomatic skills.

Sophie had remembered filial duty.

'Don't worry, Mum. I'll keep in touch. I'll be back to get my things.'

So much for her anxiety about clinging to Sophie, who had kissed her briefly and run downstairs and was gone.

William would send her back, of course, but in what condition? Her father had rejected her, she had lost her beloved job and now she was facing another rejection.

Where had she got this idea about William? Ella looked back over his stay in the house, seeking any sign of interest he might have shown in Sophie. None. None on the other side either. Sophie had typed for him, discussed difficulties in the manuscript in a businesslike manner and if she met him about the house addressed him in a teasing tone which Ella had thought not entirely friendly.

I thought she was forward when she offered to help with the luggage. I thought that was forward.

Never mind that. Think what I'm to do for her when she comes back shamed – and she's suffering enough now. How can I cope?

Suppose she doesn't come. Suppose she's too ashamed to come? Where will she go?

That thought could not be entertained.

If she doesn't come back here, I am no mother and this is no home.

She waited.

She made dinner for two and waited.

She ate dinner alone, left Sophie's helping in the oven and waited.

At half-past eight the doorbell rang. Sophie must have forgotten her key.

Ella opened the door and found Rob, looking pale, tired and unusually handsome.

Ella said the words which had been so long at the back of her mind.

'Poor Rob. My poor, poor Rob.'

She held out her arms. Rob had to stoop grotesquely to put her head on Ella's shoulder, but she managed it for a moment, then freed herself.

'Don't sympathise. I'd be bawling for hours. I couldn't get here before. I have to talk to Sophie.'

'I thought it was Sophie at the door. She isn't here.'

'She didn't come home then? Oh, Hell.'

'She came and went again.'

As Rob came after her into the brightly lighted kitchen, Ella saw what had made the change in her face. The skin was drawn tightly over her bones, revealing their severe beauty.

She sat at the table and let her bag slide from her shoulder to the floor. Then she slumped.

'Hardest thing I ever did, telling her she had to go.'

Those great bags they carry, as if they were carrying their lives about with them, thought Ella. Perhaps she had better get one.

She said, 'Was it really because of the video? Sophie said your friend found the video and that made her do it. It doesn't seem reasonable.'

Rob studied the word.

'Reasonable? No.'

'A video of Sophie and Becky walking down a street together? Couldn't you have explained, you were timing Becky's walk for the film?'

Rob looked from far off into a world where things could be explained, and shook her head.

'No. May I wait for Sophie?'

'Sophie mightn't come back. She has gone to William.'

Rob was startled into life.

'William? What use would he be?'

'I mean gone. Packed. Taken her clothes.' Faster than her father. 'I've been waiting, expecting her back. Hoping William can manage to send her back without hurting her feelings too much.'

'Send her back?' Rob was amazed at the suggestion. 'Do you think he's crazy? He won't be able to believe his luck.'

'Oh,' cried Ella. 'I can't believe it. I know she's upset, but that's no excuse. Throwing herself at a man's head like that! It's just shameless.'

'If women didn't throw themselves at men's heads, the human race would not proceed. Would you care for a drink? I have a bottle of whisky in my bag. I was going home to get drunk but I could start here.'

Drinking in order to get drunk was a shocking idea, but the thought of Rob's doing it alone was worse. She could have William's bed, if it came to that.

Ella fetched two glasses and the water jug. Rob took the bottle out of her bag, uncapped it and poured two drinks.

I'd better go slowly on that, thought Ella, as she saw how much whisky Rob had poured into her glass.

'Well, here's to better days. Or something.'

'Have you had anything to eat?'

Rob contrived a grin. The change in her face made a grimace of it.

'The Ella response. Yes, I ate at the hospital café. Misery never put me off my food yet.' She put down her glass. 'Ella, there's something I want you to know. About Sophie. About coming here. It wasn't because of Sophie. I have never. Um. To be absolutely truthful, I did put out a feeler.'

'The shirt and the necklace from Hong Kong.'

Rob nodded.

'Why did I have to tell you that? Why do I have to tell you everything? Do you hate me for it?'

Ella shook her head. She could not at this moment have named her feeling.

'Well, the response was negative and in a way I was glad. It would have been a damned shame if she had turned out to be a dyke.'

There had been a time when nobody would have offered Ella such a confidence. She regretted that time very much.

'Do not use that dreadful word.'

'The way I'm feeling, I couldn't pronounce the word gay. I'd be remembering what it used to mean.'

'Lavatory.'

'You've lost me. Gay means lavatory?'

'Dyke.' Ella decided to have no more to drink. 'Dyke used to be a very vulgar word for lavatory. You should not apply it to yourself in any circumstances.'

Becoming conscious of her stately tone, she looked with alarm at the level of the whisky in her glass. Unfortunately, Rob misunderstood the glance and refilled the glass.

'I suppose you're right. But all this liberation, this coming out. You don't liberate yourself. There's one closet you don't come out of. Never mind that. I just want you to know, I never had designs on Sophie. Wouldn't have been here, wouldn't have come to your house, ever. By the way, some people would think lavatory was a vulgar word for toilet.'

'You would not wish to call yourself a toilet.'

Rob couldn't stop laughing.

'Really, you mustn't drink any more. You'll be sick tomorrow.'

'That's the idea. Convert emotional pain into physical pain. Which passes.'

'Well, you won't be able to drive. You'll have to sleep it off in William's bed.'

'That's a strange conjugation. Conjunction. Me in William's bed. Oh damn. Listen, Ella. It's no big deal. She isn't tied to him and he's not such a bad stick.'

'I could never get him to say he enjoyed the food.'

'You saw him at his worst. He gets so wrapped up in what he's doing that he's hardly human. That's what I envy and why I give him such a bad press. He's quite amiable, really. Clean, honest, sober . . . more than I am. Paid me back my sixty dollars straight away. Thousands wouldn't. If he is a genius, he doesn't trade on it. It's just . . . you don't understand about Sophie. Perhaps a parent wouldn't see it. She's the kind they yearn after in the street. Beauty and the little extra, whatever it is. Animal magnetism to a high degree. Do you think she'd get the push from William? Not a hope.'

'Parents don't want to know these things about their children, any more than . . . the other way around.'

'That's right. The old incest tabu.'

Since she could not focus on this new view of Sophie, Ella concentrated on the words 'incest tabu'. 'The things I had about this house that I didn't know about.'

She paused and drank.

'Hate. People hating each other and I never knew.'

'Did you think you could hand out love with the clean shirts?'

'He was tying his tie.' She spoke with dreamy astonishment. 'He was tying his tie when he asked me for a divorce and his hands didn't shake.'

'Comes of having been a surgeon, I suppose. "Scalpel, please. Swab, please. Clips, please. Divorce, please." By the way . . .'

She halted and shut her mouth firmly on what she had been about to say.

'You know what, Ella. This world. This human race. It isn't divided into sexes. Everybody thinks it's divided into sexes but it isn't. It's the givers and the takers, the diners and the dinners.'

Ella said, carefully, 'If the dinner goes looking for the diner, who's the giver and who's the taker?' She added, as Rob refilled the glasses, 'We should have a cup of coffee,' but the sink seemed too far away.

Rob pondered.

'I'll think that over later.' She added profoundly, 'Resinous pines and insects.'

They should really have that cup of coffee.

'I think we've had too much to drink.'

'No, but listen. The pine exudes the resin which attracts the insect. The insect settles, the resin sets hard and there you are, trapped in the amber of someone else's passion. Trapped in amber, there you are for life.

'Your poor bloody husband, ex-husband, you know what he was? A failure. Hamfisted Harry, he was. Tying his tie, that would be the limit of his animal his manual dexterity. Got out of that hospital just ahead of a scandal, settled the mess out of court, got out under pressure. I suppose he's better as a lecturer but not that much. And there he is, the poor shit, stuck fast in the amber of your devotion. Oh God, I'm drunk. I never meant to say that.'

'Not now he isn't. Stuck fast.'

Rob muttered, 'I'm sorry.'

She looked truly wretched.

Ella now felt quite sober. Indeed, she needed a drink. There was in her mind the image of a tired old horse dragging a heavy cart, but she dismissed it briskly.

'May I have another drink, please?'

Rob poured eagerly.

'I've had my ration, that's clear.'

Nevertheless, she poured the rest of the whisky into her own glass.

'If Sophie is what you say . . .'

'Heavenly bodies. They shine on you for a while but you have to remember, night must fall.'

Oh, yes. Oh, yes, thought Ella.

She must commit those words to memory.

'Suppose she shtops . . .'

Because it isn't a man, it's a book. That's the terrible thing. If the book's a failure, will she look for another . . . writer, artist, whatever?

'You mean, when night falls for William?'

Not if, but when.

'He'd get a book out of it. You can do what you like to a writer if you don't mind being put in a book.'

Not to poets, though, thought Ella cleverly, and just as cleverly remained silent.

She said instead, 'I thought she was heartless. Heartless to you.'

'Heartless is part of it, dear. That's why night must fall. That lot have one problem and that's growing old. That's a long way off for Sophie.'

This was the future of her youngest child, alien and unimaginable to Ella.

Hamfisted Harry. Was nothing what it seemed?

Rob stood up with majestic poise.

'I am for William's bed.'

She took a deep breath and walked steadily from the room.

Hamfisted Harry. But he got the University Medal – that must mean something. Passed the FRCS exams first try.

Night must fall.

She could catch ideas as they sped past but she could not hold them. She must lie down. She thought of the stairs and decided that her bedroom was out of reach. She stood up, reeled and sat down. Even the door was out of reach.

She lowered herself carefully to hands and knees. As she advanced towards the bathroom, she thought triumphantly, 'This is how it is. Words are nothing. This is it. The truth of it.'

Clinging to the basin with one hand, she splashed cold water on her face, groped for the sponge, saturated it and held it to the nape of her neck until it seemed possible to advance to William's room.

Rob was already stretched out on the doona, snoring gently. Ella nudged her firmly across the bed, took off her shoes and wriggled under as much of the doona as was not pinned down by Rob's body.

Sleep. Refuge.

She woke in daylight, looked at her watch and wondered why it was there. She never wore her watch to bed. Then she became aware that she had worn all her clothes to bed.

The situation required thought.

Memory of the evening returned with the astonishing

discovery that she had got very drunk, too drunk to get upstairs, too drunk to get undressed.

Amazing.

And the body next to her was Rob. Unhappy Rob, for whom there was no escape.

She sat up to look down at her. Her face, loose and heavy in sleep, had lost its abnormal beauty. Ella put out a hand to stroke her cheek and let it rest on her throat below the angle of her jaw. Under the damp hair, the flesh was heavy, hot and alien, moving gently with her sleeping breath.

Ella took her hand away, not knowing why she had made the gesture, knowing that there were loves for which there were no gestures.

She looked at her watch again, this time with intelligence. Twenty past 6. Time enough.

There was something else Rob had said last night, something quite astounding.

Hamfisted Harry.

She repeated the words with vindictive delight. It wasn't a feeling she was proud of. She didn't own it as hers. It belonged with the house. This house was dead now, rotten and breeding evil. All that fuss about William's work, keeping the house quiet, keeping the volume of the radio down, not switching on the television for the midday program – devices to keep the house alive. A life-support system. William had gone, Sophie had gone.

But Sophie might come back.

That thought brought her to the present and her absurd and shameful situation, with the urge to restore normality in haste.

Moving discreetly out of respect for Rob's sleep, she got

out of bed, found her shoes and made for the upstairs bathroom.

Looking in the glass, she agreed that this unkempt, unwashed object with the dry mouth and the whisky breath was her true self but it was going to remain her secret, even from Rob.

Showered, dressed and combed, she looked at herself again with relief.

Surfaces, however false, must be preserved.

She was pressing oranges for juice when Rob came into the kitchen.

'Good morning. You slept well.'

'That wasn't sleep. It was alcoholic stupor. How about you?'

'Yes, I died too.'

Gratefully Rob accepted a glass of orange juice and sat down to drink it.

'Sophie didn't come back.'

'No. Just as well, perhaps.'

They stared at each other in silent complicity.

Rob asked, 'What would you have done if she had come in at the wrong moment?'

'Lost consciousness at once.'

Then she reflected that the remark had no connection with reality – she did not know what she would have done, at all – but was intended only to amuse Rob, in which it had been effective.

That sort of thing – not like me at all, she said to herself in astonishment.

'Pretty restricting, being a parent,' said Rob. 'That ass G.K. Chesterton saying "My country, right or wrong" is like "My mother, drunk or sober". It sounds so smart but I've often thought the second proposition preferable to the first. Do mothers cease to be human?'

'Their children would like to think so.'

In spite of her resolution, Ella felt inclined to confession. It would be good to laugh with Rob over that crawl to the bathroom. She couldn't quite manage to laugh at it alone.

No. Not even with Rob.

Rob accepted toast, coffee and aspirin but declined the offer of a shower.

'I'll make it home and change before I go to the hospital. Probably be bringing her home today. Tell Sophie will you that of course she has money coming. In lieu of notice, at least, and I'll do what I can about sick pay and holiday pay. Do you think she wants me to look for an opening for her?'

'I don't know. She was so keen on that film.'

'I'll never find another like her,' Rob sighed. 'It isn't much of a film. An unambitious little enterprise. Sometimes they take off.'

'I hope it will.'

There was a valedictory sadness in their voices.

'I owe you a few good meals, Ella. What about coming to lunch in town?'

'I'd like that. I won't be here for much longer. I have to give up the house.'

She could not keep the weariness of defeat out of her voice.

'Oh, what a rotten shame. Look, I'll give you my private number at work so you can ring and let me know where you are.'

She found a pen and a notebook in the bag and wrote her name and a number.

'Now see you use it,' she said as she handed over the sheet of paper. 'I don't want all the worry and expense of tracking you down with a private eye. Okay?'

'Okay.'

'And don't worry too much about Sophie. Truly, she won't come to any harm with William. He's a good old stick, really.'

Could not even Rob suppose that she might be feeling for herself? Feeling betrayed by Sophie?

About Rob's troubles there was nothing to be said. She went out to the car with her and waved a ceremonious farewell, hoping the gesture would be understood. Rob returned the wave as if it had been speech.

When she had cleared the breakfast away, she fetched clean linen and made up William's bed. Then, admitting her intentions, she went upstairs to get clothes and toilet equipment, hung her clothes in William's wardrobe and her toothbrush in the downstairs bathroom.

In the mid-afternoon the phone rang and Sophie spoke.

'Mum, it's all right. Everything is going really well. I thought you might be worrying but I couldn't get to a phone before. I'll be up tomorrow to collect a few things. Is that all right?'

'Rob came looking for you last night.'

'Rob did? What did she want?'

The slight emphasis on the personal pronoun consigned Rob to history.

'She talked about money due to you and she wanted to know if she should look for another opening for you.'

'Are you all right, Mum? You sound a bit down. You're not worrying about me, are you?'

No, Sophie. I am worrying about myself.

'Well, you mustn't. About the job – I don't want to look for anything until we've got this manuscript to the publisher. That's one reason I want to come up tomorrow. Can I borrow the typewriter from upstairs? I can't do a thing with William's old rattletrap.'

'I suppose so. You'd better start taking everything you want. The house will have to be sold, of course,' said Ella, hoping to spark remorse.

Sophie instead became thoughtful.

'I could do with some furniture. What about the furniture in my room? Can I have that?'

'I don't know about the contents of the house. I don't think anything's been decided.'

'Oh. Well, I suppose I can borrow the typewriter.'

'Of course you can. We don't have the bailiffs in.'

'Well, the money will be useful. She didn't give you any idea how much, did she?'

'None at all.'

Sophie, say a kind word about her, will you? Just one kind word.

'Right. See you tomorrow then. Goodbye.'

It's her age, that's all, thought Ella as she put down the phone.

At least she's no hypocrite. Any feeling she expressed would be genuine.

And come to think of it, she had lived a long time with falsehood.

• XXIII •

David put down the parcel of fish and chips and stared at Ella.

'What do you mean, Sophie's gone?'

'She's moved out.'

'For God's sake, Mum, what's happened? Did you have a row?'

Martha withdrew to switch on the stove and arrange the food on baking trays.

'No, of course not. She was upset about losing her job.'

Martha uttered a cry of distress.

'Oh, no!'

'She came home early yesterday afternoon in a terrible state. I heard her run upstairs and I went after her, knowing there must be something wrong. She was putting clothes into a bag.'

This was going to be worse than she had foreseen. 'She said she was going to William.'

This news silenced David. He frowned as if he were trying to translate it into comprehensible language.

While they were eating their fish and chips, he said unhappily, 'Couldn't you have stopped her, Mum?'

'I don't see how. Do you think I wanted her to go?'

She paused to give them time to sympathise with her solitary condition, then went on, resigned, 'She didn't stop long enough to argue.'

'But having him in the house. Couldn't you see there was something going on?'

Ella shook her head.

'There wasn't anything going on that I could see. All he did was work, and she never spoke to him except about the typing. I didn't like the way she was living, associating with people twice her age and forgetting her school-friends. I can't say he ever encouraged her.'

'I wish you hadn't had him in the house.'

'It was what she wanted. I was a bit worried about it until I saw him.'

Martha giggled softly.

'I know what you mean. It isn't Ella's fault, David. She can't live Sophie's life for her.'

David said furiously, 'She's too young.'

Martha looked at him sharply. He became absent-minded.

Ella had always had her doubts about those College camping trips.

'She's nineteen. I was worried that she wasn't taking any interest in young men.'

'He's not nobody,' said Martha. 'He's a distinguished writer. Some women . . .' She paused, rejecting what she had been about to say. 'Losing her job must have been a dreadful shock. She loved it so. How did it happen?'

This was the awkward moment. She didn't want to tell them. She didn't want to expose Rob to disgust or to pity.

'There was a crisis. Nobody's fault. Rob's friend is very jealous, unbalanced really. Always suspicious. There was a video – Max had made a video of Becky and Sophie walking together. It was just to time some dialogue for the film, that's all.'

Remembering the sunny afternoon, the laughter and the coaxing, Sophie walking hand in hand with Becky and smiling down at her, Ella felt the pain of looking into a vanished world.

She said desperately, 'It's utterly ridiculous, the poor woman must be mad.'

That memory had brought enlightenment. It wasn't Sophie she was angry with, but the first one, the first deserter who had destroyed her world.

She hurried on, 'That's all it was, just Sophie walking with Becky, but she found it and played it and she got the idea that . . . Sophie had taken her place. She took an overdose. Rob found her in a coma. She got her to hospital and they pulled her through, but Rob had to promise to get rid of Sophie that very day.'

David was picking up chips in his fingers and chewing them morosely.

'Charming people.'

'Poor wretched woman,' said Martha. 'What a terrible way to be.'

'She should never have gone near that film place. Associating with those weirdos.'

Both Rob and William had a quality that was lacking in David, but Ella's position was so shaky that she dared not even hint at that.

'You know,' said Martha, 'I'm finding this difficult to believe. Sophie is really young even for nineteen. Innocently enthusiastic, you'd say. Are you sure you have it right, Ella? She isn't just moving in with him to finish typing the novel?'

'Trust him to leave it at that,' said David.

'I don't know what's going on. She's coming up tomorrow to get the typewriter and perhaps I'll find out more then.'

But I don't feel like asking.

Martha was reflecting.

'He must be well into his thirties. She could be looking for a father figure.'

This idea at least deflected blame from Ella.

'She wouldn't need a father figure if she had a father,' said David bitterly. 'It's Sophie who will suffer from this. It's just the worst time for her.'

Not so good for me, either, thought Ella.

Coldly, she said, 'The house can go on the market as soon as you like.'

It irked her that this remark caused no stir, no sigh of relief. Apparently, that matter was already settled.

'You could manage with a smaller place, if you don't have Sophie on your hands. That's something. It would leave a bigger margin for investment income.'

'Oh, that look!' Martha spoke with exaggerated dread. 'Not tonight. No talk of money tonight. 'I'm sure it's all right, Ella. Nobody is going to be beastly to Sophie.'

Rob had said that William was a person of good

character, but would Rob's opinion weigh with David?

Last night she had feared for William.

'We'll just have to wait and see.'

Nothing like a cliché for comfort.

• XXIV •

Caroline arrived next morning. Since Ella hadn't heard the car, her arrival at the back door brought a shock of joy.

'Oh, Carrie, pet.'

'Oh, Mum.'

They hugged strenuously.

Caroline disengaged herself and said tenderly, 'Poor Mum. Try not to blame yourself too much.'

Ella stared in amazement, then retorted, 'The way you've been carrying on, you ought to be glad it's a man.'

And that, she thought later, was the shortest reconciliation on record.

Caroline stared back in disbelief, then subsided into a chair and began to weep bitterly and – there was no doubt about it – sincerely.

'How could you? How could you say such a wicked, vulgar thing? I know it's been hard for you, you've been going through a very bad time, but you shouldn't let it destroy you. Saying such wicked, immoral things – I never thought I would hear you say such a dreadful thing. And having those terrible people in the house, letting them corrupt Sophie. Perhaps you didn't see what would come of it. You couldn't have thought of anything as bad as this. You were just taking petty revenges, having these people in the house, expecting Dad to support that wretched man – '

'William paid for his own food. And if anyone is complaining about that electricity bill, what unbelievable pettiness!'

She was losing control. What could Caroline know about electricity bills?

But Caroline didn't ask. She looked for a moment shifty and uncomfortably exposed.

'Perhaps you're not sorry. Perhaps this is your way of saying to Dad, look what you've done. Now Sophie's life is ruined, look what you've done.'

'Sophie's life is not ruined. William is a man of good character and a very fine writer.'

'Oh, good character. He's shown that, hasn't he?'

Ella could not defend William's character without exposing Sophie's disgrace.

'You are talking rubbish.'

'Oh, yes.'

Caroline's tears were dried.

'That's the answer always, isn't it? I have to be talking rubbish. Any time I tried to set a standard, I got no help from you. You let that pair get away with anything they liked, you never checked them. The stupid way they talked and carried on and you just sitting and smiling as if they were being clever.'

This was a new phase. Caroline's voice had risen and was bolting with her.

'You saw to it that Dad didn't check them either. We never had a father. You saw to that. "Don't disturb your father." "Don't upset your father." "Don't make a noise. Your father's had a very tiring day." Oh, it sounded fine and considerate, but what it meant was "This is my department, and I don't brook any interference." '

There was enought truth in this to madden Ella.

'Don't you worry about my motives, Caroline. Take a good look at your own.'

Sophie had said, 'Go take a look in the glass.'

'Just what do you mean by that?'

Ella halted. She was losing Becky. She was in danger of losing Becky for good. She must make things no worse.

'Except, of course, that I'm in the wrong, as usual.'

Ella with difficulty let that pass and said more calmly, 'I think you had better go now. This is doing no-one any good.'

Comfort in clichés again.

Caroline got up and went with dignity.

Brook no interference. Brook no interference.

That wasn't Caroline talking. The feelings were hers all right, pouring out of her like blood or bile – stunned as she was by them, Ella could not deny it – but not the words. Not all this analysis either. Explaining people's motives – it sounded like Martha. No, surely not Martha. She wouldn't be holding discussions with Caroline.

Caroline hates me. Caroline has always hated me.

She sat motionless at the kitchen table. Sophie found her there twenty minutes later, still drowsy with shock.

'Hullo, Mum,' said Sophie, then repeated in a different tone, 'Hullo. What's up?'

'You just missed Caroline.'

'What rotten luck.'

Ella no longer had the right to protest at the sarcasm.

'Has she been upsetting you?'

Ella was past all pretence.

'She hates me. Caroline hates me.'

'Caroline hates everybody except Max and Becky and I wouldn't answer for them for long if they didn't toe the line. I don't know why it's such a shock to you. She's always needling you.'

'She can be a bit tactless sometimes. I never thought – '

'Tactless! Caroline's never tactless. She knows very well what she's doing. There is one thing Caroline's really good at. She knows how to put the needle in and at that she's an expert. And looking like an angel as she does it.

'But Mum, you were the one who never did toe the line. You were the expert at handling her. Do you expect her to love you for it?'

But I loved her. I understood how she felt. I couldn't let her behave badly but I knew how she felt.

'She was always under David's shadow. I understood that. It was hard for her.'

Sophie said, 'It wasn't David's fault, was it? Other people can live with things like that. I'm sorry, Mum, but Caroline's a born . . . a very nasty piece. Sometimes I wonder Max doesn't see it. I suppose that's why they say love is blind.'

A glance at Ella's stricken face informed her that parents were susceptible to the same emotional weakness. She fell silent, abashed.

Later, she asked, 'What about me? Is anyone interested in what I'm doing?'

Ella answered sourly, 'Everyone is a good deal too interested in what you are doing.'

'Hey. Is that what she was on about? She knew I'd moved out. That was quick, wasn't it?'

'These things get about, I suppose.'

'Yes. Well. About William. He's agreeable, but he says I have to think it over. He says you can't make a decision like that in a hurry, especially when you're upset. I was in a state, wasn't I?' She looked back with some amusement at this piece of the remote past. 'But meanwhile I have to find somewhere to live and he hates it at that place so we might as well join forces, sort of.'

William, it seemed, had all the vicious instincts of a conscientious school counsellor. Ella felt that socially she had no further to fall. She might blush for Sophie but Sophie could not blush for herself.

'Besides, he does need help with the clean copy. He's getting it into a terrible mess.'

She spoke complacently. Even if what Rob said about her was true, she seemed to pride herself more on her typing than on her animal magnetism. 'If we get on all right together, then we'll stay together. If not . . .' she shrugged.

This was a long way from fainting with joy on a moonlit beach. Well, that had proved to be no guarantee, either.

'What's for lunch, Mum? I'm starving.'

Seeing Ella still absorbed in thought, she opened the refrigerator, investigated supplies and said, 'Toasted ham sandwiches do you?'

As she assembled the sandwiches, she chatted easily.

'I'll be spending my days househunting and my evenings typing. Unfurnished places are much cheaper if you can find them. It would be handy if I could have the stuff out of my room.'

'I should think you could have that. I'll find out.'

I am being dismembered.

Caroline hates me and I am being cut to pieces.

'Do you think I could borrow David's good sleeping-bag? It's still here, isn't it?'

'I'm sure he'd be delighted to lend it to you,' she answered wryly.

'Good. I'll take it first and ask later. I had to go sometime, Mum, you know. You couldn't be expected to make room for me when you get your unit. It was better to go like that, on the spur of the moment. Made it easier, for me, anyhow.'

'I suppose so.'

Sophie brought the food to the table and said desperately, 'Don't let her upset you like this. She'll come back. She'll run out of excuses and she can't bear to be in the wrong.'

'Don't talk like that, please, Sophie. I don't want to discuss it.'

Sophie drew a harsh breath.

'Well, I hope you know she's buddies with Louise, and I bet that's where she got the news. David would have told Dad and that creature would have been on the phone to Caroline as fast as light.'

The voice behind Caroline: Louise. Louise having interesting, civilised discussions about her character.

Ella stared at the sandwich on her plate.

'Well, you had to know sometime, Mum.'

No, I didn't. I didn't have to know about this at all.

Caught between guilt and grievance, Sophie said childishly, 'Is there something wrong with the sandwiches?'

Ella shook her head and began to eat.

The offence was serious.

It's you and David who make her what she is. You can't help being what you are and neither can she. But what could I have done? Lucky I didn't know how she felt, for I couldn't have acted differently and I would have found it much harder.

Sophie said in a subdued voice, 'I'll go and get the sleeping-bag and the typewriter and be off.'

When Ella said 'Would you like me to drive you back?' it seemed like an attempt at reconciliation.

'If you give me a lift to the station, that would be fine.'

At the station, she said, 'Mum, you were always fair to everybody. You never favoured any one of us more than another.'

But it was life that showed favours, life that wasn't fair.

• XXV •

Ella camped in the house now, sleeping in William's bed and avoiding the upstairs rooms.

She was absorbed in making Becky's rug. She made excursions to unknown suburbs looking for opportunity shops, buying secondhand clothes of finely woven wool and bringing them home in triumph. She spent the rest of her leisure unpicking, washing, pressing cloth and cutting it into fine bias strips which she hooked into the rapidly growing picture.

Who was it that had spoken of the pleasures of the hunt? That described her feeling as she brought home an old topcoat of grey-green gabardine which would do excellently for the little stream.

She was sorry she had made that remark to Rob (of course – the pleasures of the hunt) about pale brown silk, for of course one couldn't walk on silk. Only pure wool was hardy enough for that; pure wool, however, was becoming very difficult to find. The best fabrics came from ancient garments. The next lucky find at the Saint Vincent de Paul was a man's suit in dark brown, just right for the patches of ploughed field, though it was not in good condition. She had to be careful to discard the worn areas.

While she worked, another picture was taking shape in her mind, one which would not impose such restrictions, which could hang on a wall and involve a river of pale brown silk, embroidered flowers – or crocheted perhaps in bright silks and half-seen among tufted grasses. She had only herself to please, so why not?

In that 'Why not?' there was a stirring of pleasant excitement.

Pam came in for coffee and found her in the dining room working at her frame.

'Ella, what do you think you are doing?'

'Making a rug for Becky.'

She ripped out a row of loops. The project of carrot tops for the market garden had been too ambitious. A pity, for the colour was perfect.

'Oh, wake up, Ella. Have you done anything about finding a place to live?'

'Not yet. No. I will. In a few days.'

Pam said earnestly, 'If you don't show some initiative, Ella, you'll lose control of the situation. You'll wake up and find yourself in a nice little retirement unit with geriatrics groaning around you.'

Ella perceived that this horrible prospect, which could not be taken seriously, was meant to spur her to action.

'I'll put the coffee on.'

Pam followed her to the kitchen, persisting in her effort.

'It doesn't have to be permanent, you know. Just a roof over your head for the time being. We could go round the estate agents on Sunday, if you like. Do you want me to come with you?'

That carrot colour would do for a few meadow flowers, thought Ella.

'That's very kind of you. I'll let you know.'

Pam accepted her cup of coffee in silence. Her mind was no longer concentrated on Ella's problems. Thomas was going to be married. Pam had struck up a ready friendship with the girl and could easily be directed to talk of her own affairs.

'How are Thomas and Anthea going?'

'They've decided against any sort of wedding. They're just going to the registry office with two friends, no guests, then we're having dinner together, the three of us, before they get the train. I told you, didn't I, I'm giving her her dress? A suit, actually. I've put one aside for her to look at.'

Ella smiled over Pam's happiness, but the smile revived Pam's anxiety and brought her back to the subject.

'Ella, dear. I wish you would face reality.'

'Yes, I will. Truly. Now please don't worry about it any more.'

'I wish you would start worrying about it,' said Pam, and sighed as she got up to leave in defeat.

It was necessary to break up that expanse of grey-green gabardine. The search for a certain colour and texture led her to the duster bag, where she retrieved a yellowed, shrunken pair of wool and silk knickers. As the fabric ballooned under her hands through the greying suds of their third wash, promising a satisfactory effect of froth and glitter, the muscles of her face relaxed and her mouth softened into a curve. She perceived that she was smiling.

She had remarkable success with cauliflowers and cabbages of variegated green, but the flowers of the meadow, no matter how finely she cut her strips, remained absurdly large in proportion to the vegetables. The effect, however, was not bad, primitive and amusing.

When the phone rang she was irked by the interruption.

'Mrs Ferguson? Mary Duckworth here. About your settlement.'

'Oh, yes.'

'Are you prepared to accept four hundred thousand dollars in return for surrendering your interest in the house?'

Ella said nothing. She was making a mental image of a figure four and adding noughts to it. How many?

'I don't really think you'll do any better. Otherwise the house will go on the market and you might do worse. What do you say?'

Ella said yes, and returned to her handiwork.

In the second week, she forgot that the day was Thursday. When David and Martha surprised her at work, she did not recollect herself in time and they saw they were not expected.

'Why, Ella! Isn't it beautiful! And how much you've done!'

Martha's enthusiasm was forced.

As Ella bent to put her hook and her ball of strips into the basket, she knew that behind her back they were staring at each other in dismay.

Later, as she set the table in the dining room, she heard

the refrigerator door open and close. They were checking on the food.

Did they suppose she had given up eating? Why, she felt . . . how did she feel? Better, certainly. The rug, which had been intended as an expression of grief and loss, had become a kind of comfort.

Nobody takes this away, she said to herself, seeing the moving footway which had carried them all one after the other out of her life: Mrs Barlow, Ursula Rodd and her committees, Nina, Becky, Sophie – not Pam, not David and Martha – better for them to think her a little crazy than to find her ungrateful.

They had better not find out about her sleeping in William's room for all that. That might indeed seem a little eccentric.

At dinner the conversation went awkwardly, encumbered by unspoken thoughts.

Martha asked how Sophie was faring, her tone suggesting that it was minimally better to ask than to ignore the subject.

Ella knew that she owed it to William to describe his virtuous and responsible behaviour. She could not do this without shaming Sophie further. William would have to suffer the injustice.

'David, I forgot to tell you I lent her your sleeping-bag. I hope you don't mind.'

A very lame approach to the truth, that was. Martha, however, received the message of the sleeping-bag – and nodded over it.

David said absently, 'Yes, that's all right.' He was reserved, meditating some topic he found difficult to approach.

At last he said, 'Mum,' and paused.

'Yes, dear.'

'About signing the deed of settlement. Dad wants to sign it here. In the house. Would that be all right? He's making a point of it. Mary says it would be all right. What do you say? It could be, you know, that he wants . . . it might be a move to . . . to make things better, you know.'

Remembering the note about the electricity bill, Ella doubted that. However, the children didn't have to know all the squalid details.

'We still have to talk about the contents of the house. Sharing it out. We'll have to start moving our stuff out, too.'

'Sophie wants the furniture from her room.'

'Tell her that's all right, then.'

Ella asked irritably, 'How can they settle up before they've sold the house? Where would they get the money?'

'I can't ask them that, can I? So long as they can pay it. I know she's sold her unit and I suppose they've raised a loan.'

The subject was so painful that they left it abruptly.

'What about it, Mum? Is it all right for Dad to come here?'

'Yes, I suppose so.'

'That's the end of it, then.'

Shocked at the weariness in his voice, Ella said, 'I shouldn't have left so much to you.'

'So long as I've done right by you. Mary thinks we couldn't have done any better.'

You'll never be the same again, thought Ella sadly. Never so careless and cheerful again.

'So we're all on the move,' said Martha. 'We'll be

moving, too, joining the mortgage belt now that we've paid off the unit. Do you have any idea where you're going to settle? It would be nice to be close to you.'

Ella had no idea on this subject at all. As furniture for the future, she had a remnant of pale green lamé which was to form a stylised arc of sea, the base for a foam of cobweb Shetland wool knitted rather loosely in the traditional Old Shale pattern. The rest of the design was blank as yet.

There was also the prospect of lunch with Rob, and she meant to apply for another student to replace Nina.

She understood that none of these prospects was an answer to Martha's question.

'I don't want to buy straight away. I'll rent for a while till I get my bearings.'

That was an unfortunate image, conjuring up such a pathetic picture that Martha said hastily, 'I wish Sophie would get in touch with us. We haven't heard from her at all. Can you give me her phone number, Ella?'

Helpless, exasperated, Ella said, 'She won't give it to me. I don't think she wants me to know what kind of place she's living in. She says she's out all day househunting and then typing the manuscript in the evenings. Everybody listens to you and it's very embarrassing. It's so much easier for her to ring from a callbox. You know Sophie. If she doesn't want to, she'll always find a good reason. And she does ring and chat every couple of days. I know it's ridiculous. I make meek suggestions about emergencies and she says that she'll be moving out any day and she wishes I wouldn't fuss.'

'Ask her to ring us, then,' said Martha.

'I don't want to see her with that character.'

'Oh, David.' Martha was indignant. 'He didn't kidnap her, you know.'

Another chance for the truth. Ella let it pass.

'Besides,' Martha added, 'sometimes you have to be polite to people you don't like. We're not going to drop Sophie, whatever happens.'

David had been subjecting her to a cold and steady glance.

She answered it, 'All right. You win.'

The name of the unacceptable person was not spoken.

Martha gave up all attempts at conversation and began to clear the table.

'Can you give me a carton, Ella? I'll start packing the trophies.'

• XXVI •

The voice on the phone was unexpected.

'Mrs Ferguson? This is William. William Anstey, you know. May I come to see you? I have to talk to you.'

Now she must discuss her shameless child with William. The prospect was not agreeable.

'Of course you may. When would you like to come?'

'This afternoon. I'm taking my manuscript to the publisher this morning and we'll probably have lunch together, then I can come straight up, if that's all right.'

'Yes. That's good news about the novel. You must be glad that it's finished.'

'It's a weight off the back. You don't know what a help Sophie's been. But I suppose you do know. And you too, taking me in.'

That's right. Say a kind word. You can't make me feel any better.

'It was no trouble.'

But it brought plenty in its wake.

'I'll see you later, then.'

While she waited for him, she managed to create a quite convincing aerial view of a duck on the segment of pond in the lower righthand corner of the frame. She was admiring it when William appeared, rigid with embarrassment, at the dining room door.

'I should have rung the bell, sorry. I just took it for granted, I came in the back way. Sorry. I thought you'd be in the kitchen.'

'It doesn't matter in the least. Do sit down.'

Dear me, what a hobbledehoy he was, what a large, awkward clod. The dismay she had felt at the first sight of him, since forgotten, now returned.

He stared at Ella's rug, seeming to draw reassurance from it.

'That's marvellous. Love your cauliflowers and the duck. Are you copying a set design?'

'No, I just block out the sections and make up the details as I go along.'

'Terrific. Don't stop. I like watching. No doubt you know what I've come to talk about.'

'I'm afraid Sophie has behaved very badly and put you in a most embarrassing position.'

'My position.' He stared at her and shook his head. 'I'm not complaining about my position, except that I think it can't be real. It's like the old fairytales where the idiot somehow gets it right, says the right word by accident and the door opens or the golden apple falls into his hand.'

He might be reduced to stammering misery by coming in through the wrong door, but he was bold enough when it came to unpacking his heart.

'Suddenly the tree flowers in winter in the snow.'

Ella began to be seriously angry with Sophie.

'She's put her sleeping-bag on the kitchen floor. It's the only clean spot in the house. When I go in to make a cup of tea in the morning, she's still asleep, with her hair loose, and so beautiful.'

He began to cry, quietly and neatly.

Ella hooked a line of green round the duckpond with speed and concentration.

'I'm thirty-seven.'

He had regained sobriety.

'She doesn't seem to be interested in boys of her own age. She says they are boring.'

'I don't have affairs. Don't get involved. It's too much mess and waste, waste of everything. Waste of time, too. You never get any work done.'

He added in a rush of words, 'I would be aiming at marriage.'

Ella's rug hook stopped in mid-loop.

'Have you talked about this to Sophie?'

'We haven't talked about anything since that first day, when I told her she had to take her time and think it over. I told her she could just go away without saying anything if she wanted to, but every morning when I go into the kitchen she's still there. Perhaps she's only staying till the manuscript's finished. You might see her back home today.'

I'll have a word to say to her if I do, thought Ella. Playing with a man's feelings like this.

'Even if she said yes, could it last?'

'Who can answer that?' Ella asked, with a bitterness he did not try to understand.

'No, of course not.'

Ella thought of Rob, saying, 'Night must fall.'

'Eighteen years is a big gap,' he said.

Some people didn't think twenty-eight years too great a gap. What did he expect her to do about it? Make him younger?

'Even for nineteen, sometimes she seems very innocent.'

Ella observed, 'Innocence may not be all it's cracked up to be.'

William was alert.

'Oh? Why do you say that?'

'It can be a sort of blindness, I suppose. Too close to ignorance.'

No doubt he sensed a warning in her words.

'You don't know,' he said with sudden urgency, 'just how much one wants . . . I don't know, a bit of the joy of living. Happiness. All the big words,' he added and uttered a falsetto guffaw which startled and silenced him.

'Then you had better take your chance and ask her.'

'You wouldn't be against it? I wouldn't want to cut her off from her family.'

'Oh, William. I don't think it's the most suitable marriage in the world, for you as well as her. You certainly have the right to ask her. She made the situation. I don't know about her father, what he might think.'

'She doesn't care about her father. You're the one she cares about.'

But not always, not enough.

'I'm aware that the drawbacks are obvious,' he said.

So I don't need to point them out.

'It's up to her.'

Ella got up, stretching and sighing with fatigue.

'What about a cup of coffee?'

'Yes, please. Why do you sit all day at your loom like Penelope?'

'It's for my granddaughter. I'm trying to get it finished before I move out.'

She had said that quite calmly, so the remark passed without comment.

'It's terrific. Like a primitive.'

William as a son-in-law. How odd.

He was talking like a son-in-law already. Over coffee, he said, 'The financial situation isn't so bad now, though of course there's no real security. I can sell short stories just about anywhere, I think. My second book didn't bring in much but if this one goes well it might pick up again.'

'Martha thinks you should publish a book of your short stories.'

'Martha?'

He looked attentive and almost handsome.

She said to herself, He'll live.

'My daughter-in-law, David's wife. You met her here with David. She admires your work very much.'

'Tell her I am getting one together.'

'She'll be pleased.'

Dear me, but this was heavy going.

What went on in Sophie's head? She tried to picture the beauty in the sleeping-bag who had made William cry, but all she could see was Sophie in her Girl Guide uniform, chubby and cheerful, her only care to make the A grade hockey team, her greatest charm her amiable disposition.

I cannot answer for them, she thought. I cannot take responsibility.

A combination of innocence and power might be

deadly, but William must take his chance. She thought she had issued a warning, which was the best she could do.

When William on leaving said, 'Do I have your blessing then?' she answered, 'Yes.' but added silently, For what it is worth.

• XXVII •

Seeing him in the house would be an ordeal. She didn't know how to prepare for it. She tried to picture him at the door, in the living room, but the mind's eye wasn't working. His image was fixed forever in the dressingtable mirror.

Instead she saw the living room through the eyes of the invader and noticed for the first time how dingy it appeared. She would have been happy to leave it so, but she knew that its look of sad neglect would be seen as her state of mind. People were too much interested in her state of mind. Reluctantly she moved the rug on its frame into the computer room and, feeling aggrieved, she washed, dusted and polished until cedar glowed, glass sparkled and silver shone, too brightly after all for the occasion. All we need now, she told herself sourly, is a nice floral arrangement and WELCOME on the mat.

When the doorbell sounded at 8 o'clock precisely, she

opened the door to the unexpected sight of a couple engaged in conversation.

It can't be. It can't be. The nerve of the woman. The nerve.

Louise turned her untroubled face to Ella and said, 'Good evening. May we come in?'

The shadow beside her said nothing.

Incapable of speech, Ella stood back and motioned them in with a gesture which, to her annoyance, expressed her helpless dismay.

Before they moved, David and Mary had arrived behind them. He, too, jerked with shock at the sight of Louise.

Someone must speak.

Ella managed to croak, 'Come in.'

The awkward knot on the threshold was loosened as the first pair walked past her.

David said, 'We meant to get here earlier.'

'My fault entirely,' said Mary. 'I'm to blame. I had a client on the phone and I couldn't get away.'

'Thank you for watching my interests,' said Ella, almost normally.

'It's been a privilege.'

They followed Ella into the living room where the other pair were standing, she with her hand protective on his arm. Ella was pleased to think how that gesture must irk him. She got some satisfaction, too, from the cold, hostile stare which Louise directed at Mary, who met it with an affable smile, then tapped her briefcase and said, 'Where do I set out my papers?'

'In the dining room?'

'Fine.' She said to David, 'Principals only?'

He nodded, relieved, and was offering a chair to the

baffled Louise as the principals followed Mary into the other room.

So there they were, seated one on each side of her as she read to them from a suitably imposing document the funeral service of their marriage.

Nobody could have devised this misery – not Grape Eyes, she couldn't have thought it up. Smart as she might be about microbes and such, she could never think up a thing like this. She didn't know enough about other people's feelings.

What could he be thinking? Didn't he have a thought about the first time they had signed their names together? She writing Ella Ferguson, so proud in tulle and white organza, Beryl in apricot – what a fuss there had been about those bridesmaids' dresses, redheaded Beryl wanting aqua, which made dark Marian look bilious, until she had persuaded them into the apricot that suited them both. So much work and worry had gone into that wedding, it should have lasted a lifetime. She had made a scene about the stupid toy bride and bridegroom on the three-tiered wedding cake, thinking his brilliant friends would laugh at it, though his brilliant friends had been quite an embarrassment, drinking too much and yelling and cheering at the very unsuitable telegrams they had sent. 'ON, FERGUS, ON' had been a great success; she hadn't quite known why. Her uncle had muttered, 'Medical students. What can you expect?' and sent the best man to quiet them down. How odd that medical students turned into doctors.

She hadn't wanted to throw them the garter. She had thrown the bouquet of frangipani and apricot-yellow roses to the spinsters and Marian had caught it – not by arrangement, though Beryl had been suspicious of them. She was standing on the stairs looking down at the rowdy young men, who were shouting, 'The garter. Throw the garter!' She had sensed hostility in that shouting, so that she had been quite frightened and had hidden her face as she pulled up the huge ruffled skirt and the starched petticoat – heavens, one showed much more at the beach – had slipped the white satin garter off her leg, tossed it and run, not waiting to see who had caught it. Of course she had been frightened. Sex was the great unknown. No camping trips for her.

Frightened, yet trusting.

Oh God, hold on. Don't cry. Breathe deep and steady. Tying his tie. Tying his tie. I can be as steady. Please explain the increase. Tying his tie.

The ordeal was nearly over. They had listened, read or seemed to read, signed their names to each document and that was that.

He said, tonelessly, 'I have here a cheque for your client in complete settlement of all claims.'

Mary handed the cheque to Ella. Reading the amount on it, she thought, 'No, one wouldn't feel very sentimental handing that over.'

Then they stood up and walked across the hall into Louise's living room. It was clear at once from her kindly smile of welcome that she was the hostess. And I polished it up for her, thought Ella in rage. What a fool. What a fool I was.

She sat down before she could be invited and David got up to offer Mary his easy chair.

Louise said sharply, 'Sit down, Bernard, do,' then brightly to Mary, 'All settled then?'

'Except for the contents of the house. I understand that you have agreed to make an equal division of the contents.'

'We don't have to think about that for a long time yet,' said Louise. She turned to Ella and said earnestly, 'We're going abroad next month and we'd be happy to have you occupy the house while we are away. We won't be moving in until November.'

Ella managed at last to say, 'Thank you. No.'

'But truly, you would be doing us a favour. We don't want the house left empty while we are abroad. It's an invitation to thieves and vandals. And you would have plenty of time to look for somewhere suitable to live, without wasting money on rent.' She frowned at Ella. 'Shouldn't we be trying to do what is best for everyone?'

Mary broke the silence.

'There may be other considerations beside the financial.'

'Well, it's very awkward. We barely have time – we can't find a tenant at this late hour. We have to give a month's grace as it is and we'll be gone before the month's up. This is putting us in a very awkward situation.'

What a terrible look David had for his father. Sadness and contempt.

That look must have spurred him to speech.

'Perhaps Sophie. With a few friends.'

Louise spoke decisively.

'I wouldn't care for that.' She looked around the room, making an inventory. 'Young people can be very destructive.'

David and Mary looked at her in wonder. The doctor looked at no-one while a blush mounted from his chin to his hairline.

Louise had noticed an unusual quality in the silence.

She amended hastily, 'Not Sophie's friends, of course. I'm sure they must be very nice.'

Ella had seen the blush of shame but could take no satisfaction from it because of a hideous sensation which was rising from her chest through her throat growing like a shrub, puckering and distorting her face, reddening her skin and glaring through her eyes. She got up and hurried into the kitchen.

This was madness and all her pathetic little ploys were useless against it. All she could do was hide the grotesque mask it had made of her face.

David followed and found her at the sink, holding a wet teacloth to her face.

'Mum, I had no idea. I didn't know he was going to bring her. I thought he . . . she's not real, that woman.'

She mumbled through her distorted mouth, 'It's all right, dear. Don't worry.'

'I'll get rid of them. Mary might be doing that already. Then we'll have a cup of coffee or a drink or something.'

From behind the teacloth she mumbled again, 'David. Would you all go, please? I just want to be by myself for a while. It's all right, dear. Just go.'

'Mum, are you blaming me? If I'd known – '

'No, dear, no. Of course not. David, please go.'

He put his arms round her and held her for a moment.

'I'd better look after that cheque. I'll ring you tomorrow.'

As soon as she was alone in the house, the madness walked her upstairs, fetched, packed and closed the suitcase, put the handle in her hand and walked her down again without slackening its hold. Her face was still set rigid. She had not dared to look in a mirror. She had fetched her toothbrush from the rack with her eyes averted.

She cut Becky's rug from the frame and rolled it round the balls of wool and the hook.

'I'm never coming back. Never coming here again.'

She carried the bundle out to the car and shut it in the boot.

Then she looked at the car with dread. Could she drive it safely? Could she keep the madness away from the controls?

Someone had said once, carelessly at a party, 'Drunk driving isn't so dangerous if you remember that you're drunk.' She had to have the car. She must go carefully, mindful at every moment that she wasn't sane.

Handbag, suitcase, coat. She checked the windows, set deadlatches, put out the lights and shut the house behind her.

She drove slowly and carefully and at the first VACANCY sign turned into a motel on the highway.

The woman at the reception desk looked at her with curiosity, which showed that she had done well to avoid mirrors. She noted that her hand accepting the key was steady but moved slowly, as if she thought the key might burn her. All physical details were important evidence that this was an illness, which would pass. She had learnt that it would pass.

In the strange bedroom she lay down on the bed, thinking, 'Play possum. Lie doggo. Let the time pass.' Then suddenly she fell asleep.

The sleep lasted two hours and left her wakeful in a

desolating loneliness. She had put her hand out groping for someone. No, not that one. Rob.

That came of waking up in bed with her clothes on. Trick of the mind.

Have no feeling. Play dead. Lie doggo.

She did eventually decide that she could play possum more comfortably in her nightgown, and some unmeasured time later got up and acted on the decision. Once dressed for sleep, she slept again.

By daylight she examined her face. The glare was fading but the muscles were still rigid. It was not yet fit for display.

Fortunately her voice was more manageable than her face. There were two phone calls to navigate, the first to Caroline, since there was no need to convey warmth.

'It's Mother here, Caroline.' Mum was an entity gone for ever. 'Just letting you know I've moved out of the house. I'm staying in a motel at the moment. I'll let you know when I've found a place to live.'

'You've moved out? Isn't that rather sudden?'

'I thought it best.'

'I'm sorry you feel like that about it. I'm sure the offer was kindly meant.'

Caroline no longer troubled to conceal her intimacy with Louise.

Feel nothing. Play dead.

'You'll let your father know, will you?'

'Yes, of course.'

'Thank you. I'll be in touch.'

That was that. Easily done.

Minimal human contact: cash from the automatic teller,

lunch at a cafeteria, a walk in the Gardens, which proved therapeutic and prepared her for the phone call to David.

'I've moved out of the house. I'm staying in a motel for the moment, while I'm looking for a place.'

'I'm still kicking myself for letting it happen.'

'You couldn't possibly have foreseen it.' No matter what her face was doing, her voice was behaving well. 'It made things easier in a way.'

She had borrowed that from Sophie.

Sophie.

'I can't get in touch with Sophie. She'll be ringing home and get no answer. She'll be worried.'

'That'll do her no harm. Let her sweat a bit.'

'David!'

'She won't worry long. She'll ring us when she has to. What about the furniture and stuff, Mum? You can't walk away and leave it all.'

'Nothing. I don't want anything. Let them have it. I'll have to move out some personal stuff. I'll see to it later.'

Her voice was no longer behaving so well.

Though David protested, 'You have to be practical,' he let the subject drop.

'I've lodged the cheque, Mum. I got to the bank at lunchtime. Don't forget, you're a rich woman now.'

'Always look on the bright side,' she said shakily and put down the phone without another word.

She risked dinner at the motel restaurant that night and tried the curative power of a half-bottle of claret.

When she woke next morning, she felt with relief the relaxation of her facial muscles, but the mirror reflected her face pale and puffy, still unfit to be shown to her familiars but normal enough, she thought, to pass with strangers.

After breakfast, she set out to visit estate agents.

• XXVIII •

She said to the young man from the estate agent's, 'I hadn't thought of sharing a kitchen.'

It had taken three days to change her views on money and accommodation. She was sorry now she hadn't listened to Pam – she had sent her a postcard from the motel with the message 'You told me so!', hoping it would pass for humour.

No wonder David had been exasperated with her obstinacy, poor boy.

What had she been doing, instead of thinking of her future? Hanging on to the past at all costs.

So here she was, in a room in Glebe, with a young man who clearly found it painful to watch a solitary middle-aged woman face reality. She had contemplated sharing a laundry, then reluctantly given up hope of a private bathroom and lavatory, but had continued to hope for what were known as cooking facilities.

She knew she had the young man's sympathy on false

pretences, for, as David had said, she was a rich woman now, but she did not know how to behave like a rich woman, and feared that if she broke into the enormous sum, it would crumble away.

'I wouldn't worry too much,' he said. 'There's not much cooking done. They all live on takeaways. It's not a bad place. Mr Constantine keeps up a standard. He's careful who he takes in. I'm sure he'd take you on trust, though. It has its own entrance and you can rent the garage, I'm pretty sure. You can ask him about that when he comes round on Thursday. That's his rent day.'

It was obvious that the sympathetic young man wanted to dispose honourably of Ella.

To her newly educated eye the room was not a bad one. Situated on the ground floor of the large old Victorian house, it must once have been a reception room and showed a few pleasing traces of grandeur in ceiling and mouldings. Its windows looked onto a backyard that had some claim to be called a garden.

'Very well. When can I move in?'

'We'll skip the references, I think. If you give me two weeks in advance, you can have the keys now and move in as soon as you like.'

Now she had an address and a telephone number, which had a surprising effect on her self-esteem.

Back at the motel, she began to make a list of things she must buy. Then, reflecting that money beat sentiment every time, she made a list of things she wanted from the house.

She rang David from the motel room and gave him the address and the telephone number.

'Would you fetch a few things from the house for me?'

'Sure. We'll go out there tonight and bring them round after school tomorrow.'

David made no comment, but sounded relieved at the return of commonsense.

'I didn't realise how much everything would cost.'

'No trouble, Mum. I'll put Martha on.'

Dictating to Martha, 'The single sheets out of linen cupboard, second shelf . . . the skillet with the glass lid and the detachable handle . . .' she felt humiliated that she was reading this to her daughter-in-law, not to her daughter.

You'll believe anything, she thought, before you believe your daughter hates you and your husband is in bed with somebody else.

'. . . and a couple of teatowels.'

Well, she was lucky to have Martha.

When David took the phone again, she said, 'Why don't they get you to look after the house for them? It would suit you while you're looking for a place.'

'Hollow laughter, Mum,' said David cheerfully. 'I am not popular in certain quarters. They think they were robbed and I'm to blame. I hope they are right.'

The cold, stunting wind that blew on them all chilled Ella again. She said forlornly, inadequately, 'Oh, dear.'

'Don't worry about it, Mum. We'll see you tomorrow at the new place. About half-past 5.'

The cold, stunting wind was blowing as she rang Caroline's number.

It was a relief that Max answered..

'She is not home. She will be sorry to have missed you,' he said bravely.

That's all right, Max. I am going to tell lies, too. Whenever necessary.

'I just want to give her my new address and my phone number. I've moved into a room for the time being.'

Taking down the details, Max said, 'But that is quite near the University. We shall be able to have lunch together sometimes.'

The cold, stunting wind was blowing on Max, too. He was compensating for it with a show of joviality which made him sound more foreign than usual.

'I'd like that,' she said, though the prospect of an hour's unassisted conversation with Max was daunting. Probably it daunted Max, too.

'You will keep in touch, won't you? Becky misses you, you understand.'

Poor Max. She couldn't decide how much Caroline would have told him about the quarrel. It depended on the degree of confidence she felt in her individual interpretation of virtue.

Every confidence, thought Ella sadly.

She arrived at the lodging house next morning in a mood of manufactured optimism, determined to find advantages wherever she could.

She explored the kitchen, found a numbered space in the refrigerator and another in the food cupboard, investigated cooking equipment and was glad she had asked for the skillet – it could double as a casserole – observed that there was an honour system for the telephone in the hall: a notice reading LOCAL CALLS FORTY CENTS NO STD PLEASE with a cashbox beside it, a pad and a ballpoint pen meant, no doubt, for messages – that spoke well of the management and the lodgers. The bathroom was outside the back door in a shabby extension wing with the laundry and a kind of toolshed. The bathroom was shabby, too, and draughty, but the water ran hot and, since there was only one other lodger on the ground floor, she might have it almost to herself.

She unpacked, hung up her few clothes in the combination wardrobe-dressingtable, got Becky's rug out of the boot of the car – she had anticipated permission by parking it in the garage – put it into her empty suitcase and pushed it out of sight under the bed.

Then, thinking no day could not be improved by a little shopping, she set out to explore the shops and buy food for lunch.

As she was crossing the hall, the phone rang. She moved to answer it. The door of the front room opened and a short plump man with woolly blond hair burst forth crying, 'Is my call, please.'

That he was wearing pyjamas and was still pink-flushed with sleep added to the urgency of the cry.

Ella stood back confused, expecting an emergency in which she might be of help, but as he seized the phone and said into the mouthpiece, 'Is Josef, my darling,' she hurried past, embarrassed and aggrieved. The hallway of a lodging house was hardly a private place.

The main street reminded her of Newtown, therefore of Nina – the foreign restaurants, offering Thai, Vietnamese, Indian, Greek, eat in or takeaway, food shops offering foreign ingredients, a delicatessen with a remarkable variety of cheeses, a splendid fruitshop, a useful small supermarket, a book exchange. She came back to the house feeling elated, bringing fruit, cheese, fresh bread and paperback novels and promising herself a second foray after lunch.

She found chubby Josef in the kitchen, now dressed and eating rollmops with bread and butter.

There were two small round tables in the spacious room, each with four straight chairs. It seemed that one ate there, rather than in one's room. Obeying Mr Constantine's standards, she found plates in the cupboard and began to set out her lunch.

'I am Josef. Hullo to you. I am rude this morning, I think.'

'Oh, not at all.'

'It is my darling wife. Ring me at this time every day. She make sure I wake up. I work late, come home at 3 in the morning most times. You must not worry if you hear me.'

'I won't worry now that I know. My name is Ella. Is your wife far away?'

'Fivedock.'

'Ah.'

Josef had finished with the rollmops.

'She has boy twelve. We don't suit, see.'

He took his plate to the sink. 'A big crime leaving dirty china. I don't but those boys upstairs pretty careless sometimes.'

One way of making marriage work, thought Ella, watching Josef operate the teatowel he had pulled from the rack and making up her mind to use her own teatowels and her own china, too. Mr Constantine's standards didn't reach everywhere.

On the second excursion she found a promising opportunity shop, where she bought six very pleasant wineglasses, still in their box, an old white linen suppercloth of Venetian cutwork – some of the bars were broken, but could be easily repaired – and a large picture frame which would serve as a backing for the unfinished areas of Becky's rug.

Having acquired the wineglasses she had to go out again to get sherry. It would be a nice touch to offer the children a drink – a kind of house-warming ceremony.

At half-past 5, David and Martha arrived, carried in their cartons, set them down, looked about them and were horror-stricken.

Ella changed her mind at once about offering them sherry. A whiff of pathos would finish them.

'Well, it's a good deal better than anything else I've seen, I assure you. And it isn't for ever.'

They nodded without speaking and began to unpack their cartons.

'I put in a few things,' said Martha. 'The iron – I thought you'd want that – and the transistor from the kitchen, and your sewing box.'

Her voice was thickened by a struggle against tears.

'You're an angel, Martha. I didn't think of that but I'm glad to have it.'

Praise was the wrong note. Martha gave way. She sat down, placed her folded arms on the table and rested her head on them, overtaken and overwhelmed by a fit of grievous sobbing.

That was a new sound. Both her daughters had wept with rage; only Martha wept with grief.

David stood looking at her blankly, strangely uninvolved. It seemed some limit had been reached – No Man's Land, Ella thought with dread. That had been Pam's phrase for a strained relationship: stray shots exchanged across No Man's Land. If David so much as fired a shot . . .

'My dear, what is it? What's the matter?' She put her arm round Martha's shoulders. 'Don't upset yourself like this.'

Martha had regained the power of speech, though sobs still interrupted her words.

'Oh, everything. Everything. That terrible house – I never want to go there again. I never want to see it again. Then coming here, seeing you here – everything.'

'I've asked too much of you. You needn't go there again.'

That was not the whole story, however. There was more to Martha's bitter weeping than distress over Ella's situation.

It was time to be reckless, to behave like a rich woman.

'Come on. Cheer up. I'll take you out to dinner. I owe you a good dinner, that's certain. David,' she added sharply to the defaulting husband, 'take one of those washers, will you, and wet it with cold water. The kitchen's opposite, across the hall.'

Martha stirred in Ella's embrace, found a handkerchief and blew her nose.

'Oh, I'm ashamed. Making such a fuss. But the house – remembering things, you know.'

'Well, don't start telling Mum about it,' protested David, as he handed Ella the wet washer.

'No, of course not. Self-indulgent of me. I'm sorry, Ella. You're the last I should be crying to.'

But it wasn't such a bad thing, to be cried for, thought Ella, as she bathed Martha's reddened eyes.

Martha could well have been bathing her own eyes, but she accepted the attention with a small-girl docility which was not entirely assumed.

Motherless Martha.

The restaurant was a charming lamplit room looking through a wall of sliding glass doors onto an enclosed garden. Eating an excellently cooked boeuf en croûte and drinking a superior claret, Ella was reflecting that there might be quite significant advantages in being rich when Martha broke the long silence with a sigh.

'Wouldn't it be nice to be rich!'

Ella smiled.

'The very thing that I was thinking myself.'

David said to Martha, 'That's odd, coming from you. I thought money was the root of all evil.'

'The love of money. The love of money.' Martha did, however, appear confused. 'I could spend it well if it came my way. I fancy I could resist corruption.'

'I'm happy to hear it.'

What was the undercurrent here?

Was there to be serious trouble between David and Martha? That cold stunting wind, must it blow on them too?

I've asked too much of them. I should never have involved them in my affairs.

'I rang Caroline. She wasn't home but I spoke to Max and gave him the address and the phone number.'

Martha said bitterly, 'I wonder you can bring yourself to speak to her.'

She halted then, a non-Ferguson, after all, criticising a Ferguson.

Ella said, 'This is a beautiful cheese. I wonder where it comes from. Do you think I could ask the waiter?'

The young people looked pained.

David said, 'About Caroline. I don't think it's Louise she's getting close to. I think it's Dad.'

This attempt at analysis of human behaviour was so clearly Martha's province that the women looked at him in astonishment.

'Well, I've got something out of teaching, at least. I know a bit more about kids and what stirs them and how long they remember things. I can remember Carrie doing a great drawing and trying to show it to Dad. He was busy with the mindstretching games he used to torment me with and he said "That's very nice," without looking away from this rotten puzzle. You got it right and then he put the clock on you and you had to do it faster.'

'He thought he was doing the right thing. He thought intellectual capacity could be increased by practice.'

'Didn't do you much good, did it?' said Martha. 'You took your bat and ball and went out to play.'

'Why wasn't he increasing Carrie's mental capacity?'

Martha, mindful that she was not a Ferguson, suppressed her comment.

Ella was thinking, with pain, that it was Caroline who would have profited by the exercise. The old problem of the Haves and the Havenots troubled her again.

'Well, I thought then that she was the lucky one, but I know now that for kids, being ignored is the worst thing.'

'And she's still trying? Still pulling at his sleeve to show him that drawing? Yes, things do last, longer than you could imagine. My hangup about money. It goes back to the first awful Christmas at Aunt Flora's. My trouble with money was that I had too much. Dad gave me too much and I spent up big on Christmas presents. Quite the wrong thing. Trying to buy affection, I see now, and of course that doesn't work.' She spoke with scientific detachment. 'I bought Connie a watch – Dad gave me the money for it, he didn't see anything wrong with it, maybe he should have known better. I don't know. Instead of . . . whatever I was expecting . . . there was a terrible row. Uncle Stan said she had to give it back, that it was wrong to accept presents one wasn't in a position to return. Connie wouldn't. He got so angry I thought he was going to do something terrible. Nobody was paying attention to me, I suppose they didn't notice I was crying myself to a pulp.'

Ella said angrily, 'You poor child, they might have given some thought to your feelings.'

'Well, I yelled suddenly, "I want to go home. I hate it here. I want to go home." '

'I should think so,' said Ella. 'What an insensitive person.'

Martha had paused to drink coffee and gather her thoughts.

'That was the moment when I saw the awful power of money. The yelling stopped. They all froze. Aunt Flora and Arthur staring at Uncle Stan without breathing, like people playing statues. You see, I went out with Dad once a fortnight and he used to give me an envelope to give to Aunt Flora. I'd never even bothered to think what was in it, for all I knew I was a visitor and Dad wrote letters, but I realised then that the envelope was Arthur's University course. Aunt Flora would have done anything for Arthur. They stood looking at him and he gave in. "Connie may keep the watch." It was such an effort to get the words out that you could see his jaw muscles moving, poor man. It was terrible to see somebody so brought down by a small envelope. That all came back when Ella was washing the blubber off my face. That's what Connie was doing. Dad was coming to Christmas dinner and Connie was trying to make me presentable before he got there.'

'I hope Connie showed some appreciation for the watch,' said Ella.

'In a way, yes. She did say I'd made their presents look a bit silly, but she said she'd take a watch for a handkerchief sachet every time. They didn't understand that I'd loved my presents, thought the handkerchief sachet was lovely. Oh, well.'

'Money doesn't buy affection,' said David, who had been listening with attention to the story, which seemed to be new to him. 'But it buys power, all right, and power isn't always a bad thing. Connie got her watch, Uncle Stan got his, Arthur got his University course. What's wrong with that?'

'Everyone doesn't want power,' said Martha. 'As far as I was concerned, it was the opposite. Dad wanted me to come back when he married Sally, but I couldn't, because of that rotten envelope and what it meant to Aunt Flora.'

Who had had, one gathered, little love to give Martha. Power to some, responsibility to others. Martha, thought Ella, was a really virtuous person, a lucky choice for David.

At least they were back on debating terms.

'Not a cheerful household,' said Martha. 'The first time David brought me home with him, I thought your house was the most wonderful place in the world. Perhaps that's why I'm making such a fuss.'

'I'm sure I don't know what day that was, dear.'

'It was all right, Mum,' said David. 'If there was trouble under the surface, we didn't know about it. Things went on all right from day to day.'

'I'm ashamed, though. Making such a scene. Not even my own home.'

'As much yours as David's, I hope,' said Ella, wondering that she could speak with such indifference.

Wine of course was helpful. They had drunk the last of it and finished their coffee and sat so long over their dinner that the restaurant was filling with the later diners. She signalled for the bill.

Martha said with a sudden giggle, 'Dad came to dinner with a bottle of wine and a huge box of crackers and gave us each twenty dollars for Christmas. Arthur and Connie and me. He didn't know money was a dirty word. We all sat silent, waiting for Uncle Stan to explode, but he didn't say a thing.'

'They could have had some thought for your feelings,' Ella repeated.

'He was a good, upright man. If I'd been penniless and homeless, they'd have taken me in, I'm sure, and treated me as their own. As it was, they never pretended any affection for me, which I think was a good thing.'

David and Martha held hands as they walked back to the lodging house. It seemed that some communication of importance had taken place between them. The depression which settled on them as they approached the house was for her.

'Hate to leave you here, Mum,' said David.

'It's not for long,' she answered, though she could still see no future beyond it.

Hamfisted Harry, she thought, as she sat on the strange bed, not ready yet to venture into it. That was where the money had gone, not on stock exchange losses but on a settlement out of court, hushing up some final error, the last straw. He didn't tell me and he did right. I wouldn't have wanted to know, would rather be living up to something that wasn't there. What kind of marriage had that been? The word divorce which stood stark in the future reached back into the past, how far? There might have been a moment when he had tried to confide in her and she had not listened. She did not think it likely.

That marriage had been for the future, not for the present. It had been set rigid, that first night on the beach. Nobody's fault. We would have had to become two different people. I could have loved a failure - more than a success, perhaps - but that kind of love, he wouldn't have wanted from me. Perhaps he can accept it, from her.

Don't start thinking about that one.

She found the carton with the sheets and blankets, made up the bed, made an excursion to the bathroom, got into bed and fell asleep easily, drowsy with food and wine.

She was wakened in the dark by the pressure of a full bladder, groped confidently for the switch of a bedlamp that was far away in a house no longer hers, and fell headlong into the black pit of panic. Then she remembered where she was. The memory made things no better. Terror held her.

Somewhere in the unmapped dark, there was a bladder to be emptied, a contact with reality. All difficulties can be solved, one step at a time. The light switch was by the outer door. She found it, put on the light, pushed her feet into scuffs, put on her coat and went into the hall, hoping she would not meet Josef, adding torch and tracksuit to the shopping list which continued to grow.

The hall was not quite dark. The light from a street lamp in front of the house fell through the glass panes of the door and made a pleasant pattern on the worn carpet.

One counted such small advantages.

Emptying the bladder, too, was an aid to relaxation, but the moment of terror had been so intense that she was trembling still when she got back into the bed.

On the dark she projected her planned wallhanging: the segment of sea-green lamé, the froth of creamy foam – the background sand-coloured, of course, but no shine, definitely no shine, no trace of gold. The line of sea green extending beyond the foam could wait till later. On the blank sand, beach umbrellas. There was a way of knitting a wheel shape. Mrs Wilson next door used to knit round cushion covers. They were very ugly, but reduced in size, in fine cotton, on fine needles, ribs in white garterstitch. It was all done by turning in mid-row, easy enough if one worked out one's tension. A two-inch radius, thirty-two stitches, say. Have to work out the rows, draw a circle round a coffee saucer, fold it into eight segments. While she was calculating the probable number of rows to a segment, she fell asleep.

She woke up joyful, thinking, 'I won. I handled it.'

That was the trick, to get the mind working on a small, pedestrian task, counting sheep to some purpose.

Meanwhile, today she must begin to face the problems of communal living: when to use the kitchen, when to use the bathroom, how to be considerate and unobtrusive. Certainly, if the other lodgers went to work, she must leave the kitchen to them in the morning. Reluctantly, she pulled on yesterday's clothes (an unfortunate decline in living standards, not to be repeated) and went into the kitchen to make a cup of tea before the rush started.

She left the hall door ajar for a kind of beneficent spying. Ten past 7, steps clattering down the stairs, then voices in the kitchen. Half-past 7, more steps, a little stir in the kitchen, but not much. They probably didn't make much conversation at breakfast. Some chinking of china, steps retreating up the stairs. Steps coming down, passing her door. She hoped nobody noticed that it was open.

By half-past 8, silence.

Ella had made her bed, finished unpacking and stowing her possessions and set the cartons outside on her small porch, to be disposed of when she found out what one did with unwanted objects.

What to do next?

That question must never be allowed to surface. It must be answered before it occurred.

At 9 o'clock, she ventured on breakfast in the deserted kitchen.

At half-past 9, the phone rang.

Mindful of Josef's sleep, she hurried to answer it.

'Hullo?'

Sophie's voice answered, 'Mum is that you?'

Oh, my darling Sophie. My darling child. Concern about Sophie's character was consumed in joy at Sophie's existence.

'Is that you, Sophie?'

'Well, who else? What an awful time I've had. I rang you a couple of times and thought I'd just missed you but then I thought, you couldn't be out that much, so I kept on ringing yesterday and I rang again last night and you were still out. I was sure there must be something wrong. William said to try David but they were out, too.'

'We went out to dinner together.'

'I rang him this morning before work and he told me you'd moved out.' She attempted lightness. 'To a pad in Glebe. I couldn't believe my ears.'

'It was a sudden decision. I didn't know how to get in touch with you.'

Children could vanish without trace, but not parents. Sophie, however, must have been coached by David, for she did not comment on the suddenness of the move.

'Well, that's what I wanted to tell you about. We've found a place, a whole ground floor to ourselves. A couple moving out to a house of their own and taking their stuff with them. I'll have room to store things for David and Martha and for you, too, if you like,' she said proudly.

Ella wanted to ask, 'Are you and William a couple?'

She felt sympathy for Josef, forced to live his private life in a hallway.

Sophie went on, 'I have a job interview tomorrow. It's at 10 o'clock. I could come in on the way back, if that's all right.'

'Yes, of course. What's the job?'

'Just general assistant in a film distributors. Rob heard

about the opening and put in a word for me. It should be all right.' Sophie's anger had rolled away like bad weather, leaving no trace. 'She came around yesterday with a cheque. Welcome, I can tell you. See you tomorrow, Mum.'

When Sophie's voice was silent and the strange world closed in on her again, her sense of loss was terrible.

It would not do. She must not be emotionally dependent on the children. Work must save her, even if she grew to be like Mrs Wilson next door, filling the world with Afghan rugs and circular cushion covers nobody wanted.

She would structure her life, but first she must investigate the storeroom.

She didn't face the other lodgers after all, that evening. She rang Pam and was invited to dinner.

'Bit of a change, isn't it, my cooking for you? Don't expect anything better than grilled steak.'

Pam asked no questions about the sudden move. She recounted amusing incidents from the shop, Ella made what she could of Josef's strange marital arrangements and they succeeded in passing a pleasant evening.

Pam said only, 'Do you need any help in moving stuff out of the place?' infusing the final word with dismissive contempt, as if the house itself had sinned.

'Thanks. I'll let you know.'

Children aged and moved away. Friendships aged and grew better.

• XXIX •

Sophie arrived before noon the next day, soberly dressed, even to pantyhose and shoes, and carrying a bag of sandwiches.

'How nice you look,' Ella said wistfully.

'Don't build your hopes. I'm in disguise. All to impress the new boss.'

I wish she wanted to impress me, thought Ella. There it was. She was a loser. Her prejudices were amusing. She had their affection, she hoped, but parental prestige was gone for ever.

'Do you think you have the job, then?'

'Oh, yes. It's a favour to Rob, really. I'd need to be hopeless to miss out. This place isn't so bad, Mum. I got the idea from David that it was the pits.'

'David didn't see the ones I turned down.'

In the hall, the phone rang.

'It's all right. It's for Josef.' She had made fun of Josef's love call to amuse Pam, but did not feel inclined to do the same for Sophie. 'It's a wakeup call. He works nights. It's better not to ring in the morning if you can help it.'

'Lodging house living. I thought you got to the phone rather fast.'

'Well, I think he slept through it all right but one can't be sure.'

'What are the others like?'

'I haven't met them yet. I stay out of the way in the mornings, when they're all hurrying off to work, and last night I went up to Pam's for dinner.'

'Anyhow, it's not for ever. Where do I get plates for the sandwiches, Mum?'

While she fetched plates from the kitchen, Ella was deciding what questions she might ask Sophie, how much information she could expect – she didn't want to pressure her into lying – how much information, in fact, she was entitled to expect.

'About you and William . . .?' she asked as she arranged sandwiches on a platter and set out two plates with knives.

Add table napkins to the shopping list. Worth looking in the opportunity shop for those.

'It's all a bit up in the air at the moment.' Sophie took a sandwich, opened it and inspected the contents before she took a bite.

'Don't fiddle with the food, dear.'

'But how do I know whether I'm going to like it?'

'Who's going to eat it after you've been fingering it?'

'I never thought of that. Sorry. I'll just have to chance it, won't I?'

She put the sandwich down. 'About William. He has this bug about marriage. A bit of emotional insecurity there, I think,' she added virtuously. 'He won't settle for less than marriage.'

Why had she ever supposed Sophie might be pressured into lying?

'He said he'd been up to talk to you about it. You didn't try to talk him out of it?'

What would her own mother have thought of this conversation? On that point, she did not dare to speculate.

'I didn't think it was my place. He wanted to know if I'd be hostile and I said no. I think he is a good man. I don't think it would be a good marriage, because of the difference in ages, but you both know that. As for asking if I'd turn my back on you, I wouldn't be doing that, whatever you did.'

Sophie nodded but looked discontented.

'It isn't a thing to rush into. A bit irresponsible, I think. How do you know how you'll be feeling in two years' time?'

'Perhaps your feelings aren't the only things that matter.'

Sophie looked as if she had opened a sandwich and found an entirely unacceptable filling.

Ella thought suddenly, I don't believe a word of this, even if she does. Women haven't changed so much. I think there's a voice in her head saying 'Mrs William Anstey', and once you hear that voice it's all settled. The rest of it is wriggling out of the responsibility. The terrifying responsibility.

Sophie had finished her sandwich.

'Well, I've said six months. Trial period. I suppose if it works for six months it could work for ever.'

Ella began to wriggle, too.

'I don't see why you have to marry at all, at your age. There are so many people you haven't met yet.'

Sophie scowled.

'I can't stand being fussed at. Listening to people talking a lot of rubbish. William's a serious person. He doesn't talk rot.'

Perhaps you haven't heard him at it yet, thought Ella.

Was it romance Sophie was speaking of? Courtship? Matters which had monopolised the minds of girls of Ella's generation?

Come to think of it, that had not been a happy time. It had been full of false starts, heartburn, disappointment and anxiety. One took this falling in love for granted and it hadn't done much for the quality of life. Ella had been lucky to have her moment on the beach. She hadn't had to talk herself into anything out of a sense of duty to a word.

'If you've made up your mind, I hope things turn out well for you both.'

'Love you, Mum.' Sophie came to kiss her cheek and went back to her lunch.

'You'll need your father's consent, won't you?'

The mouthful Sophie was chewing seemed to have turned bitter. She swallowed with difficulty.

'A fine one he'd be, to talk about difference in ages. He'd hear a few words from me if he tried.'

Ella was about to protest but she saw in time that Sophie's eyes had filled with tears.

'Sophie dear, don't fret so. Don't upset yourself like this.'

'Do you think it's easy, seeing you here, living in a room?'

'I don't have to live in a room for ever. I've plenty of money to buy a place of my own.'

'It's no use, Mum. I hate them. Just hate them. You can't talk me out of it so don't try. You just make it worse, being noble.' She wiped her eyes. 'Well, down to practicalities. David said we can take the furniture from our rooms. One of the boys at the house is going to borrow his father's van. He knows how to pack stuff, he's worked with his father, and one of his friends is coming to help, so I'm going to move out my stuff and David's, too, and store it for him. They can hardly move for cartons in their place, with his books and stuff. I shouldn't be doing anything for him, he's being such a curmudgeon, but blood's thicker than water, as they say. Can I get you anything out of the house, Mum, while I'm about it? I could store things for you, too. There's a big closed-in verandah we're going to use for storage. There's plenty of room.'

Ella was shaking her head.

Sophie drew a deep breath.

'What we all think is, that it will be tough getting hold of anything once that vulture moves in. There are things there that belong to you, no argument. Like the food processor and the kitchen knives and cooking gear. They're yours. They were presents.'

And from whom?

Ella continued to shake her head.

'I don't want anything. Thanks for offering.'

I am alone with this, she thought bleakly. No-one can know the horror I am fighting.

'Well, they're not getting the rose rug. I'll take that and keep it for you till you want it.'

'Of course. It has your good pink skirt in it.'

'It has a lot of our lives in it.' She added with bitter resentment, 'Why do they want that house, anyhow? It's too big for them, I don't see how they can afford it. Martha says it's a ritual takeover, a payback because you told Dad to go. Though I don't see what else you could have done. Martha says people will squander money on gestures like that.'

It was reassuring that Sophie's worldly wisdom came from Martha. That made her air of confidence less alarming.

'If I get the job - well, I'm pretty sure of it but they're ringing to confirm it next week - I'll be starting work at the end of the month. William wants to go away for a week, a few days anyhow. Kind of honeymoon, I think. Honestly, Mum, he is something else.'

Sophie's face was softened by an expression which might have been amusement, though Ella hoped it was tenderness.

'Do you think I might have your telephone number?' Ella asked meekly.

'Oh, sure.' She began to search her bag for pen and paper. 'I won't get lost again. Promise.'

With the slip of paper waving from her fingers, she looked about - for the little Buddha which pinned down messages on the side table. Visibly put out, she dropped it on the unfamiliar table in front of her and got up. It was clear this failure in sophistication had disconcerted her.

'Thank you, love. I won't use it unless I have to.'

'Better for me to ring you,' agreed Sophie. 'William wants to come around. We'll fix something up.'

'Sophie . . .' she said, as Sophie kissed her goodbye.

'All right. I take back *vulture*. But you can't stop me thinking.'

When Sophie had gone, Ella set up the rug, balancing the improvised frame between the two straight chairs, found a program of classical music on the FM band of the transistor radio and set to work.

This required resolution. Everything she did now required resolution: going to bed, getting up, bathing, dressing, washing out clothes, going out, coming in - not much resolution, but always a little, like a slight, continuous abrasion that caused discomfort - she couldn't call it pain.

She didn't want to finish Becky's rug. It was a tenuous connection with Becky; when it was finished, even that connection would be broken. She worked at it with determination, thinking of the wallhanging she intended to make for Rob. If it turned out as badly as poor old Mrs Wilson's rugs and cushion covers, Rob would have only herself to blame.

She smiled, thinking of Rob. The smile had come of itself, not requiring resolution.

The kitchen was not where one cooked, but where one ate. The lodgers - Mr and Mrs Braddon, the two mature singles, John and Sylvia, the two university students, Luke and Phillip - began to arrive at 6 o'clock, bringing food in boxes and paper bags, cold cuts and salad in plastic tubs.

Meaning to behave with consideration, Ella confined her cooking to one gas ring, eating small made dishes with homemade salad and one of the excellent breadrolls she bought every day from the hot bread shop.

She did not understand at once that loud asides about gourmets and five-star restaurants were not friendly, that people who ate meat pies brought home in paper bags did not enjoy the smell of sautéed veal kidneys and mushrooms simmering in red wine.

The comments came from the young men, but as soon as she knew they were hostile, she feared that they expressed the feelings of them all. None of the elders showed any disapproval of the attacks but went on stolidly eating fried chicken and hamburgers.

Eating dinner in the kitchen that evening was a test of social nerve. She swallowed her savoury dinner without tasting it, thinking she was at fault, out of place.

The Braddons were a middle-aged couple, younger than she, locked away in some private grief or anxiety, a sick child, perhaps, or a failed business. They were eating a confection of noodles out of paper tubs. She had seen these tubs in the supermarket and had read the printed instructions with astonished interest: one poured boiling water on the contents and waited five minutes for a delicious meal. If, as she feared, it was poverty that forced Mrs Braddon to serve such a meal, Ella herself was indeed at fault. She could almost forgive the young men their resentment if the misery of the Braddons had moved them to it.

But it wasn't that. No. What she heard in their jeering tone was the opinion that she was an inferior person, who should not be eating superior food.

This insolence from young men was disconcerting. The only young people she knew were her children's friends – had Alex, Stephanie and Laura disliked her, secretly, as these young men did openly?

She reflected that it wouldn't have mattered in the least if they had. She couldn't imagine concerning herself about their opinions. They came and ate, minded their manners, said thank you and went off to their matches and their parties and if they thought her inferior, they did well to keep their opinion to themselves.

What should she do? She might compromise. Sylvia, a teacher obsessed by political ambitions, ate grilled chops and boiled vegetables before she set out for an evening meeting. It was at the stove, where she was frying wiener schnitzel in the adaptable griddle, that Ella had heard about the political ambitions. Sylvia had eaten early and was washing up when the young men arrived. Was that a matter of convenience or an exercise of social skills Ella had yet to learn?

She didn't intend to live on grilled chops. Besides, she felt sure it was too late for compromise, that attitudes were now fixed and she was a social outcast.

Next evening and thereafter, she cooked dinner early and carried the tray to her room. This meant she could drink wine at dinner, which she would not have ventured in the kitchen, but the two glasses of wine were no substitute for society.

At least, the prospect of the little unit was becoming more acceptable.

Josef ate dinner elsewhere – with his darling wife, she hoped. She was glad there was one lodger she hadn't offended.

The room opposite Josef's was a public room with a television set and a gas fire. Mr Constantine held session there every second Thursday to collect rents and hear complaints and requests. He was a swarthy, middle-aged gentleman with classical features, acne scars and excellent manners. Ella handed over Josef's rent in an envelope, negotiated the rent for the garage, settled her score and asked if it would be possible to have a fire in the grate in her room.

'Of course,' said Mr Constantine. 'It was used last winter but you must tell me if the chimney isn't drawing.'

He gave her the address of a wood and coal merchant, told her where fuel should be kept, in the bins in the shed beyond the laundry, and promised to split kindling for her.

His kindness was almost as disturbing as the hostility of the students. A little of it might have been directed at them, for they were waiting within earshot to settle their accounts, and he paused for a moment on the offer to split kindling.

She was very glad that the outrageous thought quite passed them by.

• XXX •

Why hadn't she thought of the sewing machine?

Becky's rug was finished and spread on the floor, ready to be lined with the heavy cotton folded beside it, but her portable electric sewing machine was still in the little room Sophie had used as a study.

She could have asked Sophie to fetch it. Sophie would have thought her the more sensible for the request. Now she could not ask any of them to go back. She knew she had been asking too much of them. David and Martha had certainly reached the limit of their patience, though they tried to conceal what Martha would call their negative feelings, and she would not involve Sophie any further in the situation which had made such a sad change in her. Enough harm had been done.

All she had to do was drive up to the house, unlock the back door, walk past William's room to the study, pick up the machine and walk out. That was hardly even entering the house. She was within her rights: the month's grace wasn't up. She could ignore anyone who came to question her - very bad manners, but manners no longer applied.

It hasn't happened for a week. If it happens, I know how to control it. I have the better of it.

The house looked empty, every door and window shut. She drove in level with the kitchen door, for easy loading, since the machine was heavy. The room which had been David's, then Sophie's, then William's, then her own, was bare now, stripped of furniture. The room next door was undisturbed. The sewing machine was there, on the floor beside the bookcase. She bent to pick it up, then straightened.

She had remembered what Sophie had said about the rose rug, words which had been moving when she spoke them. How seriously had they been meant? Had Sophie remembered them and taken the rose rug?

She went to look for it in the living room.

The thing was waiting in the living room, where that creature's acquisitive glance had drifted and darted like a poisonous, transparent sea creature. It was drifting there still; it touched the clock.

A glorious, liberating surge of feeling lifted her, made her tall and powerful. She went into the kitchen, took the heavy meat mallet out of its drawer and carried it back to the living room, where she set the clock on the carpet and joyfully beat it to death. It died with a small, plangent sound which caused her great satisfaction. Then she turned to the pictures, swinging the mallet lustily to shatter the glass in each one.

The glass in the upper doors of the old cedar corner

cabinet split with a delightful cracking sound. She opened them and surveyed the rows of wineglasses. The Stuart crystal had been a wedding present. The memory of the wedding renewed her strength, which had been flagging, vandalism being unexpectedly strenuous. She put the claret glasses on the floor and began to batter them. The carpet was frustrating her efforts. She placed them one by one on the heavy, low coffee table and set about them. The effect on the coffee table was more than she could have hoped.

Her strength was gone, now.

Hastily, she emptied the shelves, made a pile of the fragile glasses and tipped the coffee table over to crush the pile. That worked well.

She sat down, panting, conscious of a trickle of moisture between her legs and of a post-coital langour.

Then the panic began. She advanced from glorious irresponsible infancy to five-year-old terror as she began to think of consequences and wonder how to escape them.

It would have to be a break in. She would have to fake a break in.

There had been a break in once. The thieves had made a hole in a kitchen window to reach the latch. She must be careful not to cut herself – a cut hand would be a giveaway. One of the intruders had cut himself – she remembered how nauseating had been the sight of blood drops clotted on the windowsill. She didn't have to reach through, groping for a latch, just make a hole with a stone from the garden as they had done, then come in again through the door. No use thinking how tired she was. It had to be done.

This was like being in one of Rob's films, making it up and acting it as she went.

She found a heavy stone in the grassed slope behind the cultivated garden - what luck she had brought the car to the door, out of sight of the road. The sewing machine. Remember the sewing machine. She fetched it and hid it in the boot of the car. She attacked the kitchen window with the stone. The glass was too tough. The job was beyond her strength.

She was exposed to view from the house at the foot of the slope. With a giggle she told herself that Meg would be up in a minute, offering to help. The giggle frightened her.

Stop wasting time. It didn't have to be the kitchen window. The living room window was sheltered from view by the rockery and the upward slope to the road. She fetched the small hatchet from the garden shed and attacked the living room window, where she made better progress, though the hole was larger and not as neat as the one the thieves had made. Everything took practice. They were professionals, after all.

Should she put the hatchet back? No, leave it there. Wipe the handle, wipe the handle.

Indoors again, she sat looking blankly at the disorder. Hurry, for God's sake. Other people had keys. If anyone surprised her - she had just walked in and discovered the damage. Vandalism. Shocking. How can people do such things?

Don't start giggling again.

Money. There wasn't any. Yes, the housekeeping purse in the kitchen drawer - they'd have found that.

Don't go running backwards and forwards to the

kitchen. Think. Liquor behind the solid cedar doors of the corner cupboard – they'd steal liquor. She opened the cupboard, found, besides the open bottles of whisky and gin – she took the time to empty those onto the heap of ruin – a full bottle of whisky, one of brandy and one of Tia Maria – leave that one. Not sufficiently anonymous. Thieves wouldn't care for Tia Maria.

Now to the kitchen for the housekeeping purse – her own handbag, where was that? On the floor of the study – fetch it first. The housekeeping purse and a bag for the bottles.

She emptied the money from the purse into her handbag, dropped the purse, open, in the doorway to the living room – a good touch, that, put the liquor into a plastic bag and looked around her.

Inadequate. Unconvincing.

What else did thieves do?

No, she couldn't quite come at that.

Graffiti. That's what they did. They wrote on walls. A nice finishing touch which would wreck the striped Regency wallpaper. Great.

Back to the kitchen. She fetched the marker pen from the memo board and came back to set about the task.

Now this was danger. What would she do if she was interrupted? Thrust the pen down the front of her dress? No. Drop it on the carpet.

As soon as she had printed the first FUCK, in bold letters with her left hand – she knew she was in deep water. She didn't have the necessary vocabulary. The only other dirty word she knew was SHIT; one couldn't fill these empty spaces – she hadn't realised how much empty space there was – with repetitions of FUCK and SHIT. She printed SHIT beside the cabinet. The word looked absurdly small and lonely. She had only made things worse. FUCKING BASTARDS. That was better. That filled a space. What now? Why hadn't she listened more, read more modern fiction? For the first time, she was seriously unhappy, wretched and disgusted. She had gone beyond other limits than those of vocabulary. In the large vacant space to the left of the door, she printed FILTHY GOBSUCKERS, dropped the pen, picked it up to wipe it and dropped it again.

She looked about the room. The window was shut. She had forgotten to open the window. What a giveaway that would have been. She raised it with a frantic jerking effort, picked up the plastic bag with the liquor, fetched her handbag from the kitchen and fled, letting the back door slam shut behind her.

Why wasn't the key in the ignition? Of course, it was on the ring with the house keys. She had had to unlock the back door, hadn't she?

Where were the keys? Had she automatically put them back in her handbag, or had she left them somewhere in the house? She could not remember. She did not dare to open her handbag for fear of learning the worst.

Everything would not be lost. There was another key taped under the car. She would have to ring Caroline and tell a tale. Well, you'd better get used to telling tales.

I came to fetch the machine, saw the damage and was so upset that I . . . she opened the handbag. The keys were there.

Her annoyance with herself over this unnecessary piece of drama was helpful. She sat behind the wheel recovering her composure, telling herself she was safe now, that if anyone came, the discovery story would stand. Of course, there was the small matter of the bottles of liquor in the plastic bag on the seat beside her. Criminals needed an eye for detail. She got out and hid them in the boot.

Experienced now in driving in a state of strong emotion, she started the car and drove safely to the lodging house and into the garage.

Once indoors, she looked about the room with joy and relief.

Sanctuary. Home.

• XXXI •

She waited for the news to break.

She knew now how people managed to live with a guilty secret. Joyfully. With exultation. The shattered living room was a private landscape she could command, where she breathed safe and free, the fear of madness gone for ever. Any social awkwardness, any evasions required of her would be trivial compared with that happiness.

Still, she waited for the news to break.

She lined the rug and put it away in her suitcase, meaning to ask Max to deliver it for her as soon as she knew how the land lay.

Sophie rang to say that she had the job and that William wanted to come and visit.

She did not mention the break in.

David and Martha took her to dinner at a pizzeria. They did not mention the break in, but there was a reserve in their manner which suggested unspoken thoughts. Perhaps they knew about it and were suppressing the knowledge, thinking it would distress her. Short of asking if they had heard of any good break-ins lately, there was nothing she could do about that.

She acquired merit at the lodging house through her willingness to answer the telephone. The first evening she had climbed the stairs, feeling slightly foolish, to call out, 'John! Telephone!', he had come running and, flustered with guilt, had said 'Sorry!' as he passed.

When the call was finished, he had knocked on her door, looking harassed, and apologised for the inconvenience.

'An emergency at the Home. If I know a call's likely, I wait downstairs.' He paused. 'I'm a social worker, work at a youth refuge. Things do come up, unexpectedly, and I need to go in.'

The thing which had come up unexpectedly was clearly a cause for anxiety.

'You don't need to apologise. I'm only too pleased to be helpful.'

And more thankful for the human contact than she wished to admit.

'Truly? That's wonderful. There have been problems about the phone.'

'Well, it would never worry me to take a call for you, I assure you.'

'Oh, great. It's really not often. I have to be going.'

She wondered, as she watched him go, what the trouble was that creased his forehead. Perhaps one day he might talk to her about his problems.

Mr Constantine had appointed himself her protector. He came from the house he occupied, two doors away, to supervise the delivery of the fuel, split kindling and even set her first fire.

Didn't those wretches ever go near the house?

It was Caroline who rang at last, nearly a fortnight after she had murdered the clock.

Lucky it was Caroline. Hidden feelings were the norm there.

'Mother?'

'Yes, Caroline?'

On either side a perfect measure of courtesy.

Caroline, however, now showed some hesitation.

'I don't know whether you've heard, there has been a break in at the house.'

'No. No-one has said anything to me about it. When did this happen?'

The sharpness of her tone was no affectation. It said with real annoyance, Why wasn't I told of this before?

Because it isn't your house and it isn't your business. How long it took to learn that.

'We aren't sure. Sophie was there at the weekend, not last weekend, the one before, moving out some furniture and she says everything was all right then. Louise discovered the damage when she was showing some friends through the house. It was a dreadful shock.'

Good.

'Sheer wanton destruction, glass shattered in all the pictures and filth scribbled all over the walls. Thank goodness that was washable and we've managed to clean it off.'

What a pity.

'Every glass smashed from the corner cabinet. There was hardly anything taken. The police say they must have been looking for cash and small valuables and got spiteful because they didn't find what they were after. Just a little bit of money out of the housekeeping purse and a couple of bottles of drink. And then doing hundreds of dollars worth of damage. You can't understand these people, how their minds work. We were wondering . . . there has to be a list for the insurance, of course.'

Ella said nothing. Caroline's hesitation was now explained.

'I'm afraid I'm not much help and of course Louise doesn't know how many glasses there were.'

'How odd,' said Ella coldly. 'I thought she would have counted them.'

Caroline sighed.

'You'd be collecting half of the insurance, of course. It would be a help if you could make a list of the glassware.'

In her voice, there was a note of grievance, not against Ella. She didn't like the task she had been given, and no wonder.

'I'll do my best.' She added boldly, 'I must have been there later than Sophie. I went up to get the sewing machine. Let me see. On the Tuesday. Everything was all right then.'

When I went in, that is.

'Oh. I didn't know you'd been in the house. We'd better tell the police that. They're trying to fix the time of the break in. You don't mind if I tell them and they come round to see you?'

'No, not at all.'

She hoped she did not sound faint.

Well, this was what you took on when you turned vandal. Nobody can prove it. I was there, I collected my sewing machine, I left.

Why had she said she was there?

You had to keep as close to the truth as you could. Besides, she hadn't much liked the way Caroline had reported 'She says everything was all right then'. Why 'She says'? Oddly put.

I don't regret it. I'll never regret it.

When she had put down the phone, another thought occurred.

Insurance money. That would be fraud. Like people burning down their house to get the insurance money.

How easy it all was, to get drunk, to go mad, to vandalise, to commit fraud.

Perhaps she had always had criminal tendencies; they hadn't surfaced before because they weren't relevant, didn't suit her lifestyle.

If she refused to take her share? Better morally, perhaps, but not legally.

If it came to the point where she had to confess, to avoid criminal action, she would tell that person. What he thought didn't matter.

Disgraceful pair, making a catspaw out of Caroline, getting her to do their dirty work.

She kept asking herself what she should do and knew she would do nothing.

The police had ways of getting the truth. They set traps, they asked trick questions.

Say as little as possible, stay as close to the truth as you can.

She must have read this advice somewhere. She had never prepared herself for a life of crime. Say as little as possible, she repeated mentally as she waited for the dreaded call.

When the phone rang late that afternoon, it was Caroline who spoke, too indignant to preserve her dignified manner.

'I thought I should let you know at once. Dad isn't going to claim on the insurance. He's quite firm about it. He says it isn't worth the trouble. Hundreds of dollars worth. And the clock. They smashed the clock. I don't know what's come over Dad.'

Perhaps he has got a message, thought Ella.

She said, with sympathy, bringing Caroline's grievance into the light without compunction, 'What a pity they didn't tell you that before.'

'Yes. Well. You had to know about the damage, of course. It's your property as well.'

I can bear that, easily.

'Yes, of course. Thanks for letting me know. Goodbye, then.'

There was one friendship that would not flourish for long.

• XXXII •

The ring came at the front door before lunch.

Ella, who was practising controlled breathing as she came up the hall, saw Josef's tousled head looking out at his doorway and called out, 'It's all right Josef. I'll get it.'

Panic, eagerness. That wouldn't do.

She opened the door and thought she was looking at David.

'Mrs Ferguson? Detective Constable Vernon. I think you are expecting me.'

'Yes, that's right. Come in, please.'

The impression had been momentary, a matter of figure and stance as he stood, his face obscured, with his back to the light. It was still disconcerting. It emphasised the decline in her social standing and might offer a dangerous temptation to relax and lower her guard.

It was a matter of movement, too, she saw as he walked with her down the corridor and into her room.

'I didn't realise you had your own entrance. I'm afraid I disturbed the fellow next door.'

'It's about time for Josef to get up. I suppose it might have made him wonder if you'd been in uniform.'

'Rattling my handcuffs.'

This would not do. She must not be put at her ease – though that was clearly the young man's intention. He radiated reassurance like a friendly dentist.

'I won't keep you long, Mrs Ferguson. You will know we are investigating a break in' – he took a notebook from his pocket and turned its pages like an ordinary policeman – 'at Number One Woodrow Avenue Acacia Heights. Your previous home, I believe.'

'Yes, that's right.'

'We are checking dates, trying to fix the time of the break in. Your daughter says the house was in order when she went in to move some furniture out on the second of the month. You paid a visit to the house during the relevant period, I believe. Can you tell me the date of that visit?'

'It was after Sophie had been in, because the furniture was gone. It was the Tuesday – yes, it must have been the fifth, then. I went to fetch my sewing machine.'

'What time of day was that?'

'In the afternoon. Early afternoon. Perhaps half past 2.'

'And everything was in order then?'

'Yes.'

When I went in.

'I see.'

He closed his notebook and said confidentially, 'By the way, what's a gobsucker?'

She started, blushed and stared at him, incapable of speech.

There was nothing in his face but friendship. The conspiratorial grin he wore was almost a wink. You and I are having a fine joke on the world, it said.

'I couldn't say.'

Clinging to a straw of truth, she added, 'I've never heard the word.'

'No, I suppose not.'

He stood up and said earnestly, 'I'm sorry to say, Mrs Ferguson, that we haven't much hope of apprehending the culprits. There was too great a lapse of time between the break in and the report to the police. If we could fix the time of the offence we could interview a few likely suspects, but as it is . . .'

Go free.

'Well, I'm sure you did what you could.'

'Oh, yes. We try.'

But we don't always try our hardest.

'Well, thanks for your help. Don't worry, I'll see myself out.'

You'd better get out before I kiss you, thought Ella as she opened the hall door for him and said goodbye.

'Nice young fellow, that,' said Josef in the kitchen. 'Family?'

When Josef wanted to know something, he asked.

'No, just a friend.'

Was there no such word as gobsucker, then? She was sure she had seen it written up somewhere – that or something very like it. Well, lucky that ink had been washable.

Now she could see to it that Becky got her rug. When she

had eaten her lunch of fruit and cheese she rang the University and left a message for Dr Vorschak, asking him to call her as soon as it was convenient.

She didn't know what to expect of Max. He had made the effort to bring Becky to see her, but he hadn't repeated the visit and he hadn't honoured the lunch invitation either. She thought it was a matter of good intentions defeated by adverse circumstances. She couldn't expect him to destroy his marital peace on her account.

The phone call at least came promptly.

Max was jovial.

'Why, Mother, this is splendid. How are you? How are things going with you?'

'Very well, thanks. The reason I rang, Max. I've been hooking a nursery rug for Becky and now that I've finished it I'd like you to take it to her. Would you mind calling round for it? Seeing that you're so close, I thought . . .'

Max paused too long.

So that she will always have something from me, so that she will know I love her. Don't deny me that.

'Of course. She will be very happy about that. This afternoon? I am here till 5. I could come then.'

'That would be fine. Do you need directions?'

'No, I have the directory.'

'Please come to the side door with the little porch. You can drive right in.'

She put down the phone and thought about that pause for reflection. It seemed sinister, though Max had been friendly.

How had she ever got to be the villain in this drama?

It was the money, no doubt, the long, bitter struggle over money.

Sometimes she could understand Martha's dislike of the getters and strivers. That struggle had made a sad change in David, which could explain Martha's depression. As for Max, he was probably friendly with that one . . . no use speculating.

She wasn't going to unroll the rug and sit crying over Becky all afternoon, either. It was her farewell to Becky; that had to be endured in silence.

Shopping was the only resource. She decided to award herself the crimson bowl she had been hankering for since she had seen it in the window of Kitchens Plus. That would encourage her to spend the rest of the afternoon polishing the utilitarian wardrobe-dressingtable combination where she intended to place it.

That program proved satisfactory. There was nothing like a job of polishing for working off mental anguish. She was standing back to admire the result of her work when Max knocked at the outer door.

'Wherever you are, Mother, you make a home. Those curtains must be of your making, I think.'

'They are sheets, really. You couldn't get such designs in anything else. You think it works? It's not overpowering?'

This was a serious question needing an honest answer. She had been working to transform the room into a setting where she could invite the young people to dinner without shame. Success was essential; if the effect was amateurish, she would be touching the string of pathos and making them miserable. If she was successful, of course, they would fear she was settling in, rejecting the nice little unit they talked of so fondly. There was too much sensitivity about, altogether, but knowing her children, she thought greed would prevail and they would forget their worries for a homecooked dinner.

Max, endearingly, was giving serious consideration to the curtains.

'Perhaps, if your colours were not so subtle. No, it looks very effective. The height of the ceiling is the good point of the room. You accentuate that with the vertical drape. Very good, I think.'

'I got the grandfather chair at the local antique shop. I couldn't do it, of course, if the landlord weren't such a nice man. He's been very helpful. Well, Becky's rug.'

His reaction to the rug, when she unrolled it, was satisfactory.

'Enchanting. Enchanting. You said a nursery rug. I was expecting Little Bo-Peep.'

'I hoped it would do for more years than that.'

'I am sure that it will. What a beautiful piece of work. I hope very much, you know, that she has inherited your talent.'

Ella was thinking in astonishment, 'Talent?' – a word she connected with Rob and with William – when Max astonished her further.

'But of course I cannot deliver it for you. You must bring it to her yourself.'

'Do you mean now, this evening?'

'Why not this evening?'

'Caroline won't be expecting me.'

'There is such a thing as the telephone, is there not? You must have a telephone here.'

'In the hall.'

'Then I shall use it.'

She heard Max say, 'Just a friend. With a nice surprise.'

He should give her warning.

Was that tactlessness – always a possibility with Max, though not usually to this extent – or was it deliberate unkindness?

Unkindness from Max to Caroline was something new.

Travelling beside him with her passport rolled on the back seat of the car, she reflected that Max was not making things easy for her, either. Whatever his intentions, the best she could do was make it clear to Caroline that she had no part in them.

'Max took me quite by surprise,' she would say. 'I wanted him to deliver . . .' No, leave it at that. 'Max took me quite by surprise.'

It was the worst scenario.

Caroline in her best hostess gown came smiling into the hall to greet the visitor, and halted, looking shocked.

He could have spared her that, thought Ella, but Max, who had always registered and suffered every atom of Caroline's pain, did not intend to spare her. With his arm round Ella in a most unusual gesture, he said jovially, 'Here's Mother come to see us, with a lovely surprise for Becky.'

'I've made her a rug.'

'She's in the living room.'

She led the way.

Becky in pyjamas and dressing-gown was building a

tower of blocks, which collapsed as she stood up shouting, 'Grandma!'

'Come and see what Grandma had brought you.'

Glad to be rid of her awkward burden, Ella spread the rug, to which Becky paid no attention, since she was rolling on the floor, giggling in an excess of delight.

'Oh, I don't see you. I don't see you for a very long time.'

'Come and give me a cuddle then.'

Sitting in an armchair and taking the little girl on her knee, she hoped that this might reach Caroline later, though she couldn't be expected to smile over it in a moment of defeat.

'It's very pretty,' said Caroline, looking at the rug.

'Pretty is not the word,' said Max. 'It has the charm of the primitive combined with the skill of execution. It is unique.'

Now you're being clever at her, Max. That's enough.

He added, 'She will come to love it later.'

Ella hugged Becky's warm, heavy little body while Becky, still giggling with delight, nuzzled against her shoulder.

'I'd rather she loved me now.'

'We want Grandma to come and see us much more often, don't we, Becky?'

'Yes, yes. Yes, yes, yes, yes, yes.'

Caroline said, 'It's time she was in bed.'

Becky was gracious.

'Grandma may put me to bed tonight.'

'If that's all right with Mummy.'

'She's been on the pot. She just has to have her teeth cleaned, that's all.'

'And a story,' said Becky.

'I can manage all that. Say goodnight to Mummy and Daddy, darling.'

She took Becky's hand and led her away, eager to leave the couple alone and let Caroline have her say. Max's behaviour had been devious and inconsiderate. Perhaps Caroline wanted to tell him so.

When she came downstairs after tucking Becky in and kissing her goodnight, she found Caroline dishing up roast chicken while Max opened a bottle of wine, both in silence, showing no sign either of war or of friendship.

No Man's Land.

At the dinner table, in spite of the constraint in the atmosphere, she felt remarkably at home.

But this was home, the very sitting for the domestic dinner table – guilty secret (hers, this time and she'd never regret it), buried hatred (still Caroline, alas), while Max was playing her own part as the embodiment of the three wise monkeys, hearing no evil, seeing no evil, speaking no evil.

Virtuous Upbringing. That was its name. Pam had brought back a postcard of that panel, from a temple in Japan, with the carving of the three wise monkeys. 'Virtuous Upbringing' it was called.

'Don't be rude to Caroline, Sophie.' 'David, pass Sophie the bread. You shouldn't need to be asked. You should be watching.' 'Yes, Dad.' 'And Sophie, you shouldn't be stretching after it, you know. You should ask.' 'Yes, Mum.'

While inwardly the separate worlds were turning . . .

Just as well one didn't know.

They had minded their manners and cleaned their plates. The rest she couldn't answer for.

And how much was Max carrying in silence?

Hamfisted Harry. If Rob knew that name, so must Max, unless he had shut his eyes and his ears. If he hadn't managed to do that, he had certainly shut his mouth. There was more to Max than met the eye.

'Have you made any plans for the future, Mother? I suppose you won't want to live in a room for ever. Though you have made it really very charming. You must see it, Caroline.'

'It's an interesting experience. I'm quite comfortable, really. No, it won't be for ever. David and Martha are househunting, you know, and I'd like to buy something near them.'

She wished she hadn't said that. Caroline's mouth had tightened to a line of pain.

'Of course. They are such a support to you, you must want to be near them. I wish we could have done more.'

Caroline looked up.

'Do you think you could clear your things out of the house soon? It's very awkward, you know, when Dad is trying to let it.'

'But that is one thing we can do for Mother. We can pack her things and store them for her here.'

His impervious cheerfulness was beginning to fret Ella, too.

'Would you mind calling me Ella, Max? I would prefer it.'

That didn't ruffle him, either.

'Of course. I am honoured. It is more modern, is it not?'

She must stop this discreet sniping at Max in Caroline's defence.

There it was – she could never be immune to Caroline's suffering. Whatever blight had fallen on her, whatever pain it was that could get relief only in giving pain to others, Ella suffered them, too. One felt just as much for the emotional cripple as for any other handicapped child.

Between the chicken and the mousse she gave up at last. It was out of season, the complex of guilt and sympathy, love and frustration she felt for Caroline. Time to be done with it.

'This is a good chocolate mousse. It isn't my recipe, is it?'

'No. It's out of Margaret Fulton. Max likes the orange flavour.'

'Oh.'

It was one of those dinners where one is truly grateful for the wine.

Max drove her home.

During the journey they spoke little. As he stopped the car at her door, he said, 'You must come again very soon, Ella.'

'I have to be invited, Max.'

'But of course you will be invited. I shall telephone you next week. What is the best time?'

See no evil, hear no evil, speak no evil.

• XXXIII •

She invited Sophie and William to dinner.

Her own sensitivity prompted the invitation. She could accept the irregular couple on her premises but not on theirs. She understood that the prejudice was absurd; though she was prepared to indulge it, she was not prepared to admit it.

Late in the afternoon, Sylvia knocked at the door, opened it and looked in.

'Will you be in this evening, Ella? Wow, you have been making some changes. How does Connie feel about it?'

'He helped me to move the furniture.'

'Favourite inmate, you are. You won't be for long, by the way, if you keep the stove going for hours. What are you doing, cooking a casserole?'

'It's all right. We have an arrangement. Fifteen cents an hour, or part thereof. He's more worried about cleaning the oven than about the gas. I've promised to see to that. Mrs Abercrombie doesn't do ovens.'

'He's a good soul, really. What I came in for, if a man named Ross rings and asks for me, will you take a message, or take his number and say I'll ring back?'

'Yes. No trouble. If there's a call, I'll leave a note on the pad.'

'You're an angel. Have a nice dinner.'

Guarding the telephone was quite the easiest way of becoming an angel Ella had encountered.

Sophie and William arrived soon after – if that was William. Love and money together might not have turned the frog into a prince, but they certainly brought the story to mind.

New clothes made a difference, of course. *He was wearing real shoes.* The silky red hair which had given the incongruous touch of prettiness he now wore in a stark basin cut which made him look like a character in a historical film.

Could one tell a man one loved his new hairstyle? Probably not.

'William's put on his television gear in your honour,' said Sophie, making Ella aware that she was showing an unflattering astonishment.

'Every inch the famous author,' she said.

'That is rather premature,' William said.

Ella remembered Rob's words. 'Sometimes you think he's joking and then you realise that he's dead serious.'

William was holding a rectangular parcel and awaiting his moment.

Before he handed it to her he swooped boldly and kissed her on the left eyebrow.

Claiming bridegroom status, thought Ella, smiling to

herself as she took the parcel. Faint heart never won fair lady, as they said.

Her smile widened in pleasure as she unwrapped two framed prints – finely drawn, delicately coloured, precisely detailed illustrations of botanical specimens: The Waratah and The Flannel Flower.

'Found them in a junk shop. They looked like your sort of thing, so I had them reframed for you. I'm afraid there's been a bit of vandalism, though. There are page numbers in the corners, they must have been cut out of a pretty valuable book. I hope you don't have a conscience about that.'

'None at all,' said Ella serenely.

'No. I wouldn't have done it myself, but seeing that it's been done . . .'

'Where do you think I should hang them?' she asked.

'I brought picture hooks and wire. Sophie couldn't remember whether there was a picture rail.' He found this inattentiveness surprising. 'We brought the hooks and the wire in case there was one.'

'They are in my bag, with the wine,' said Sophie. 'I am developing squaw characteristics.'

Ella was holding a print against the window wall.

'What do you expect, dear, when you carry those great bags about with you? Asking for trouble, I should have thought.'

'Do I detect a certain animus against men, Ella?'

She turned to look at him, saying briefly, 'Not if they're braves.'

Sophie's little crow of laughter announced the morning.

'One of Mum's remarks. I haven't heard one for months. You sound like yourself again.'

'Well. That's the place for them, isn't it? You must have been thought-reading, William. You even have the colours right.'

'Nice curtains, Mum.'

'I think they go well. We'd better leave the pictures till after dinner. If you'll put a match to the fire and open the wine while I serve up.'

Cooking being still a suspect activity, she was eager to take her dishes out of the oven before the lodgers arrived.

'Cute little teawagon, Mum.'

'It's what they call a traymobile. It has to be a side table.'

Serving dinner at a table as small as a large desk, while preserving the formality due to the meal, required thought.

'There is room for the plates and the glasses and the pepper and salt. Everything else will have to come from the side table.'

Sophie was studying the traymobile.

'Saint Vincent de Paul?'

'That's right. But the mahogany chair is from a real antique shop. At a real price.'

William occupied the mahogany chair at one long side of the table. The traymobile was drawn up against the other, within Ella's reach for serving.

The arrangement did well enough. There was no note of pathetic makeshift to harrow the feelings unless one looked for it. As she had foreseen, the food monopolised the young people's attention, so that there was little conversation till they had reached the fruit and the cheese.

'Ooooh, that was lovely, Mum,' said Sophie, suiting her tone to her childish display of appetite.

'I'm limited to casseroles, I'm afraid.'

'They'll do.'

'And to feeding two of you at a time.'

'And that'll do, too.'

At this emphatic rejoinder Ella turned to her in alarm.

'You haven't quarrelled with David and Martha?'

'The sooner big brother realises that I'm not twelve years old, the better.'

William said, almost with humour, 'I am afraid to go there. I think he may challenge me to a duel. I did not know that brothers still felt so chivalrous about the honour of their sisters.'

'Mum, what's eating him? If he's just carrying on like this about William, then truly, he is sick. And he isn't. Narrowminded, pigheaded, overbearing, but not sick.'

'Sophie dear, please make it up. I really can't bear it if you two are estranged. It seems as if that's the last thing, as if everything had come to pieces.'

'Oh, we're not estranged. He told me what he thought of my morals and I told him what I thought of his intellect, delivering my last shaft from the safety of the doorway, as I thought I was in danger of physical violence, but whatever is eating him, he'll have to get over it and I'm sorry he's rude to you, William, but you have to forgive him, because he's my favourite sibling.'

'I can't blame him for thinking me an unsuitable match for you,' said William. 'I bear him no grudge on that account.'

'I didn't get to the match bit. The climate didn't seem propitious.'

'He's been under a lot of strain lately, you know, and I don't think he's happy in his job.'

'But he wouldn't be taking that out on me. That's the kind of stupidity . . . I don't know. We'll just have to give it time and stay firm. If anyone asks, Mum, please make it clear that I don't accept invitations without William.'

'Is that for Max and Caroline, too?' asked Ella, seizing an opportunity while she considered the implications of Sophie's announcement.

'I'm not expecting any invitations there. Catch Caroline giving her blessing to an irregular union!'

After a considerable pause, Ella said thoughtfully, 'She seems to have become more tolerant lately.'

'I am sitting here,' said Sophie wretchedly, 'wondering how to get my big foot out of my big mouth. I am truly sorry, Mum. But do you know, even if it wasn't Dad, I don't think I'd approve. Funny the things you find out about yourself. I suppose I've been too close to that one.'

William looked happy.

That was the story with all her children, thought Ella. They knew a true lover when they met one and they looked no further.

This match, after all, was promising well.

'Caroline's entitled to accept her father and his domestic arrangements,' she said. 'I hope you will, too, in time.'

No mention of Caroline's shameful intimacy with Louise. Speak no evil . . .

'I went there to dinner last week. Max drove me up there to give Becky her rug. If you'd seen Becky when I walked in! She was delirious.'

Becky.

'Well, if they ask us nicely. I suppose if you can, I can.'

William said with some feeling that he was prepared to accept any friends he could get.

'You are sure to have a friend in Martha,' said Ella.

That brought the conversation to William's work and the prospects for the new book, a topic which, with the placing and hanging of the prints, occupied them for the rest of their visit.

When they had left, Ella stacked the dishes on the traymobile, wheeled it across to the kitchen and set about the washing up with the feeling that the effort had been worthwhile.

Now for David and Martha.

She must stop shielding Sophie, who didn't need shielding, at the expense of William, who did perhaps need it.

If the subject comes up, she promised herself, I'll tell him just how well William has behaved. Next time, certainly. Without fail.

• XXXIV •

Martha noticed the new prints as soon as she came in.

'Just the right finishing touch. Perfect. Where did you find them?'

'I didn't find them. They were a present from William. He came across them in a junk shop and had them framed for me.'

'Oh. They look exactly the sort of thing you'd choose yourself.'

'That's what William said.'

This was her opportunity. Again, she let it pass.

'David, have you and Sophie really had a quarrel?'

David, who was studying The Waratah, turned away from it, grinning.

'Not exactly a quarrel. We had an energetic exchange of views. I said I'd like to knock some sense into her silly head and she said all I had in my head was the stuffing they put in cricket balls and the covering was just as thick. She threw that over her shoulder as she left. A nice turn of phrase, I thought, and delivered on the run.'

'What was the use of shouting at her?' asked Martha. 'You won't turn her off him, you'll just make her more determined.'

'No use at all, but I enjoyed it. I've had my say and now I'm prepared to resign myself and be polite to the bastard.'

Being polite to the bastard was a very good prescription for family life, in Ella's opinion.

'I'm glad to hear it,' she said. 'I'm sure William will be glad to hear it, too. He's afraid you're going to challenge him to a duel.'

That did bring a smile, which improved the atmosphere, so that they sat down to dinner in harmony.

'Oh, this is nice,' said Martha. 'You can't really talk in a restaurant.'

'Don't get this food, either,' said David, who was applying himself with energy to the dish of osso bucco and saffron rice. 'This is great, Mum.'

Martha persisted, 'But we do need to talk.'

'Yes. Well. The thing is, Mum, that I want to give up teaching.'

'You must give up teaching,' said Martha. 'You can't spend you life at a job you hate.' She said to Ella, 'I've been telling him that for ages.'

'I want to go back to studying. I want to study accountancy.' As he pronounced the word he looked apologetically at Martha.

'All right. I know I was being ridiculous.'

'Suppose you finish your dinner,' said Ella, seeing a debate in prospect. 'It seems a very good idea to me.'

'Yes. A pity to waste this.'

Over biscuits and cheese and the last of the wine, he began again.

'I want to be an accountant. I haven't fallen in love with money, I don't think it's the greatest good, but keeping your eye on it, watching where it goes – that seems like a useful sort of job. It's figures I like. Can't handle people but I'm certain I can handle figures. Martha would have to keep us while I'm studying.'

'You know I don't mind that. I do wish it was something else, but it's your choice.'

'Apart from anything else, I don't know enough. I want to learn more. There's always something new to learn about money.'

Ella said, 'I don't see your problem.'

'We meant to move to a bigger place, but if I give up work, we can't afford to move. We argue this round and round. It's now or never for me. We can't start a family till I'm established. If I put off the move any longer we'll both be too old.'

He paused and took breath.

'So what about joining forces? Getting a house together? You'd have a decent margin for investment, we wouldn't be lumbered with a mortgage.'

'And mutual support,' said Martha. 'That's important, too. We've been looking at a house, we think you'd love it. It's a big old weatherboard place with fruit trees in the garden.'

A living house, a house with footsteps and voices – Ella wanted this so much and she could not have it.

This is where I pay, she thought. I thought I had got away with it, but the bill always comes in. My darling children, I can't live with you because you don't know me. I'm a vandal, a fraud, a mad woman.

'It needs a bit doing to it,' said David, 'but it's livable and structurally sound.'

Her silence was disconcerting them.

'We wouldn't impose, Ella. David and I would manage the cleaning between us. I suppose you'd have to be cook, but I'd be kitchenmaid. Why shouldn't it work? We're all reasonable people, aren't we?'

On that subject, Ella could not answer for herself.

'It needn't be forever, Mum. If you'd really rather have a place of your own, we would raise a loan and buy you out, as soon as I have the qualifications and get a job. We'll do that in any case, as soon as we can. I'm not going to waste time, you can be sure of that.'

Don't put it like that to me, David. Don't tell me you need my help. I have to say no and I can hardly bear it.

They looked at her in silence, mortified by the memory of their enthusiasm.

David said at last, 'What about Sophie, Mum? I don't see how that affair can last, and where is she to go if it breaks up? I know you'd always give her a home, but she mightn't feel like asking you. She might be embarrassed.'

In spite of her distress, Ella found time to wonder what could embarrass Sophie.

'I think it will last, you know. William is a more responsible person than you think. He is the one who is holding out for marriage.'

Martha uttered a sound which, though sad and helpless in tone, was still a giggle.

'So she'll be keeping him, I suppose.'

They were recovering from their disappointment, or perhaps had not given up hope of persuading her.

He managed to smile over his words, saying, 'I do think that is different, though I admit I don't quite see how. But even if he is responsible, she isn't. If the affair breaks up and she starts drifting among those characters . . . Wouldn't it be better if there was a home base she could come back to? There's something very wrong with Sophie, Mum. You tried to warn us, to tell us she was in a bad way over Dad, but we just didn't know how bad.'

Martha said as no doubt she had said before, 'There's nothing we could have done about it, if we had known.'

'There's not much doubt that it was Sophie and her pals who broke up the living room. The police gave Dad the idea that it was an inside job - not in so many words, perhaps, but he could tell by the questions they were asking. Who had keys to the house? Who might have a serious grudge? It looked to them like a cover-up, somebody trying to fake a break in to cover malicious damage. I tell you, Dad was stricken. He asked me if any of his children could hate him so much. Well, it wasn't me and it certainly wasn't Caroline.

Malicious damage. Nasty words but she had to admit they were accurate.

'Sophie didn't do it. I was there after Sophie took the furniture. Everything was all right then.'

David shook his head.

'Sorry, Mum, but that's what you would say, isn't it? If you went in and found the damage and knew she'd been there, you'd cover-up for her.'

She was not such a brilliant liar as she had supposed.

They had heard the falsehood in her voice and had misinterpreted it.

'Perhaps she thought she was doing it for you. I don't know. It's hard to take, hard to understand.'

Tracked down by Fate, Ella said flatly, 'I did it.'

'Oh, come off it, Mum. That's going a bit too far.'

Martha however was sitting very still, except for her slowly nodding head.

'I did it, I tell you. I went to get the sewing machine. I didn't mean to go near the living room – well, I did it. That's all.'

Now she was naked, the last shred of parental dignity ripped away, a madwoman laying about her with a meat mallet.

David protested, 'They say there was filth scrawled on the walls.'

Gobsucker. Lucky that ink had been washable.

'I did my best, or my worst.' She added angrily, 'You should have known it was me. It's always the injured party. Did anyone have a grudge? Yes, I had. Well, there it is. I did it and I can't say I'm sorry.'

She was sorry, however, that she had tried to cover her traces. That was the really humiliating part. 'Being a mother doesn't turn you into an angel.'

Martha said softly, 'We have never known till this moment how terrible this has been for you.'

David's thoughts were unreadable.

Martha said, 'It was only a bit of glass. Not like destroying people.'

Her eyes were on David. She knew there were better things than glass at risk.

She said again, 'I think it was therapeutic. Feelings can

be beyond words. They still have to be expressed or they'll do permanent damage.'

Therapeutic. Now her behaviour was classified. There was a place for it in the inventory of human nature.

David came to put his arms round her.

He said only, 'Well, we'll just have to put up with you for the sake of your cooking,' but his voice was as expressive of love and pity as was Martha's face.

'If you want to live with me, you have to know what I'm like.'

Instead of answering, he tightened his embrace to a hug, then let her go.

'I think we had better keep this to ourselves,' said Martha. 'There are certain people who might not understand.'

'Or might understand too well,' said Ella.

'There is that, of course.'

'I can't have people thinking Sophie did it.'

Martha said, 'The fiction will stand.'

David nodded.

'Dad's only too anxious to believe in the vandals. I don't think he's told anyone else what he thought. He didn't explain why he wouldn't claim the insurance and he was under pressure there. He was too shattered, I think. I can convince him.'

'It will all be forgotten,' said Martha. 'We are going to be the villains of the piece. They will be quite sure we were feathering our own nest, if we set up together.'

Ella said, 'You must talk it over with Max and make sure that he understands what you are doing. After all, anything I own will be a matter of inheritance, eventually. Becky's interests will be involved, so it's important to have it all clear.'

'Now I know where David gets it.'

'I'll do that, Mum. Keep him in the picture.' He began to smile. The smile broadened. 'We'd better keep an eye on the lavatory walls in the new place.'

'And that,' said Martha, 'will be the last word said on the matter. You will come and look at the house with us, won't you, Ella?'

Yes, yes, yes, yes, yes.

PENGUIN – THE BEST AUSTRALIAN READING

BOOKS BY JESSICA ANDERSON IN PENGUIN

Tirra Lirra by the River Jessica Anderson

For Nora Porteous, life is a series of escapes. To escape her tightly knit smalltown family, she marries, only to find herself confined again, this time in a stifling Sydney suburb with a selfish, sanctimonious husband. With a courage born of desperation and sustained by a spirited sense of humour, Nora travels to London, and it is there that she becomes the woman she wants to be. Or does she?

Taking Shelter Jessica Anderson

In a novel about and across the generations *Taking Shelter* has our attention from page one.

A group of people, young and old, are drawn together in their quests for permanence, tenderness and love in an era when there are no rules about the age, gender, or the faithfulness of lovers. Written with keen perception, wit and emotional honesty.